THIS BOOK SHOULD BE RETURNED ON OR BEFORE THE LATEST
DATE SHOWN TO ANY LANCASHIRE COUNTY LIBRARY

NLA

Lancaster Library
Market Square
Lancaster
Lancs.
LA1 1HY

1 3 OCT 2005

2 6 JAN 2005 0 7 NOV 2005

- 9 OCT 2004

07 DEC 2005

0 9 MAR 2005

2 8 JUN 2005

1 5 OCT 2004

0 4 NOV 2004   0 9 AUG 2005   2 7 APR 2006

1 5 NOV 2004

1 7 MAY 2006

1 7 JUL 2006

AUTHOR	CLASS
PRUNTY, M.	F

TITLE

Superstar lovers

SUPERSTAR LOVERS

London-reared of Irish parents, **Morag Prunty** edited several young women's magazines in London, including *More!* and *Just Seventeen*, before moving to Ireland in 1990 to relaunch *Irish Tatler*. She is now a full-time writer and lives in County Mayo with her husband and son. *Superstar Lovers* is her fourth novel.

MORAG PRUNTY

SUPERSTAR LOVERS

PAN BOOKS

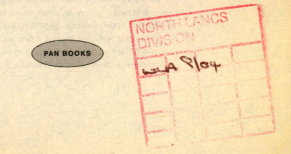

First published 2004 by Pan Books
an imprint of Pan Macmillan Ltd
Pan Macmillan, 20 New Wharf Road, London N1 9RR
Basingstoke and Oxford
Associated companies throughout the world
www.panmacmillan.com

ISBN 0 330 41910 2

A CIP catalogue record for this book is available from
the British Library.

Typeset by SetSystems Ltd, Saffron Walden, Essex
Printed and bound in Great Britain by
Mackays of Chatham plc, Chatham, Kent

for Niall

Prologue

Molly felt the longing stretch across her stomach, as she did at this same time every week. The knowledge that soon the passion of her addiction would be released, the craving realized. She didn't mind the wait, not now that she had become organized about it. There were ways, she found, of making these things last. She had trained herself to make sure that the time she had to fill between fixes was more a matter of hours than days.

Sometimes on the way down to Fonzie, Molly wondered if she really felt right being so dependent on him and what he provided. But then, Molly always decided, she wasn't doing any harm to anybody and how many vices had that boast? Perhaps if she hadn't acquired this habit, life might have opened up for her more. But she was happy enough the way things were, cocooned as she was in her own little world. She needed to escape. And that's all it was, surely? Everyone needed to get out of themselves now and again. Didn't they?

Molly's step quickened as she reached the door, and all doubts were forgotten as the end came within sight.

Fonzie reached down to his secret shelf and put the gear on the countertop.

'*Hello!*, *2Day*, *Heat*, *Now*, *VIP* magazine . . .'

As she reached over to grab them, the kindly young newsagent put his hand gently over Molly's and she knew there was bad news coming.

'*Woman* is here, Molly, but I'm afraid aul Rita Cooney got the last *Woman's Own*.'

A blow, certainly, but not enough to warrant the extent of his seriousness.

'And . . .?'

A pause as they both prepared themselves for the worst.

'There's been a delay on the teen mags. *BIG* and *Smash Hits* . . .'

Jesus, no! The cover story on Alfie! She had seen it flagged in last week's *Hits*!

'They're not here, Molly. They arrived late at the distribution house in Dublin. Won't be here until early next week. I'm sorry.'

Molly gulped back her disappointment. Fonzie knew how important these magazines were to her and sometimes that made her feel vulnerable in his company.

'No problem,' she said brightly, handing him his money, 'sure they're only magazines.'

'That's right,' he replied.

But they both knew there was more to it than that.

PART ONE

MEMORANDUM

To: Lucy Lemon – Editor

From: Hettie Flinthrop – Celebrity Co-ordinator

Re: MoniKa/Alfie Smith At-Home Shoot

Lucy! *So* exciting about MoniKa/Alfie shoot next week! Justin (Mon's agent) just rang to say that on reflection they've decided to donate the money *themselves* (want to see all those smiling little faces – you can't blame them!). So if we can send the cheque directly to McIvor Management that would be great. I know you had reservations about the £500,000 tag but it *is* an exclusive and the house *is* meant to be fantastic!

Hugs! Hettie

1

It hadn't worked out the way he had expected at all, this marriage business. But then, Alfie wondered as he settled back in his plane seat, what had he actually been expecting? Perhaps that was the problem, as the words of his mentor/ best man the night before what was supposed to have been the happiest day of his life came back to him: 'Have you thought this through, Alf? I mean *really* thought about what this means?'

Of course he hadn't. What was there to think about? MoniKa was, by agreement of the world's fashion press, 'the most beautiful woman in the world' and he was in love. They had been dating for a year, as much as both their busy work schedules would allow. It had been the most successful year of his career to date, with four number-one singles, a platinum album and awards ceremonies so numerous that they blended into one another – along with the places, the parties and plane journeys, until the only stable thing he could remember for the year 2001 was MoniKa. He had been playing the Point in Dublin the night of their first anniversary. One of the journalists interviewing him in his hotel suite before the concert had brought along that day's edition of the *Sun* newspaper, which had dedicated six colour pages to *A Stormy Year for Alf and Mon*.

It was full of the usual lies. January, the two of them holding hands, walking down Bond Street, trying to blend in with dark glasses and combats, with a picture insert of a dancer he had briefly encountered with the quote, 'Secret love rat Alfie dumped me for Supermodel'. Fuzzy snaps of both of them with agents, friends, cousins purported to be evidence that they were cheating on one another. Throughout the twelve-month period they had allegedly been one or the other gay, cheating, violently arguing, having affairs and ultimately (December), with a chart of their joint increased earnings over the period, *The greatest publicity stunt ever staged*.

Alfie was offended. He was always offended when people didn't think he was genuine. Fakeness – the giant ego, the tantrums, the pouting pretentious disease of modern celebrity – was something that he had always determined to keep at bay. He succeeded, in his own mind, through the only escape routes open to him: giving to charity (for which he was accused of publicity seeking), continuing to work as hard as he could (greedy), trying to form and maintain meaningful friendships with his peers (gay) and avoiding reading the papers. He knew he was still a down-to-earth young man. As down-to-earth, certainly, as was possible given the first-class/five-star/ Versace-freebie lifestyle which, despite himself, he had found to be the inevitable remit of a guy in his position.

In the early days, it had been impossible to maintain any level of normality. Not that he had wanted to back then. He hadn't started out in this business to live a 'normal life'. No matter how much it was all about the music now, it hadn't been in the days of U&Us. Not by a long shot.

U&Us were not a manufactured boy band. Not at first, anyway. They had been formed a full school year, a lifetime when you are eighteen, before the local talent competition, which had put them in view of Dave Davidson. Dave was a Seventies throwback. A one-hit wonder from Wigan, he had never got over his sole appearance on *Cheggers Plays Pop*, and was looking for a way to oil his way back into the world of 'showbiz' without compromising his moderately successful position as head of marketing in a Northern advertising agency. Dave picked up on these five good-looking lads and courted them into allowing him to be their manager. He was a rug-sporting, loud-shirt-loving poncified bullshitter. But he was no fool when it came to turning a few bob, and Alfie was no fool either. While the others wanted to hold out for a response from record companies to the demo tape they'd borrowed a grand each off their parents to record, Alf, one year older than the others and therefore their appointed 'leader', talked them into going with Dave. It paid off, and after the usual round of teeny school-disco gigs, courting magazine editors, dance classes, singing lessons, wardrobe and hair overhauls – all financed by Dave – they got a record deal and the band took off.

The next four years were the biggest wake-up call five

teenage boys could ever have. Singing, dancing, snogging girls, hanging out together were normal recreational activities for lads their age. Add international travel and cruising around in limos, then becoming pop stars was surely just an elongation of their youthful fantasies. Playtime with a very grown-up bankroll. For the first year they lived the dream, faced the press jointly with beaming boyish grins that said they couldn't believe their luck. They loved their fans, they loved the music, they loved being on the cover of the teen magazines. They were grateful, truly grateful, to their manager, to the record company, to the fans. This was their wildest dream come true. The best thing that had *ever* happened to them. But at eighteen, not enough had happened for them to measure up against. The shorter the period of wanting something, the quicker the gratitude fades.

They could not have known that when you do anything long enough and with enough intensity, it becomes tedious. The gratitude wore off by year two. If they whinged at their mothers for getting them out of bed at eight a.m. after a week of half-term lie-ins, now they found themselves being roused at five by yet another cooked breakfast in a hotel they couldn't name, in a city they had barely heard of. If their parents vaguely nagged them about 'getting girls into trouble', the management, which now totalled a team of six – a public relations manager, a tour manager, a floating 'representative of the record company', two full-time security minders and Dave – had them under permanent surveillance to ensure that they went nowhere near any of the underage girls who followed them in crowds. If their teachers had gently goaded them into 'studying harder', now they had demanding daily rehearsals with fierce yelling tutors threatening them with public humiliation if they didn't perfect that step, hit that high note, smile, smile, smile all the time.

'SMILE, you ungracious little shit! There are five thousand fans out there who have paid money to see you. Smile, sing, shuffle – I've told you a million times, Alfie, you moron!'

In the end they all knew it didn't matter if they couldn't sing or dance. Only the smiles were important. The fans weren't there to hear the music. They just wanted to see the glossy pictures they had plastered to their bedroom walls come to life. The audience became nothing more than a shivering wave of noise. Girls wept and wailed and wet themselves: a far cry from the coy nervous seductions of their local discos. They went through the motions on stage not for the fans, but for fear of their management. Each fantasy they experienced – the hotel suites, designer clothes, thousands of screaming fans, chart success – wore them out with the rigour of their exhausting working schedule and turned into a cynically viewed duty. It was something they had all wanted, but not wanted enough to warrant the discipline and 24/7 commitment that had been hoisted on them. A more experienced manager might have understood the benefits of letting the boys go home more often, allowed them to incorporate their family and friends into their entourage. But Dave was greedy; there was always another gig, another video, another single. This was a short-term money-making opportunity and he was determined to milk it.

Year three it really started to fall apart. They missed their families. They had bought houses they had never visited, cars they had never driven. They needed to let go and enjoy some of the fruits of their labour. Led by Alfie, the band threatened to go on strike and Dave finally conceded to arrange a concert in Leeds, followed by a week off. The night went brilliantly, but the following day each of them was called at home and told that there had been a change of plan. They had gone to Number One in Denmark, and a car was coming to collect them to take them to the airport for an impromptu publicity tour.

Alfie refused to get into the car. He lay on the sofa of the new suburban home he had bought for his mother while the family pleaded with him to go. But he stayed firm. The limo driver waited outside the detached house for two hours, until he knew it would be too late to make the flight. The phone rang and rang and rang, but each time Alfie grabbed it and clicked the receiver off. He went up to his room and pulled the curtains and sat in a bedroom he had never been in before. His mother had decorated it like a hotel, with a four-poster bed flanked by flouncy curtains and a salmon-pink carpet that still smelt shop-new. The en-suite bathroom even had a basket of shampoo and bath-foam sachets nestling by the side of the oval-shaped bath; a designer shaving range and an unopened packet of razors were arranged neatly on a chrome shelf by the sink. Alfie imagined his mother threatening his younger brother if he so much as went near them. While his siblings sat downstairs, glued to MTV Europe for news of his disappearance, Alfie locked himself in the room. He dug his face into the sheets to try and find something that smelt like home. Something from before. An old pizza box under the bed, the odd Top Man sock mysteriously mismatched with one of his sister's, a half-empty bottle of CK flung into the corner on an old Union Jack bean bag. Some reference point to remind him of who he was before he became a pop idol. His old CDs were filed neatly on a desk next to his bed under a brand-new miniature stereo. His mother had hoovered and dusted and decorated away his first eighteen years, replacing them with this new glamorized version of life he hadn't known he was trying to escape until now.

As much as Alfie felt estranged from his old life, he knew he had been the one who had chased it away.

His family begged him to go back. He was letting his fans down, letting Dave down. 'After all the hard work he's done for you,' Sharon said. Alfie knew it would only be a matter of days before the crafty bastard had got to his mum.

'He got paid for it.' Even as Alfie said it he was aware of how precocious it sounded. He was talking like a seasoned whore. At twenty-two it wasn't normal to have such first-hand experience of contracts and marketing and percentages. He wasn't going back to U&Us. He wasn't even going to think through why. Alfie just knew it was over. That evening he called his mother's solicitor and gave him Dave's mobile number. *Alfie Quits U&Us by Mobile!* the headlines read the next day. The truth was Alfie didn't even know who his own solicitor was. He knew that he must have been introduced to the guy somewhere down the line, but he had met so many thousands of people in the past four years, he could only remember the occasional pretty face and names more famous than his own.

The next few days were hell. Journalists camping outside the house; his brother and sister had to stay home from school and his mother ordered their groceries in over the internet.

The *Alfie on Booze and Chocolate Binge* story was courtesy of a Tesco delivery boy who was paid fifty pounds to show the tabloids two bottles of dry white wine and a family fun-size bag of Mars bars.

'Pop singer Alfie Smith locked himself into his half-a-million-pound mansion this week and comforted himself over his U&Us sacking by bingeing on chocolate and booze. A source close to the family said: "Alfie loves his chocolate and often orders in family packs which can contain up to twenty bars." Also in the large delivery from a well-known supermarket in Leeds were several bottles of wine. "Mrs Smith regularly buys drink," our source told us.'

Accompanying the story was a picture of Sharon Smith in her housecoat putting a few beer cans in the wheelie bin. The photographer had had his long lens trained on their side entrance for almost forty-eight hours. He had endured the tabloid-savvy Sharon coming to the side entrance in a neat twin set and lipstick with sealed rubbish bags and waving and smiling nicely for almost two days. She hadn't reckoned on him sticking it out that long. The picture was taken at five a.m., after a sleepless night of worry. The caption read, *The party is over for Sharon Smith*, and the picture was repeated in the women's section over a small filler piece asking various 'top hairdressers' how long it was respectable for a woman of Sharon's age to let her roots 'go'.

She cried when she saw it. A 'kind' neighbour felt it was her 'duty' to drop it in the door. Alfie knew it was time to act. He wanted to go out there and fling himself on the nearest photographer – at least to tell them all to fuck off and leave his family alone – but he knew that wouldn't make them go away.

So he donned a Gucci leather coat over his trackies, slid on a pair of shades and went out to talk to them.

They hurled questions at him and he answered them nicely. He was sad to have left U&Us. He left by mutual agreement – they could make of that whatever they liked. He wished the boys and Dave every success in the world. They were a great bunch of people, and he would be forever grateful to the management and the fans. Yes, he was very sorry that his fans were sad and that they felt he had let them down. No, he wasn't on a break and no, he was never going back. No, he didn't have any plans for the near future beyond spending time with his friends and his family. Yes, it was worth watching this space. He waited until they had run out of every possible line of questioning. Yes, he did like chocolate. Yes, he did drink beer. No, he didn't take drugs. Yes, his mother was delighted to have him home. No, he didn't know when she last had her roots 'done'. On and on, and Alfie stayed calm and helpful and charming. It was the only way he knew, instinctively more than through training, to make them go away. As they left, he followed them down to the bank of a hundred or so weeping, shivering, hopeful pubescent and teenage girls that were contained by two policemen in a neat semicircle around the entrance of their short drive. He autographed every single album, T-shirt, pair of knickers, vest-top and poster handed to him. Then, when he was quite happy that they were all happy, he walked back to the house.

The following day there was one newspaper and a handful of girls outside. The day after, four or five girls called to the door. After that, peace.

MEMORANDUM

To: Timothy Macmillan – Publishing Director

From: Lucy Lemon – Editor

Re: MoniKa/Alfie Smith At-Home Shoot

That toe-rag Justin was just on to me demanding a car in
addition to the £500,000 'charidee' donation which I
am not at all sure his client isn't planning to spend on
handbags – *if* she gets to it before it goes up McIvor's
nose. Needless to say she was pitching way out of her
league – a soft-top Jaguar MX4 in fuchsia pink. I told
him to fuck off, that she wasn't Madonna. Having said
that, it's a cover story, it's an exclusive – and we need it.
Didn't you say you had somebody out at Volkswagen
who was looking to give a high-profile freebie? Sorry to
do this to you, Tim – I know Hettie is a colossal pain in
the hole, I keep trying to reign her in and put all agent
negotiations through me, but to be honest, she is *not* the
brightest button on the blazer. What can we do though?

We might have the brains but she's got the bloody contacts.

Best, Luce

2

Corrine had called her daughter 'Sapphire' after her own stage name. It had a glamorous, one-off ring to it. Sapphire was born with her mother's luminous blue eyes. Then they turned brown, and the delicate promise of Corrine's second coming morphed into a rather plain and podgy twelve-year-old – further evidence in Corrine's chequered life path that the best-laid plans can fall foul of expectations. The name had stuck to the child better than to herself – despite the fact that Corrine still had those jewel-like eyes that suggested something of great value lay behind them.

'We'll call you "Sapphire",' Wilson had said as she slid one morning from his bed and struck a pose by the window so he could drink in the sight of her young slim body. Waist-length hair draped across her breasts, her legs open slightly, part invitation and part innocence.

'Why?' she had asked him. She knew why, but she never tired of people telling her how beautiful she was and she was especially proud of her eyes.

'You *know* why.' Wilson was like that. He never gave her the satisfaction of compliments. He may have been older and uglier, but he was famous. The fact that he was with her was compliment enough.

'But the hair, darling, has just *got* to go.'

He was always so camp. It's a wonder nobody guessed. Certainly not her. But then she was only fifteen. What did she know back then?

She knew she was beautiful. Not tall, as tall as beauty was defined on the catwalks these days. Or skinny, but she was neither short nor stout. Her face was her greatest asset, and that is how beauty should be defined, she told herself now as she studied the cruel carnage of age on her body, stretch marks, the deep groove of her Caesarean scar, veins threatening to push through her lower calves. But Corrine's lips were still full, though lined slightly at the edges, and the eyes still had it.

'She's a star; she has that indefinable quality,' Wilson had said to Karl from KLM Management at that first meeting.

'Can she sing?' Karl had asked, the two men talking about her as if she wasn't there. Corrine didn't mind. Still didn't mind now, thinking back, that they had treated her as little more than a mannequin. She had wanted to be famous, believed she was special. In those days it wasn't like it is now, with every two-bit kid on the block wanting their fifteen minutes. Only the genuine articles made it back then. She was 'different'. She looked different. This was her destiny and these two men were going to help her fulfil it. If they wanted to pretend she was their puppet then that was fine. She knew who was really pulling the strings. A beautiful, perfect fifteen-year-old body sharing itself with a squat thirty-year-old rock singer, who even his greatest fan would be at a loss to describe as handsome.

'That doesn't matter,' Wilson had waved the question aside, 'she has *presence*.'

'She has too much hair,' Karl had said.

'She's booked into Keith at the new Smile salon in Knightsbridge. I've told him to make her look totally "now". You sign her up and I'll write the material.'

Wilson was the greatest songwriter of his generation. He was to remain so for generations to come. He was no oil painting, but that only made his popularity and chart success all the more remarkable. He had talent, and he was willing to harness it to turn a suburban teenager into a pop star. Corrine had thought the sweating and sobbing that was their supposed sex life was a small price to pay. In public he walked proudly with his hand around her waist, exuding lecherous self-congratulatory delight. In private he cuddled and cried and complained that he 'couldn't'.

'I don't know what's wrong with me,' he'd say, his puggish face crumpled in pained disappointment with himself, 'you're so beautiful.'

She would feel a little bit of love for him when he said that. Enough, at least, to stay, and long enough to get what she wanted.

Ten hit singles and sufficient industry savvy to make it on her own.

In any case, by her eighteenth birthday, they had both

had enough. Corrine of playing arm candy, always taking second billing at parties and premieres: 'Wilson and his girlfriend Sapphire.' She was a star in her own right now, as talented and enduring as him. With three whole years being Top Of The Pops, Corrine knew everything. She had that much in common with her fans.

Wilson too needed to move things along. Being with Sapphire had helped him lie to himself, and to his public. But Wilson was starting to realize he didn't really need to do either. After three years trying to train his sexuality down a straight road he decided to give up and started exploring the gay underworld of Eighties London.

Corrine got another eight years out of it before the hits petered out. Then her real age was revealed and the scandal of her past under-age affair with Wilson. It wasn't such a big deal back then, and it didn't do her too much harm. She had been taken advantage of. Led astray. Manipulated. Abused. Wilson took the flak gracefully, admitting that he knew her age but saying that their friendship was largely platonic. He announced that he was gay and started to wear a lot of sequins on stage. She had done him a favour, really.

Karl didn't renew her contract after that, and she got signed by a large US label who put the album out cheaply. Three mediocre albums later and it was all over.

Wilson had made sure her future was secure in those first three years. He knew. The pretty little pop singer, make her and let her break herself. She was so young, she was bound to underestimate him. With her first big advance, he made her buy a house for her parents in their name. She had wanted a car, even though she couldn't drive.

'You're an only child, chicken.' (She hated it when he called her that.) 'It'll keep them happy and it'll all be yours in the end, so what's the difference? You've got to think of the future.' Or rather, he had to think of her future. Wilson didn't want that on his conscience as well.

He had been right, of course. If her parents hadn't died and left her the house, she would never have been able to afford the place in Ireland.

Ironic that by the time it was over – after ten years, at least five of them riding high – her early, grudging investment was all she had left. That and the pile of tatty memorabilia in the attic, which she was clearing out for Sapphire's new 'den'.

Corrine wanted to give the twelve-year-old her own 'space' at the top of the grand Georgian two-storey house.

'But I've plenty of room down here, Mum.'

The house was rambling and there was only the two of them in it. But the truth was Sapphire seemed to be getting more clingy as she got older, and she was getting on her mother's nerves.

Sapphire had not been planned. Corrine had followed her then boyfriend to Ireland only a few weeks before she had been conceived. Sapphire's father was a talented but hapless recording engineer called Crimp who was working with the Irish rock band Godot at the time.

As Corrine's pop-star celebrity had faded, she fell, by accident, into journalism and discovered that she had a talent for writing. Having been on the receiving end of interviewers for years, magazine editors found that she had a unique ability to turn in insightful, intelligent interviews without attracting threats to sue. Finding that she had more of an ability to write than to sing, Corrine published a novel, which enjoyed very good reviews in the 'serious' papers and sold reasonably well. While she was frustrated at not earning the money she had earned in her early music days, Corrine none the less enjoyed the credibility that writing gave her. Being perceived as intelligent by the right sort of people was surely a progression from the shallow fame of her youth. It was the ultimate sideways move, and allowed her to fuel the idea that she had moved out of the industry by choice, in order to pursue a higher art form. 'Novelist' had a cache about it that 'ex-pop-singer' undeniably lacked.

Corrine continued to do her journalism. She had no choice. It was, and would remain to this day, a constant source of puzzlement and disappointment as to how little money she had actually earned during her days as a successful pop artist. Her early career had more or less carried her through the leaner years. Once Wilson was gone she had nobody really to advise her and by the time she had paid various managers, security and personal assistants their cut, she barely had enough to secure the deposit on the flat in Notting Hill. Songwriting royalties was the only way, she learned too late, of making money in the music business. Otherwise you were just a puppet on a salary, like the people in the office. Corrine needed the money she earned from journalism to keep her going.

Then she met Mal, Godot's charismatic lead singer, and it seemed like everything might be about to change.

Godot were, quite simply, the biggest rock band in the world. And what had earned them that position was not just a combination of powerful lyrics and emotive melodies, but their seemingly grounded, publicity-shy approach to fame. Of the four, Mal had the most appeal because he was the hardest to reach. Corrine was one of a handful of journalists in their ten-year career whom he had deigned to meet.

Up to that point Corrine had never had a crush on anybody in her life. She left that to the other person. There was more to be gained in having people fall in love with you than the other way around. She still could not say for sure that she was in love with Mal, but she knew, from that first moment, that she wanted him. He was certainly the first man whom she felt was great enough, beautiful enough, powerful enough to contain her. Perhaps even worth giving something up for.

Mal emptied the hotel suite as soon as she walked in.

'You can all fuck off now,' he said to the hangers-on that were there to protect their charge from the evil threat of media. Only the raised eyebrow of a seasoned fellow band member indicated he knew what was more than likely on Mal's mind.

'Do you want coffee?' he asked, indicating that, although he was enormously famous, he still knew how to pour his own coffee.

Corrine wasn't taken in by such homely tactics, but there was plenty else to be impressed with: a powerful imposing physique, a slightly scruffy, understated manner and one of those mismatched, striking faces that looked as if the features had been struck into the bones with a hammer. Corrine saw straight through him. The hair seemed unkempt, but it was carefully contrived to look that way. His T-shirt was crumpled and over-washed, but there was a cashmere thrown on the back of the chair that was worth at least two hundred pounds. This was no sweaty bog-boy. He was trying too hard. But the fact that he was trying at all meant that the game could begin.

'Tell me about your wife.'

That was her first question. Brazen and designed to put him on the defensive.

'She's my rock,' he said. A standard press answer. Rehearsed. Everyone knew that Mal Doherty screwed around. Probably, almost certainly, his 'rock' knew.

Corrine didn't even write it down. She just sat and silently stared at him, letting him tie himself in knots bumbling on about this woman, Helen, whom he pretended to care about. A more experienced interviewee would have known that instigating awkward silence was a standard journalism tactic, designed to make the subject ill at ease and babble themselves in and out of self-revelation. But for Mal, there was more to it than that.

'I met Helen before this all happened. She's the mother of my children and I love her.'

Everything he said sounded defensive, so he'd say it again to try and make it more convincing. 'Helen this, Helen that . . .' He kept repeating her name, trying to bring her into the room. As if reminding himself of his wife would somehow protect him against this terrible helplessness that was overtaking him just being in the presence of this woman. Mal had chosen to do the interview because he was curious about this pop singer turned music journo. He fancied her. And what he fancied, he generally took. But he was careful. He always chose. That was important. It was his rule, his way of keeping control of his comings and goings. He loved Helen, and while he liked to spread himself about – what man wouldn't in his situation? – he always kept it strictly physical and saved the emotional stuff, the important stuff, for his wife. She was the only woman who really rocked him, and he intended to keep it that way. Until now. Corrine was doing something to him that was beyond his control, and he could feel himself falling into her eyes.

So the inevitable happened, and the affair progressed. It was as passionate and painful as most serious affairs, and centred on the oldest theme. He loved her, but he wasn't going to leave his wife.

She said that was all right, but only because she didn't believe him.

Corrine was as deluded as every mistress, except that she had less patience than most. She ended it after six months, convinced he would fall apart and follow her.

Mal did fall apart, and it was his oldest, closest friend who suspected that an affair was behind his sadness. It just so happened that that person was also his wife.

Helen didn't say anything. She knew that Mal had a weak, artistic ego. He was the kind who would tell her everything she didn't want to know, then expect her to comfort and console him.

So she left the twins with their nanny and toured with Godot for the following year. No gaps for girls left open. Mal didn't mind. Falling for Corrine had lessened his appetite, and he was happy to concentrate on work, and then curl quietly into the safe care of his family.

Once Corrine realized that she was being blocked at every angle – with all their previous aiders and abetters ignoring her calls – her determination to reach him grew. She craved him. In the months they were apart, she began to see how being with Mal would be the answer to everything. His wife was an ordinary woman. She didn't understand him. That wasn't her fault. Corrine was his soul mate. She was different. He was different. They were meant to be together. She could write brilliant novels, and he could write brilliant music. They could be brilliant together. All she needed was to find a way in, and that was where poor Crimp came along.

He wasn't hard to find. All she had to do was investigate who would be working on Godot's next album, then seduce one of them. Crimp was the sort of easy-going guy who would let a girlfriend of two weeks tag along. He didn't care that she was a big-cheese journalist, or an ex-pop-star, or a novelist or even a beauty. She was just some bird who wanted to come along to Ireland for the ride. Corrine despised him, but she slept with him anyway because the rented cottage in Wicklow felt empty and cold, and she had experienced a brief and uncharacteristic crisis of confidence in her decision to leave her life in London behind and chase Mal.

By the time she got over it, she was pregnant.

'Come down to the studio today, babe, yeah?'

Crimp had been cajoling her to go into Dublin for weeks, and she kept steadfastly refusing, insisting that she was writing and would rather stay in Wicklow and work. In reality, he wanted to show the lads in the studio what he had tucked away back in the cottage, and she knew he'd be bragging and bandying her name about in front of Mal, which was perfect.

Three weeks passed and there was no phone call.

Four weeks, six.

On the day Mal finally rang her, Corrine was standing in the hall of a house she didn't own, in a country she didn't know, holding a positive pregnancy test in one hand and a fag in the other.

'I can't talk now,' she had said. Stunned by the bad timing of both, she had hung up.

Twelve years later, it was as if all the glamour and mystery of those days had never happened.

MEMORANDUM

To: Lucy Lemon – Editor

From: Timothy Macmillan – Publishing Director

Re: MoniKa/Alfie Smith At-Home Shoot

Got the first figures through and they are looking worse than we thought. Going down by the minute. This is really a disaster, Lucy – and seemingly the McIvor contract is watertight – so there's no going back on the £500,000, even though they reneged on delivering Alfie. I have never had so many letters of complaint. It seems Alfie has a huge fan base and they are not taking this well. We have two readers threatening to sue on grounds of emotional distress and the legal boys are taking the threats v. seriously. I know you're angry and want to give Hettie the chop, but frankly, this might not be the right time. She's our only real celebrity contact, and, especially after this, we'll be hard pushed to find another. We need her, for the time being anyway, to help us firefight as the only way I can see out of this mess is an exclusive with Alfie.

Let's see if we can turn this around,

Tim

3

19 January 1980

Dear Anne,

I hope you got over the bad spell of weather all right and that the baby is well. I cannot wait to see her again! I will get the bus down for a visit when the snow clears.

Best wishes to you and yours,

Miss Mannings

PS I am not in Tangier.

Molly studied the postcard sent to her mother by the old neighbour a few weeks after Molly was born. On the front of the postcard was an aerial-view photograph, probably taken in the 1960s, of a beach scattered with a few high-rise hotels. It must have looked impossibly exotic at the time. Certainly, it had caused huge amusement in the Walshe household: the very idea of the retired spinster who had worked in the local post office all of her life bothering to postscript the card, imagining that the recipients might think that she had taken herself off somewhere foreign. It had caused Jack Walshe, Molly's father, such humorous diversion from his many ailments that he had framed it and put in on the mantelpiece, where it had lived, behind the Child of Prague, for as long as his daughter could remember.

'Tangier!' he still exclaimed from time to time.

'She never went further than Galway in her life.'

'No, Mary. That's not fair, she was in Bundoran once.'

'That's right. She was getting treatment for the knees.'

'Did she send us a postcard from there?'

'She did surely, Jack. It said: "PS I *am* in Bundoran." '

Then the two of them would collapse again.

Margaret Mannings had always been a kindly woman by all accounts – but mad for the Church and always into everybody else's business. She had been a neighbour of her mother's family when Mary was growing up and after she had married Jack Walshe and moved back from England to open the B&B 'Miss' Mannings had stayed in touch.

'I'd have probably never married your father only for Miss Mannings,' Molly's mother was fond of telling Molly.

'She saw me kissing your mother in the park one night, and told the priest on us,' her father filled in.

'They came down and told my parents. I was eighteen. I'd have never lived it down if I hadn't followed through on him. I never kissed another man before nor since.'

'Not indeed that you ever wanted to!'

'Not indeed that I didn't get plenty of offers!'

Her parents were like that. Still madly in love and on top of each other all the time. They doted on Molly, of course, being their only child. But at the same time, she knew they were wondering when she was going to move away and get on with her life. She was twenty-three, and her mother had been married at nineteen.

'That Mallarkey lad above in Newstop is cracked on you.'

Molly would shrug.

'Jesus, Mam, you'd think you wanted rid of me? Is it the room you want? Because I'll move out for the summer season if you want. I can kip down in Aoife's.'

'Don't be ridiculous. I just want you to be happy, and you can't be happy stuck here with your mam and dad all the time.'

But that was the problem really. Molly was happy. The B&B was big – seven guest rooms in all. She had tea- and coffee-making facilities in her bedroom, and an en-suite shower *and* a TV. You didn't get much more independent than that! In the summer months Molly was quite happy to get up at seven and help her father put on breakfast for the guests.

Molly enjoyed her job in the chemist's; she had her gossip magazines every week to look forward to, and Killa was a great town. OK – so it wasn't Galway or Dublin. There were only six pubs in it, but they were packed during the summer with visitors. And if people came here on their holidays – there must be *something* special about the place. The winters were long enough, but there was always plenty going on, and Moran's had extended out the back and were planning to turn their function room into a proper nightclub. Since Molly had started working, she'd met all kinds of interesting people from round about.

Everybody needed a prescription sooner or later, and where Molly thought she had known everybody there was to know from school and mass and growing up in the area, she had found all kinds of new faces were starting to crop up in the surrounding areas that Flynn's chemist supplied. There was Corrine, for instance, who came in at least once a week for shampoo and cosmetics. She was very stylish and Molly often minded her twelve-year-old – a lovely little girl called Sapphire – while Corrine headed off for the night with her new boyfriend, the local DJ Father Enda.

Mr Flynn was a great boss and let Molly run the cosmetics counter in whatever way she saw fit. The reps came up from Dublin to see her, and she was in charge of buying all the stock. It was quite a responsibility for a girl of her age and she took it very seriously. In such a small place, you couldn't afford to go recommending a lipstick that didn't suit or selling on some 'miracle' wrinkle cream unless you knew for sure it was going to get results. So Molly made sure she was fully informed about every item she stocked. She ran an 'open house' policy as far as cosmetics were concerned. Encouraging the customers to come in and 'experiment' under her expert guidance, and rewarding purchases with a 'goody bag' of new samples. Two years ago she had sold more make-up than any other single chemist in the country for a big cosmetics company, and had been rewarded with an overnight trip to Galway staying in a swanky hotel and attending a make-up seminar by the American make-up artist Julian August. A framed certificate, signed by the man himself, sat on her glass counter and Molly used it as inspiration on tough jobs like, say, showing Rita Cooney, for the umpteenth time, how to conceal the map of raised moles that peppered the vain old woman's face. In the summer just past, Molly had set up a nice little sideline in making local girls up for their weddings. And not just the brides. Mothers and bridesmaids often brought a good few hundred euros into her back pocket. Then there was her friend Aoife Breslin, who worked as a model up in Dublin. She persuaded Molly to help her organize a fashion show for her mother's shop. The first Breslin's Ladies' Wear Spring/Summer International Fashion Show had taken place at Donlan's Hotel and had been a huge success, raising over fifteen hundred euros for the local Under Sixteens' G.A.A. Team. Molly had helped dress the girls (a selection of the town's best specimens plus Aoife's new friend Karla, a stunning six-footer from Lithuania), and done all of the make-up. The clothes weren't great; the 'international' end of the collection basically comprising some German mother-of-the-bride suits which swam on the girls. But the atmosphere was electric, with gasps of pride from the proud parents, plenty of 'g'wan, ya good thing's from the lads of the town, and a disco afterwards that raged into the early hours.

They were already planning the next Breslin's Autumn/Winter show, and Aoife had great plans to bring down a rake of girls and a top DJ from Dublin. What with that, and weddings booked for almost every Saturday between now and Christmas, Molly had enough on her plate without thinking about lads or moving out of home.

And she would have been more than able to avert her mother's niggling if it weren't for the issue of Miss Mannings' money.

Miss Mannings had never married. The prognosis on her lifetime's single status was obvious to everyone but herself. Even as a young woman she had favoured a brash outspoken pragmatism that any man would have found hard to live with. Through her teens and early twenties, her parents had tried to fix her up with every neighbouring farmer. But even they recognized that Margaret's greatest selling point was a hefty physique, ideal for baling hay and birthing calves, but not apparently advantageous to the marital duty of conjugal relations. She was also prone to speaking her mind in an age where open expression was considered anathema to successful marriage.

So Miss Mannings stayed at home with her parents until they died, and got herself a job in the local post office where she dreamed of foreign travel. She collected postcards, communicating with regional post office workers from around the world, fantasizing in turn about some gorgeous postcard hunk turning up in Killa one day and whipping her off somewhere impossibly exotic. Of course, she never let on. To the world, Miss Mannings remained the plain plump old busybody, the very antithesis of glamour. Nobody could ever have guessed the yearning for excitement and romance that she carried about with her all of her life.

Until after she died. Thousands of postcards were found in her small cottage – many of them from pen-pal lovers, written in reply to a woman who had clearly presented herself to them as a flaxen-haired twenty-five-year-old sex kitten. Perhaps, people commented as word of her secret life spread, that's who she really was all along. In which case a few shortsighted farmers had missed out on a golden opportunity.

Then there was the will. To their amazement, Miss Mannings had left a portion of her savings, some five thousand pounds, to Jack and Mary Walshe's infant daughter. It was a ludicrously complicated document but it stood up to legal scrutiny, as did its proviso that the money was to be given to the child when she was eighteen and the money spent on 'seeing the world'.

Molly, like any teenager, had wanted to blow it on outfits and make-up and buying burgers for her friends in Caffola's, but her parents had held firm to Miss Mannings' wishes. So the money sat there, in the Credit Union, accruing interest. Almost nine thousand pounds it totalled now, and most of the time it was just something that was there. Like an old forgotten photograph, or an ornament that has been in the house so long that you no longer see it. Molly never needed extra money. She had enough for everything she wanted, and she got all the cosmetics she wanted for free! But every once in a while, like today, she would be wiping down the mantelpiece and take the card out of its frame and try to will herself into wanting to go to Tangier.

'I am *not* in Tangier,' she would say to herself, trying to drum up a bit of what Miss Mannings would have felt. A curiosity, some little pellet of desire she could build on. But there was nothing there. A vague regret perhaps, but nothing tangible and strong enough to make her want to do anything about it. So she would clip the card back in its frame, put it back behind the Child of Prague and forget about it.

Until the next time. Which was to come sooner than she thought and from a completely different place.

Offices of *2 DAY* magazine
'Britain's *BEST* celebrity weekly!'

MEMORANDUM

To: Hettie Flinthrop – Celebrity co-ordinator

From: Lucy Lemon – Editor

Re: Alfie Smith

Fucking find him. NOW!

4

'What have you done with the potatoes, Sim?'

Helen was having a handful of VIPs over for supper that night.

'They cooked.'

Sim smiled broadly at her, as if the power of her goodwill alone had boiled the water.

'Good. Where did you put them?'

'In stew. I put them in stew. Nice.'

Pheasant slow-cooked in old port ruined with a layer of disintegrating spud. Fuck.

She turned the heat off and grabbed a serving spoon and started to scrape wildly at the offending vegetable.

'I did wrong, Miss?'

Sim's face collapsed, and she looked tearful.

'No, Sim, it's fine. Really. Pass me the bin.'

Sim looked confused.

'The bin. Over there. Rubbish! Rubbish!'

And as her new housekeeper sauntered across the kitchen to get the Brabantia, Helen stood in quiet despair, watching as lumps of watery mash fell onto her Manolo mules.

Actually, it wasn't fine. Helen craved good 'help'. At times like this, when she had a lot going on, the effective running of her home seemed paramount and it took on a physical longing.

Perhaps it was, as only the wealthiest élite will admit in the company of one another, away from the horrified ears of the politically correct or the hopeful empathy of the moderately wealthy, that 'one simply *cannot* get the help these days'.

While the twins were small Helen had run the house herself, with help from various housekeepers and babysitters from the local village. Ironically, now that the fundraising was taking up most of her time, she found she needed help around the place more than ever, though the twins were big enough to look after themselves.

Money was not a problem, or space. It was time. Mal didn't want any 'strangers' living in the house. So then Helen had to oversee the building of a guest cottage on the grounds of their Wicklow estate and as was always the case when they had to employ people to do things for them, there was the 'money is no object' issue.

As well as being a high-profile fundraiser, Helen gave heavily herself to charity. And there was nothing she hated more than being ripped off. The way she looked at it, twenty grand skimmed off the top of a job to pay for the builder to upgrade his five-year-old Mercedes was not an act of charity. People who had plenty of money to be getting along with, but less money than her, were the worst offenders. She had met people who had nothing, travelled to some of the projects she helped raised money for. She had met families that had no food, no clothes, no home and been taken at face value. Then she gets some builder, who lives in a six-bedroom house in Naas, spinning her a line about needing an extra thirty grand to 'finish the job' and getting all 'tight bitch' on her when she objects to putting in Royal Doulton bathroom suites, which she knows well were seconds he got for free and is going to try and charge her full price for.

They would never pull that shit on Mal. But then, Mal was protected by the celebrity aura thing. He walked into a room, and outside of their close circle, people just stared at him open-mouthed. They forgot about bathroom suites, or thirty grand to finish the job, or preparing the dinner, or hoovering the hall, or whatever it was they were supposed to be doing. All they could compute in that moment was 'I am standing in a room with/building a house for/mashing potatoes for/hoovering the hall of *Mal Doherty.*'

Helen had been watching this for years: people suddenly thinking in hushed tones; becoming overwhelmed by the fact of his fame and temporarily losing track of themselves. It was always the problem with staff. There was a danger that, no matter how educated or seemingly pragmatic they were in the interview, when it came to actual contact with the enigmatic Mal Doherty, they became distracted – in some unfortunate cases, like the undercover fan from Germany posing as a qualified nanny, dangerous. Helga had literally flung herself at her hero's feet, dropping Fionn as she fell. They had to call the police to remove her from the house and Helen had spent the night in Crumlin children's hospital. They hadn't pressed charges. It wasn't worth the publicity. Helen dispensed with any thoughts of hiring a nanny after that.

With housekeepers, Helen would bring them in from any country she thought might not have heard of Godot. Sim was from Thailand. But after just a few weeks living in Europe, and with the help of MTV, she knew who she was working for. She was smitten, and it didn't make Helen's life any easier. Sim meant well, Helen knew that, but meaning well didn't make the beds or prepare a meal for three wealthy businessmen and their wives from whom she was trying to extract sponsorship. Being in the home, in the presence of the great Mal Doherty, wouldn't be enough for these guys. Men like this didn't take time out from a hectic schedule and staff up their private planes for a plate of mash. She'd have to phone Thierry, their private chef, and get him in at the last minute. There'd be dramas and tears, and much clanging of saucepans, but in the end their plates would be piled with some complicated confection that only a Michelin-star chef could have produced. It was a shame because Helen had wanted this evening to be a low-key family affair centred around a home-cooked meal. When you have untold wealth, simplicity takes on real value.

Mal was home at the moment. When he wasn't touring or recording, which was about one-third of the year, Mal was hanging around the house. Playing with new gadgets in his studio or sucking up to the twins who were increasingly trying to distance themselves from their famous father and carve out their own identities. Being married to Mal wasn't like being married to other men. His contribution to running the household was, frankly, nil. She managed the money, keeping tabs on the various accountants, advisors and managers who kept the whole Doherty wealth ball rolling. As for house management: cooking, making sure the driver had a sandwich at lunch-time, checking the twins for hash (no) and condoms (yes) before they went out, calling the house-messaging service that fielded crank calls, paying cash to the man who delivered their organic foodstuffs once a week, and the million and one ways that Helen kept their lives running with minimum interference from the outside world, Mal didn't even know it was all going on. He was an artist. He wrote songs that were brilliant and brought them in loads of money. When he came home he wanted to enjoy the family life that his touring and recording paid for. That the two-thirds of his year that he spent working contained certain recreational 'benefits' was not something either of them openly acknowledged. He was always glad to be home, happy to be cocooned in the warm, clean, safety of family life.

Helen had met Mal in the days before he was famous, when he was part of just another struggling band who were fuelled entirely by their own egos and self-belief. He was a good-looking wannabe rock singer, and she was a good-looking waitress who did a bit of modelling to make ends meet. When the band got signed to a small London label she was delighted for him. From a respectable middle-class family, who were reluctant observers of their daughter's romance with this 'rough-neck' from the Northside,

Helen herself secretly believed that, with his good brain, Mal would eventually go to college and get himself a proper job. They were both young. There was time to waitress and model and muck about with mates with guitars before they settled down. Even at that young age, Helen knew enough not to express her conventional aspirations to Mal. Best let him get the whole music thing out of his system, and then they could move to the suburbs. When Godot's first single became a huge hit, she was surprised. Their first album went platinum, and she panicked slightly, not knowing quite what it meant.

They married on a beach in Florida during Godot's first American tour. Mal had arranged the whole thing, priest and caterers and all. Or rather, his manager had. It wasn't what Helen wanted, and she thought she would have major explaining to do to her parents when she got home. But Mal was on the cover of *Rolling Stone* that month, and Helen learned then what it meant to be with an enigmatic international rock idol. The beach wedding was what Mal wanted. And what Mal wanted, Mal got. That was the new rule. Their entourage numbered some thirty people. Managers, make-up artists, technicians, musicians, stylists – thrown together in a tour bus, all caught up together in the glory of this new successful fate. They all knew about this 'surprise' wedding, and not one of them had thought to tip Helen off. Mal Doherty wanted to take her as his wife. Of course, they had talked about it before then. But none of the other people involved could have known that. All they knew was that, at that moment in time, Helen Dunleavy was the luckiest woman on earth. When she called her family, expecting the worst, they too were delighted for her. Everyone in the whole world, it seemed, thought it had been a marvellous gesture. So that was how Helen had played it ever since. She was the luckiest woman alive. If she had doubts or misgivings about Mal's loyalty or fidelity, she put them aside. If she was irritated by his lazy, sometimes sullen attitude to his home life, Helen had no end of female friends to advise her on 'how lucky she was' that he came home at all. To subtly offer the implication that, if he was unfaithful, he never did it on his own doorstep. She knew that, essentially, he loved her and would never abandon her and the children for some supermodel floozy. There had been that one time, years ago, when she knew he had fallen in love with somebody else. They had never spoken about it, but Helen had played the dutiful rock-wife and followed him on tour – almost a year away from her children but it had been worth it to secure their future. The charity work had gradually grown, and Helen now had something of her own to concentrate her energies on. When Mal was at home, he played second fiddle to her fundraising, like she had done for years to his music. He didn't seem to mind too much and said he was proud of her, even and especially in interviews and at public events. At concerts, all over the world, he ended each with a homily to his 'wonderful lady' and asked people to dig deep and give to her causes in containers at the door. She had to have the containers designed and produced and the exits covered by volunteers at every event. He got the glory – but Helen got the money, and she got to hand it to the people who needed it. There was more satisfaction in that than she had ever imagined possible, and it drove her to do more.

While Mal was at home in Wicklow, Helen made the most of his presence to benefit her causes. Everyone wanted to meet him, but it was the corporate chairmen, the politicians, heads of state – those people who were interested in adding the glamour of the artists, the cult of celebrity to their coterie of 'friends' – she needed to get on side if she was truly to make a difference in her work. This was networking at its highest level, courting and cajoling through the promise of friendship and 'home-cooked' meals.

Thierry was briefed over the phone and arrived at six, two hours before the guests were due. His commis followed him laden with two crates of ingredients. He was in confrontational form, as he always was when called in on short notice.

'You say you want simple. I give them chicken. It will be shit. They will eat shit. Mr Important Person, here is a plate of shit for you to eat. And for your wife? Some shit also.'

Sim had never met Thierry before and stood shaking in the corner. This was all her fault. She wasn't sure if he was there to cook or to punish her. In Thierry's case it was nearly always both.

Helen smiled. 'Thanks for coming at such short notice, Thierry. I know you'll do something wonderful.'

'Ah yes. But I can do something wonderful if I have ingredients. I can call Paddy and say what you have for me? You have some grouse? Some pig? You kill pig for me and cure for three days maybe? I roast in garden. I pick fruit from garden for compote. We build pagoda and eat under stars. Is beautiful. Is simple.'

He looked tearfully at Helen for a moment, lost in the fantasy of what might have been, then flung the saucepan he had just removed from the cupboard (for he worked while he ranted) across the room. Sim whimpered and his commis, well used to it at this stage, raised his eyes to the ceiling, and got on with unpacking the boxes.

'Why, Helen? WHY? You give me no time. I go to supermarket. SUPERMARKET! Imagine Thierry in supermarket? IN *DUNNES STORES*, HELEN! I get chicken. I cook chicken – not from Paddy who make chicken, who *love* chicken, who *feed* chicken. Paddy with his yellow chicken with the fat boobies and the lovely flavour. Hmmmm – is like butter. Not these chicken from supermarket, they *sa-ad* chicken. They full of the hormonals. They taste of shit. So tonight I give your guests this shit to eat and they says, "Thierry. We heard he is great chef and he cook us chicken what taste like shit? Whass going on?" Is not worth it, Helen. Is not worth it to me – great chef. Is last time, Helen. Is last, *last* time I do this for you.'

Helen tried to look as penitent as she could. This was why she preferred to cook herself. In truth she was fed up with having to face into attitude every time she wanted something done. If she wanted attitude, all she had to do was talk to the twins. But she didn't have time to argue, and she still had to go upstairs and make herself look respectable, not to mention pep-talk her surly husband into behaving himself tonight.

She walked over to the hysterical chef and held both of his hands.

'You're a genius, Thierry. An Artist. I promise, *promise*, I will never do this to you again.'

He melted, as he always did. As the guests would tonight, opening their hearts and their wallets. When she needed to, Helen knew she could really turn on the charm. It's just that sometimes, just sometimes, she wished she didn't have to.

NOSEY PARKER

'I'M JUST HONEST – THAT'S ALL'

Our man Honest Ron Parker reports on the stars and their scandals

PUT THEM IN THE VOMIT COMET RON!

This week's candidates are newly-weds MoniKa and Alfie Smith. Readers this week, and next week, and every week for ever f****** more in all probability, were treated to a truly nauseating display of celebrity w*** as their 'intimate, family' wedding was splashed all over *2Day* magazine. Paid a reported one million pounds for 'exclusive coverage', this is a typical example of how today's celebrities are taking control of the media while genuine investigative reporters like myself get left out in the cold. When they are starting out they are all over us looking for free publicity, then when they 'make it', they try and charge us a million quid to see them go 'I do'. Well, I don't, Alfie. Buy it, that is. This paper has too much integrity to pay jumped-up little boy-banders who already have far more than they deserve. So you can take your dicky bow and your stick-insect wife and you can shove them up your a***!

THE VOMIT COMET: WHERE THE STARS BECOME *REAL* STARS AND FLOAT AROUND IN OBSCURITY FOR EVER!

Alfie says: 'I'm giving the money to charity.'

We say: 'Don't make me vomit, mate!'

Do you want to see Alfie and Mon in the Comet tomorrow?
Phone 080027821 for Yes, 080027822 for No and 080027823 for Not Sure.

(Calls charged at a rate of £5 per minute.)

5

Wilson slid his feet out from under the sheets, and into the security of his slippers, which he left in exact alignment just poking out from under the Cath Kidston commissioned valance every night. Except they weren't there. Stephen had moved them again. Of course, he shouldn't have had to put them there himself in the first place. Strictly speaking that was Carol the housekeeper's job. But sometimes, if you want something done right, you have to do it yourself. This was the third night in a row he had woken at three a.m. to find his boiled cashmere mink-lined comforters moved. Hidden. Confiscated. The third night in a row he was faced with the prospect of having to pad down to the kitchen in his bare feet. The slipper-hiding had started some six months ago, but had stopped of late, and Wilson had been lulled into a cruel sense of security. Now it was happening again. It really was too, *too* much. Last night he had picked up a crumb on the six-corridor journey which had imbedded itself painfully into his instep.

'I have dropped arches,' he had said to Stephen moodily the following morning, 'I'm in agony.'

A pause for effect elicited nothing.

'Some people think it's not important, but it's a serious condition. The specialist told me.'

Stephen had barely raised his eyes from that month's *Wallpaper** magazine. He didn't care. Nobody cared. Wilson thought, I could chop my own foot off here and now, and nobody would even notice.

'I can't walk barefoot – even on carpets. The specialist told me.'

Still no reaction.

'I could permanently damage my feet.'

Stephen took a mouthful of Special-K but kept his eyes firmly on this magazine.

'I'll end up in a wheelchair.'

Nothing.

'That's what the specialist reckons, anyway.'

Of course he should have said, 'Stop hiding my fucking slippers, you arrogant little cunt!' That's what he would have said if it was anyone except Stephen, and they would have jumped. Staff, the vast number of medical 'specialists' he paid to diagnose-up his minor ailments into 'serious conditions', even his manager who had put up with decades of abuse knew better than to defy his old friend when it came to his 'little indulgences'.

'It's the small things that matter to me,' Wilson was fond of stating publicly.

'All this –' he had stated grandly at their Spring Ball for five hundred of their closest friends, sweeping his arms across the marquee laden with out-of-season delphiniums and an indoor lake inhabited with swans, tamed and trained especially for the occasion, 'means *nothing*. I could live on a council estate in Colindale once I've got a few of my favourite bits and pieces and my boy with me,' and he had looked lovingly across at Stephen. Everyone at the table had nodded assent, apart from the one person who wasn't so independently rich and famous that he couldn't actually mentally and emotionally process what life on a council estate in Colindale was like.

'Yeah, right!' Stephen announced sarcastically.

Not for the first time, the sceptics who had believed that Wilson's relationship with his feisty good-looking fitness instructor would 'never last' froze in their seats awaiting a 'scene'. Live swans over your black-tie gourmet dinner came at a price and their generous host's tantrums were legendary.

'I mean it, Stephen. Take my slippers—'

'Oh, not those *fucking* slippers again.'

'So they were expensive. Boiled cashmere, mink – I had them made,' he added, quite unnecessarily, 'they needed a special medical instep built. I have dropped arches.'

One aspiring actress actually reached over and gripped Wilson's hand in acknowledgement of his bravery. 'I had a bunion removed last year,' she whispered, then winked and mouthed conspiratorially, 'We'll talk later', no doubt hoping the chiropody bond would be enough to secure her a place on the couple's annual yacht weekend in Antibes.

'Tell them how much they cost, Wilson.'

The fifty-seven-year-old's forehead twitched behind the botox.

'That's not the point.'

'It is if you live on a council estate in Colindale.'

'They were three thousand pounds,' he muttered. The cost of one trained, rented swan, the collective company thought. Cheap at twice the price.

'But the point is I *love* those slippers—'

'Yeah – and if you had them and me you'd be able to live anywhere.'

'Once you've found love, it doesn't matter where you live. Am I right?'

Wilson was addressing everyone at the table except Stephen. This last statement rang bitterly true to the table of ten who had clocked up twelve divorces with a value of seven million in alimony between them. Stephen's sneer sliced through their sycophantic nodding.

'Of course, dear. Versailles? The yacht in Antibes? The Riyadh in Tangier? Shall we take a suite in the Plaza this Christmas? Doesn't matter where you live. God, Wilson, you do talk a load of crap sometimes.'

The new-best-friend actress decided, prematurely as it turned out, to take Wilson's side.

'I know just what Wilson means. When you're in love with somebody, it doesn't matter where you are as long as you're to-ge-ther.'

And she made the mistake of pointing at the two men at opposite sides of the table and bringing her fingers together over the last word.

'That's right. I *heard* you bought a little shack in Peckham with the grip after Mr Hollywood dumped you.'

One false move and she plummeted down the social

ladder taking the weekend in Antibes and a long-lens topless-on-deck shoot in *Hello!* magazine with her.

Wilson laughed and the rest of the table followed. It was wicked, but she had walked right into it.

'Love is *always* in context. Would I be with you if you were a plumber with a two-up, two-down in Orpington? Let me think about that for a minute . . .'

And the assembled company inwardly winced knowing full well what the honest answer would be and praying that he'd lie. Not just for Wilson's sake, but for the sake of every rich fool who believed they weren't loved for their money.

'I don't *think* so!'

'So you're with me for my money?'

'Partly.'

'Mostly? Fifty / fifty?'

'Sixty / forty.'

Everyone was smiling like they understood the joke, but none the less keeping their heads down in case they'd be asked to join in.

'No, scrap that. On reflection, darling, I'd say it was more seventy / thirty.'

'Ouch – that hurts.'

'You don't *look* hurt, dear,' and Stephen turned to the actress: 'Do you think he looks hurt? I don't think he does.' Displaying uncharacteristic wisdom, she excused herself on nose-powdering grounds and didn't come back for dessert.

'I'm crying inside.'

'Torn up, I can tell. Isn't the botox great, though – the way it hides a multitude of emotions?'

'Are you calling me emotionless?'

'Emotionless? No. A tad *cold*, maybe.'

'So now I'm cold. I am *not* fucking cold. Ask anyone here. Am I a cold person? Karl? You've been my manager for forty years. Am I cold? Am I? Am I?'

'What the fuck would they know? They don't have to live with you.'

'And just *what* is that supposed to mean?'

'You want me to tell them? You want me to spill it all out here in front of everyone?'

'Spill out what? I've got nothing to hide. I'm an open book.'

'Nothing *worth* hiding, you mean.'

'Except, it seems, my fucking cashmere slippers which, by the way, were missing again last night.'

'You see . . .' Stephen said, looking around the table, 'what I have to put up with. Petty. Spoiled. It's like living with a child.'

'Aha. Now we have it. Except you're not – isn't that the thing? Are you? And that's what this is all about.'

'What?' Stephen said.

'*You* know what I mean.'

Stephen let it go – whatever it was – and the evening continued without feathers flying, of the swan *or* boa variety.

That was the way it had become for this couple of ten years' standing. Sniping at one another in public; able to start a fight knowing that the propriety of privacy would prevent them finishing it. At home they kept the lid firmly screwed down on the real story. Stephen hid Wilson's slippers, and Wilson lit his daily cheroot over the breakfast table and gleefully blew smoke over his fitness-obsessed partner's muesli.

Aside from the single issue that divided them, the fifty-something singer / songwriter and his younger partner were doing pretty well. They had certainly been 'married' longer than most of their friends.

Wilson had picked Stephen from a cast of thousands of good-looking fitness 'specialists' whom he had employed throughout the eighties and nineties. Their job was to 'police' his drinking and smoking, contradict his (largely accurate) self-deprecating comments about himself by pretending that his limp, ten-minute daily 'work-out' was showing results, and backing up the various ludicrous diet plans which he never stuck to. Mainly their job was to look cute in a leotard then lie back and think of Gucci.

Stephen had walked out of their first session before Wilson had even had the chance to reach into the 'gifts for lovers' drawer he kept in the gym.

He had been professional but firm.

'I'm sorry, but I only work for people who are serious about their bodies.'

Wilson had played the cute, flirtatious card by assuring this well-hung young newcomer that he might not be serious about his own body, but he was extremely serious about his.

Stephen had given him a look that suggested he had never heard anything quite so lecherous and revolting in all his life, and refused his fee.

Wilson had been hurt. He had developed a sixth sense

around who would and who wouldn't over the years. All of his boyfriends had been short-term. Slags and money-grabbers in the main. If there had been a jot of genuine affection between them, he hadn't spotted it. Wilson was philosophical and resigned about his physical appearance. He knew he was no oil painting, but he was talented and rich. He could have been a good-looking painter and decorator and would he have been any happier? He'd never know. He loved people. His mother, his house-keeper Carol and Karl, his manager, in a funny brotherly way. He shared and expressed love, his fantasy of it at least, through his powerful ballads and that made him loved and appreciated by millions of people all over the world. The fact that he was a small, stout, ordinary-looking man only increased his popularity. How many people enjoyed that adulation? It wasn't intimate, but then that was a sacrifice he was happy enough to make.

His decision not to pursue Stephen was wise, as it turned out. They had met again at a party thrown by Madonna, who Stephen had been working with while her regular guy was on leave. He had looked stunning, in low-key well-cut Prada. Wilson had the same suit in his vast collection, but had needed it custom-built to fit his short legs and torso. Stephen's was straight off the peg. Model size.

Stephen had waited patiently outside the constant circle that surrounded Wilson at these events and reintroduced himself with a warm politeness that was neither fanatical nor ingratiating. He put himself on the line by admitting that he knew very few of the celebrities and their hangers-on who were at the party, generously giving the feted celebrity space to either humiliate or accommodate him. Wilson chose the latter, and they sat and talked for the rest of the night.

'So you only work with beautiful people?' Wilson confronted him.

'That's right – and those people who want to be beautiful.'

'The ugly ducklings – like me?'

Stephen smiled. 'You're hardly a duckling.'

'I'm hardly a fucking swan either.'

'Are you fishing for compliments?'

Wilson was taken aback.

'Because if you are, I have to say I loved your latest album.'

Wilson waved it aside, as if it didn't matter.

'You're waving it aside as if it doesn't matter, and let me tell you, Wilson, it's *all* that matters.'

Stephen went on and Wilson listened, which, he noticed in that moment, was something he very rarely did. Nobody ever said anything much he thought was worth listening to.

'Only the really beautiful people know how unimportant beauty is. That's the con. You get born with it, or you pursue it, then you get it and it means nothing. See, every person in this room tonight – look at them,' and the two of them looked across at the glitzy and the glamorous, real and fake, 'not one of them wouldn't trade the way they look to be able to do what you do. They all want what you've got, Wilson.'

Wilson couldn't help himself. 'But I want you.'

He had to wait three weeks before the relationship was consummated.

'Let's just be friends,' Stephen had said, and Wilson had to curb his foot-stamping, instant-gratification instincts for the first time in years.

Stephen didn't want anything.

'I have enough money,' he said. 'I have everything I want.'

Nice sentiments, but Wilson had the upper hand on money versus morals. Stephen meant well, but at the end of the day, if one Prada suit is nice, then this season's entire Prada/Gucci menswear collections will be even better. Times them by three for the yacht in Antibes and hanging ready-to-wear in your suite at the Plaza, and you have really made an impact.

Wilson's money wasn't the whole story, but it had made a difference. If it hadn't, Wilson himself wouldn't have been happy. It was his contribution. Stephen's contribution was something else. The first night they spent together Stephen traced every inch of his older lover's body with the flat of his long elegant hands. Across the soft mound of his belly, along the mottled, freckled flesh of his arms to the stump of his neck. Wilson writhed, flinching with shame until Stephen's persistent comforting touch made him relent into trust.

Money had secured him his man, but the friendship that grew between them had made him stay. They had gone through Wilson's mother's death and lost several close friends together. Bought and sold houses together. Learned to ride horses, water-skied, given up sunbathing, smoking, drinking, mid-morning donuts together. They had thrown parties, travelled the world, lived the last ten years in fitness and in wealth together. They had had their ups and downs, but the ups were high and the downs largely petty affairs based on boredom easily assuaged with another trip, another tour, another party.

Now there was this rift. Born out of a serious issue that seemed, to Wilson at least, not entirely in his control. What do you do when your lover wants something that money cannot buy? Even after all this time, Wilson did not know the answer to that one.

As he stubbed his illegal breakfast cheroot out in his coffee saucer, and looked across at his lover, Wilson felt a sudden stab of fear that he might be on the brink of losing him.

6

'Excuse me, sir?'

Alfie pushed his sunglasses right up to the bridge of his nose and half turned towards the air hostess. Please God, don't let it be now.

'Could you please put your seat back up, sir? We're about to land.'

He had to stop himself giving her his special celebrity smile. The one he kept for nice waitresses and doormen to let them know he was 'one of them'.

Of course, Alfie wasn't one of them. If he was, he wouldn't be giving out winning smiles like they were candy, and people wouldn't respond to them as if they were just that.

It was one of those affectations that Alfie was becoming aware of in these past four hours since he had decided he didn't want to be famous any more. Like feeling a small pang of chagrin at having to buy his own airline ticket, and queue at the check-in desk. Not having a runner around to fetch him his breakfast from the cappuccino bar. God – I am a spoiled bastard, he thought as he willed himself into not giving a winning smile to the girl serving him. There was a thrill in this invisibility, but only when it was taken in the context of who he was. Part of him longed to say to the passenger sitting next to him: 'I'm the pop star Alfie Smith and nobody recognizes me. Isn't it *great!*' But of course, that would defeat the object. There was always the possibility that the tweedy man next to him might be some kind of an intellectual who had never heard of him. And how would that feel? he wondered. Would he be disappointed? Relieved? He had half a mind to strike up one of those peculiarly intimate aeroplane conversations.

'What are you doing in Dublin?'

'Just over for the day on business. And you?'

'Oh, I'm an international pop idol running away from my fame. Dublin was the first flight out and the only place I could go where I didn't have to show a passport.'

No, it wouldn't work. But Alfie was so excited. He didn't want anyone to know where he was, but at the same time he was fit to explode with how easy it had all been. He wanted to *tell* somebody, and had to keep reminding himself why he was doing this in the first place: to escape from everybody knowing everything about him.

And it had been easy. He had woken at four a.m. in the house in Holland Park and gone downstairs to fetch himself a glass of juice. MoniKa was fast asleep and the house was silent. He looked out of the kitchen window; the street was empty, and Alfie knew that London was asleep. His fans were dreaming instead of screaming and he felt safe. On his way back up to bed Alfie noticed that the breakfast things were laid out for the following day.

A plate of croissants arranged in a neat pile in the centre of the table and a bowl of washed strawberries. Then he remembered. At eight a.m., *2Day* magazine would be arriving to photograph 'Alfie and MoniKa in their elegant London home'. MoniKa would be playfully feeding him croissants and he would be smiling and they would look like a couple in an advert for low-fat butter. The caption would read, *'Alfie loves his morning croissant, but supermodel MoniKa has to watch her weight so she prefers fresh fruit.'* In less than four hours this silent sanctuary would be teeming with people. Alfie stood barefoot and naked in his new home and it was as if he was watching the following day unfold in front of him as a three-dimensional film. There would be a photographer, his assistants; a stylist, her assistants; a hairdresser, more assistants. MoniKa's loud homo make-up artist filling the air with his camp squawking and glittery powders. He'd be made to try on every item of clothing in the house. The drapes would be rearranged; there would be a person to spray the strawberries with water so they looked 'fresh'; a person to rifle through their kitchen in search of 'interesting implements' for the 'Alfie loves to cook – here he is peeling an artichoke' shot. Florists would arrive with vases full of complicated arrangements which they would have to pretend were theirs and would be allowed to 'keep afterwards'. The following day, his mother Sharon would arrive for a day's shopping in town. A driver and a security man would have to be laid on for herself and her new daughter-in-law, and at the end of the day MoniKa would give her a vase full of the free flowers, and Sharon would say they were 'perfect' and perpetuate the lie that MoniKa had picked them out for her personally.

After the frantic media circus that was their wedding, the young couple had spent ten days on a remote Caribbean island. Hidden from the world, they had swum naked, made love, prepared meals from the hamper of simple fresh ingredients left at the door of their beach house every morning. They were back two days, and while Alfie was not fool enough to have expected the idyll of their honeymoon to be continued into everyday married life, he had hoped that the house in Holland Park would become a space where they could hide away together.

If his vision of the *2Day* shoot made it clear that his home life was going to be a trashy publicity affair, it was coupled with a powerful, sudden clarity that this was not a life that he wanted.

⬬

After leaving U&Us, Alfie had spent a year hanging around his family at home. For the first few months, he got invited to the parties and the premieres, but when the PRs and party planners realized he wasn't going to come, the invitations stopped. Eventually, more quickly than he had expected, his life slipped back into more or less the way it had been before, except there was more money and every day was the weekend. He filled his mornings watching TV, afternoons at the local gym and evenings preparing meals and helping his mother around the house. Sometimes he went down to the local and met a few of his old schoolfriends, but conversations always came back to U&Us and

Alfie grew tired of their laddish jibing. He wanted to move on, but he didn't know where.

The band broke up shortly after he left, and Alfie watched them all slip, one by one, into obscurity. Two of them ended up in rehab. The others learned that while their good looks and moderate vocal talents worked collectively, it took more than a pretty face and an ability to harmonize to turn an ex-boy-band member into that Holy Grail of teeny-bop talent, a George Michael. Only one of them had that elusive 'star quality'. Dave Davidson knew it, and somewhere underneath the ennui that was gradually taking him over, Alfie knew it too. Ironically it was his ex-manager's pestering that eventually coaxed him back into the limelight.

He rang and rang and rang until finally Sharon was pleading with Alfie to take his call.

'I've a meeting set up with Wilson,' Dave announced triumphantly. 'He has a track left over from his last album and he wants you to record it.'

'Fuck you!' Alfie responded. But the following week when he was in London, shopping for clothes in Knightsbridge for want of anything better to do, Alfie found himself passing the grand Georgian building off Grosvenor Square that he knew housed the offices of KLM, Wilson's management company. He wandered in on a whim.

'Wilson about?' he asked the receptionist.

Even after Alfie's 'resting period', there was no need to ask 'Who wants him?' A phone call was made and Alfie was picked up by car and taken to the mansion in Hertfordshire for lunch.

Wilson had taken Alfie under his wing (metaphorically and actually as he had two custom-built angel's wings flanking the front gates of his estate). Alfie moved into a guest cottage on the estate and, for six months, he lived the gay couple's life of luxurious, protected celebrity. He started to write his own songs alongside the Godfather of Pop, and Wilson brought in a piano teacher to teach him the rudiments of music. Stephen, delighted to have 'someone who is *serious* about their body' to train, put him on a high-protein diet which, coupled with a rigorous weight-lifting routine, turned him into a veritable Adonis. More importantly than all of that, Wilson taught him that it all was about the music. The outrageously indulgent lifestyle of the world's most enduring and legendary pop star was something the old man was philosophical about.

'You've got to enjoy the ride, Alfie. You've had a taste of it, now you need to decide if you want to take it on to the next level. Do I wish the press would leave me alone sometimes? Yes, I do. Am I prepared to trade all this in lead a more "ordinary" life? Frankly, no. I write and perform songs. It's my job and I love it. If the papers want to dig up some rent boy I buggered in 1985 – well, then I've just learned to ignore it. Go to the odd premiere, throw the odd party – give them something to write about, then they leave you alone for a while.'

Alfie's friendship with Wilson hit the headlines after the three men attended an AIDS benefit in London's West End. Alfie hadn't wanted to go.

'I can't face it, Wilson. Can't I just stay here?'

'Sure you can – but I'd say, shit or get off the pot.

You've got the bones of a decent album which we can sign any day you want. My management boys are all geared up for a re-launch. If you want to go ahead with getting your stuff out there, you'd better get prepared for the pariahs' son. Anyway, fuck them! What are they going to say?'

ALFIE STEPS OUT FOR AIDS

Fuelling speculation that ex-teen-star Alfie Smith is part of a love tryst with songwriter Wilson and his lover Stephen Silke, the three men arrived at last night's AIDS benefit in London's Four Seasons Hotel in matching suits.

Alfie was fuming over breakfast the next day.

'Well?' Wilson asked him, smiling coyly. 'Are you?'

'I knew it . . .' Stephen added before he had time to answer. 'Haven't I said it to you, Will? With looks like that – it's such a *waste*!'

Alfie shuffled uncomfortably, unsure of how to respond without upsetting his friends.

'Well?' Wilson asked him again. 'Are you a filthy, depraved, moral-flouting . . .'

'. . . bum-banditing, pillow-biting . . .' Stephen helpfully added.

'. . . homosexual?'

'No,' Alfie answered quietly.

'Are you sure?' Wilson tortured him further.

'I mean – absolutely *certain*, now?' Stephen went on.

'No twinges? No secret little fantasies you want to tell your Uncle Wilson abou—'

'I am *not* gay,' Alfie said a little too assertively. 'Definitely,' he added more quietly, lest they thought he was protesting too much.

His hosts exchanged crestfallen glances.

'Well, then. What's the problem?'

Alfie was flummoxed.

'Well – *this* is the problem,' he said, waving the front page over the table.

Wilson took a generous bite of Danish pastry. 'How so?'

'Look at him!' Stephen said, raising his eyes at Alfie. 'Sugar-loaded carbs. Pure poison. You'll have a heart attack, Wilson. I'm *telling* you!'

Alfie was infuriated by their laissez-faire attitude.

'It's all right for you guys – this story – but what about—'

'Your public image?'

'Yes!'

'Your poor mother?'

'Yes!'

Wilson put the Danish pastry down, somewhat regretfully, and Stephen snatched it away and finished it.

'Grow up and chill out, Alfie. Sharon won't give a shit, unless you're gay and you haven't told her.'

'I'm not g—'

'We *know*. So she'll call you all upset, and then *you'll* be all upset, then she'll get *more* upset. For fuck's sake, Alfie, *this* . . .' and he grabbed the paper and screwing it up, chucked it on the floor, 'is just the beginning. You'd better get used to it. It's meaningless crap. Those poor bastards are just doing their job – so just do yours. Calm your mother down and shrug it off when she calls. In a few months' time you'll be out with some dolly and you'll be "Love Stud Alfie".'

'I was "Love Stud Stephen" back in the early days – do you remember, darling?'

'Yes, dear – you media slut, you.'

'Now I'm just plain old Stephen Silke.'

'Respectability is a terrible thing.'

'It's my age. Do you think I should step up on the facials?'

So Alfie made a deal with himself that he would be like Wilson and shrug it all off. He was re-packaged, re-launched, earned his first full million, and then some. He took control of his career and, as far as he could, of his life. That was the hard part. Wilson was an old hand. Settled. Alfie was too young to lock himself away in a mansion. He was rich – but not rich enough yet for the extravagance required to buy privacy in a world full of people who wanted to follow his every move. In any case, it would have been foolish of him to pretend that there weren't parts of it he didn't enjoy.

Sometimes he would come off stage on a high and it really did feel like he owned the world. The tour crew would be buzzing backstage waiting to tell him how brilliant his performance was – then they'd hit some club in a new city and there'd be free drinks, drugs if he wanted them, and he'd have the pick of every woman in the place.

Everyone was his friend, and sometimes he believed it was because he was special and it was what he deserved. When he had tired of all that, he had met MoniKa and, despite constant press intrusion, it had felt, for a while, like she was a stabilizing influence. Like they could find their own path through the chaos and create something intimate and exclusive. Alfie hadn't realized it until now, but he had wanted that 'thing' to be their home. In less than four hours, his illusion was going to be shattered.

For the second time in his career, Alfie didn't stop to think about the consequences. He just threw a few things in a gym bag and walked out of the house. He saw a lone cab trundling along the empty street, hailed it and went to the airport.

Dublin airport at eight a.m. was something of a shock. With only hand luggage, Alfie was through customs and standing in the middle of the wide arrivals hall unsure about what to do next. People were tutting and pushing past him and he felt horribly aware that without the cachet of 'quirky' fashion-icon celebrity, his striped woollen hat and old-man's overcoat probably made him look like a class-A nutter. Nobody was 'noticing' him. It was a strange feeling. Lonely and frightening. In front of him was a rotating Adshel lightbox and Alfie suddenly came up against his own wistful face on the cover of his latest album. Then it was gone. Then a car, a cereal, a woman in a bra – then his own face again. Now you see me, now you don't. Now you see me, now you don't. Now I am standing in front of myself. Now I'm gone again. But I'm still here, looking at a woman in a bra. Now I'm back again. Alfie found himself transfixed by the moving image, unable, somehow, to move his feet. Paralysed with panic, he became aware of an airport security man looking at him. Alfie was sensitive to being spotted, but not in this way. Security men were usually working for, not against him. He knew that he must look suspicious, and that if he didn't move away, the security guy would come over, recognize him and then? With a concerted effort, Alfie deliberately lifted one leg, then the other, until he found himself walking briskly towards the exit marked 'Taxi'. He stood, shuffling and mumbling to himself 'Hurry, hurry', at the back of the short queue, then threw his bag into the back of the large sedan before it even had time to stop.

'Where to?' the driver asked.

It was only then that Alfie realized – he hadn't the faintest idea where he was going.

The Smith Household,
Holland Park, London W11, England

To: mnKa@hotmail.com
From: Hettie@2day.co.uk
Re: Meets this afto?

Hey, Monny! Hettie here! Just catching up 2 C how U liked the shoot? Everyone thinks you and Shaz looked soopa-sexi and the house looked FAB. Gave Justin a tinkle this mo but he hasn't got back 2 me so I thought I'd send you a little 'e' to C if you fancied a meet up in Carluccio's this afto?

Hugs and kisses Hettie.

7

'Mummy! Mummy! Enda is on the radio, Mummy!'

Corrine felt middle-aged. The child she had reared was heading towards her teens but, while bright academically, Sapphire was young for her age, still playing with dolls and constantly seeking out the company of her mother.

'Don't call me Mummy. I've told you a million times, it's not my name.'

'Sorry, Corrine.' The child looked hurt. She was large and ungainly and wearing a pink lace-collared jumper of her mother's from the late Eighties that style-conscious Corrine had repeatedly tried to throw out. Sapphire was standing at the bottom of the ladder which led to the attic, shouting up.

'Will I bring the radio up so you can hear him? Will I?'

God, this fucking place, Corrine thought.

She was still rifling through her old stuff, willing herself to throw some of it out. In her hand Corrine was holding her first album. A photograph of herself at sixteen with a wide bleached streak obliterating one eye, the other heavily made-up and the self-explanatory title 'SAPPHIRE' splashed across it.

The album had gone to Number One. She had been a pop phenomenon in her mid-teens. So it was history, but it was still surely something? Interesting at least. But here, in this shitty little backwater, nobody cared. 'Father' Enda gets a radio show and everyone was beside themselves listening to his amateurish fables about 'being good to your neighbour' in between ancient Enya tracks.

Corrine had started an affair with an ex-priest from the district of Killa in which she lived. Enda was dull and earnest, making outdated attempts to act like a 'lay' man after his twenty years in the priesthood by growing his hair long and saying 'groovy' a lot. A word which he had ample opportunity to utilize in his programme, *Sounds of the Spirit*, on the local radio station. There was a lot of Enya although Christy Moore's dreary political warblings were also favoured. When he wanted to push the boat out and play something really 'groovy' you might be treated to a bit of early Van Morrison or a U2 ballad. Enda was inexperienced sexually and irritatingly innocent. Sometimes in his company Corrine felt slightly sick at having sunk so low as to get involved with a man merely because he was available and she had found herself living in a remote place where the pickings were so thin that an ex-priest with a ponytail was a 'good' bet. But then Enda was madly in love with her. And even if his infatuation was based on the false image she presented to him as a vague, willowy 'creative', it was better than being alone.

Once Sapphire was independent enough, Corrine planned to sell up and move back to London. She would re-launch herself as a journalist, maybe even write another book. Sapphire was resolute that she wouldn't board at school, and while Corrine's investments were running low, the Killa house and the land she had incidentally acquired with it had shot up in value due to their stunning views over the lake. She had kept and rented out the flat in Notting Hill – that in itself was now worth a fortune. It was time to cash in and re-create her life. Twelve years was long enough. Sapphire had had her turn. Corrine had sacrificed enough to be a good mother. It was time to get her life back.

Clearing the attic was the first step.

'Sapphire – come up and look what I've found.'

'But Enda's show, Mummy. Enda's telling one of his *stories*.'

<hr>

'*There's this guy, right, a really cool dude by all accounts,*' Corrine could hear Enda cooing in the distance, '*and he has this motorbike, yeah?*'

Enda had 'run it by' his 'lady' two nights ago, and Corrine had nearly vomited then so she wasn't about to listen to it again. '*Loves his motorbike more than anything . . .* blah . . . *runs over an old lady . . .* blah, blah . . . *has bike crash . . .* blah . . . *old lady's daughter helps him . . .* blah . . .' Moral: love your fucking neighbour as per usual, then.

'Enda can tell you the story later, darling. Come on up here and see what I've found.'

Corrine wasn't a bitch. She knew how to be nice to her child. She was a mother, after all. Sometimes she felt so stressed out, so claustrophobic – especially now, towards the end of the summer holidays when she had been with Sapphire, day in and day out for weeks on end – that she became aware she had barely spoken a kind word to her. Then Corrine would take the big twelve-year-old into her bed where they would watch TV and munch through a big bag of crisps together. In a conscious effort not to criticize Sapphire for stuffing in fistfuls at a time and dropping oily crumbs in the bed, Corrine would stroke her hair and tell her daughter she was pretty, even though they both knew it wasn't true. When she fell asleep, Sapphire was too big to carry into her own bed, and so unable to rest comfortably alongside the lumpy pubescent in her small double, Corrine would go and sleep in the cold spare room next door. She would wake in the mornings, chilled by the morning light through the curtainless windows and try to quell the feeling that had taken her over in the night. During the past two years, with increasing regularity, Corrine had woken in the mornings instantly angry. Like she had been injected with some kind of hate-poison. She directed her thoughts at tangible things and built on them: the ignorant little backwater in which she lived and its hick inhabitants; the dreadful boredom of trying to fill a day in rural Ireland; do-goody Enda and his bloody fables; the injustice of her own lousy love life; this wretched house and its endless supply of 'small' jobs that needed doing. Any complaint to distract her from the negative thoughts about Sapphire that seemed to dog her every moment. That the child was fat. That she was ugly. That she was altogether an inferior specimen to her glamorous, talented mother. That she was a clingy stupid child whom Corrine would be stuck with for the rest of her life. Corrine knew it was wrong to entertain such negative attitudes towards her own daughter, and so she just carried them around as facts about Sapphire that she simply knew. But in knowing them there was pity, then pain. In the pain, resentment. Then guilt. Then anger. Pity, pain, resentment, guilt, anger – not exactly a winning combination for a happy life. Corrine tried to stay around the middle of the scale, loitering in resentment which was easy enough to cover up. Pity was pointless and anger wasn't great, but if she had to choose between the two, she'd sooner lose her temper than, God forbid, have to listen to Sapphire whingeing. And that, Corrine knew more than thought, was the whole problem, really. Since Sapphire had been born, Corrine's whole life, as she saw it, had been subsumed by this other person. This tiny new life had overwhelmed her. In the beginning, with a feeling of maternal love. Nothing had ever felt more complete to Corrine. No man had ever filled her with this extreme feeling of joy, of wonderment, of unconditional, absolute love. She felt miraculous, the recipient of God's glorious gift of life. Another human being that was totally in her care. She was completely in the thrall of this tiny, breathing, burping miracle. More amazing to Corrine still was how she felt herself. The fear and the humiliation of the pregnancy faded away and took with it everything that had ever happened to her before Sapphire was born. The pop career, the book, Mal Doherty, even the father of the child and his concerns that she might expect him to hang around, all became insignificant. Everything apart from the love she felt for her child in that moment got swept off to a faraway place called history.

The infatuation lasted, in one form or another, through Sapphire's infancy and into early childhood. Corrine moved around in the first few years. Back to London before the birth, and into her parents' home in Golders Green. Her father had died a painful death from cancer that had run almost parallel to the first seven months of her pregnancy, and her mother was eager for the distraction of her first grandchild.

When Sapphire was two, Corrine decided, on a whim, to explore Ireland. It hardly made any difference where she lived, now that she had her child. Besides, Sapphire had been conceived in Wicklow, and there were tax-free incentives for writers. Corrine was thinking she might like to write another book. She found a cottage close to the city centre in Dublin and her arrival was heralded with a couple of articles in the gossipy Sunday papers. *English Pop Star Moves to Dublin.* It was a long time since Corrine had been described as a pop star, but Ireland was more than happy to recycle old celebrities in order to fill the social pages and 'people' newspaper sections. Corrine enjoyed the attention and, arriving at openings and launches with Sapphire on her hip, enjoyed a small resurgence in celebrity. Although it was always as 'Eighties pop star' and never 'writer'.

Perhaps Ireland had enough of them already, Corrine thought, or perhaps the perky little journalism grads were patronizing her. Either way, she managed to get herself a regular column in a Sunday broadsheet and knock one particularly cocky blonde off her perch. Over the first few months of hanging out in Dublin, Corrine kept an eye out for Mal, but she never saw him. She did, however, meet his wife Helen at an around-the-table lunch discussion for a women's magazine, where six women's views on the subject of Family Life in the Nineties were being discussed and recorded for publication. Corrine nearly died when she was introduced to her ex-lover's wife, but her embarrassment wore off quickly as she noticed how – well – ordinary Helen was. Certainly, she was nothing special looks-wise. Corrine established that she did bits and pieces of charity work. No wonder Mal was so bored with her he screwed around.

After the lunch, Helen made a point of coming over and talking to Corrine.

'You did an interview with my husband some years ago? It was a beautifully written piece.'

Corrine feigned surprise that *this* was Mal Doherty's wife! That he had talked *so* much about her in the interview! That she was *delighted* to meet her! Helen was friendly, but Corrine recognized an element of caution in her manner. It was the veil of politeness that protects fame from foe. Helen invited Corrine to a lunch she was holding for a few 'friends' the following day. It was in a restaurant, albeit a very good one, but it was not in the house. Doubtless there would be some sort of do-goody charity connotation. Corrine saw this for what it was: the other women would work in PR and business; people that Helen liked, but didn't quite trust enough yet to let into her home. This, everyone at the lunch would understand, was the 'C' list. Ordinary mortals had to earn their way into the inner sanctum. 'B' was mentioning Mal openly in conversation, although at this stage you would be unlikely ever to meet him. 'A'-list membership might never come to those people not directly initiated into fame themselves, and if it did, you could be sure that you were an exception. Corrine knew that she was being relegated and was riled. Quite apart from the fact that she had fucked this woman's husband, not to mention virtually usurped the very high position from which Helen was now looking down on her, Corrine had known fame. Big time. She wasn't about to sniff around some wannabe wife bitch's hemline for scraps of celebrity. Not her scene. Not by a long shot.

When Corrine didn't turn up the next day, Helen rang her in the afternoon to apologize. She had mentioned seeing Corrine to Mal, and he had seemed very upset that Helen hadn't known that she was the singer Sapphire. Of course, she must come out to the house for supper. Mal was away, at their house in Mayo, working on his own for a few weeks – would Corrine like to come around on Saturday? About nine?

Sure she would. Except that she would prefer to go down to Mayo and find Helen's husband. Which she did.

Having baby Sapphire with her while she was re-opening the affair was both a good and a bad thing for Corrine. On the plus side, she was able to keep her overwhelming feelings for Mal under control; no matter how much she loved him, she had this child to love too. It enabled her to put Mal in second place, a position he had firmly placed her in and one which he deserved to suffer himself. Against that were the negative practical elements: nappies and naps. It was the start of the tantrum season. But Mal and Helen's house was a large ex-convent, big enough to both contain and entertain, and when needs be lose a lively toddler. Newly purchased, and not yet inhabited for any length of time by Helen and her brood, it was grand and impersonal, which suited Corrine fine. Mal had turned as white as a sheet when she had knocked on his door, Sapphire curled prettily in a perfect curve between her neck and hips. Strong arms and plenty of cleavage. He must have heard she'd moved to Ireland? She was working on a new book – needed to get out of the city. She was looking for property to buy in the area and hey – huge coincidence – she heard he was down here working and so she thought she'd drop by. Ultimately, it was bullshit that neither of them cared about as they became instantly lost in the shock of how much they still wanted one another. Almost five years had passed yet the concerns that from time to time would have dogged their respective fantasies, the fear that childbirth had slaughtered her sexuality, that Corrine would hate him for the weak way he left her, evaporated into the drowning need of one body for the other. It was the beginning of five weeks of bliss. And Corrine included Sapphire in that, which, of course, was what hurt the most when it didn't work out.

Corrine bought a house in the area. A nice big old

house that needed some work, but not so much that she couldn't pay for it. Sapphire settled into Killa, toddling along after the older kids as they explored each other's territories. Corrine was polite but kept aloof enough from the locals. It wouldn't do for them to start noticing her relationship with their local celebrity – Mal – when he came back down. Which he surely would. Soon.

So Corrine waited. The whole summer she waited and there was no sign of him. Then there was a sign. A big brazen red and black one outside the convent that said 'FOR SALE'.

The weak-willed shit had sold out again. Over the coming ten years, they did see each other again once or twice. At a gallery opening in Galway which she just happened to be passing. Ireland was like that. In any ten-year period, if you moved around at all, you were bound to bump into the same person at least twice. Another time, she literally walked into him on a street in central Dublin. They exchanged pleasantries and after five minutes, as she was walking away, he grabbed her urgently and said, 'Sorry.'

'For what?' she'd replied. And that was the last time they had spoken.

How much the bitterness of her non-relationship with Mal, or the death of her mother, or moving away from her new 'audience' in Dublin – losing her column – to settle in this rural backwater affected Corrine's relationship with her daughter would be impossible to gauge. It was certainly not something she dwelled on herself. Except that the love she felt for her daughter disappeared somewhere between her fifth and sixth years. That's not to say, she told herself, that it wasn't there. Sapphire was her daughter. That she loved her was a given. It was just that she could not feel that love any more. On looking at her, hearing her voice, answering her questions, imagining her daughter's future, Corrine felt nothing any more but irritation. She told her that she loved her often, because Sapphire asked her all the time. 'Do you love me, Mummy? Do you love me, Mummy?' 'Yes, yes, yes!' At the same time she would look at this overweight, unattractive child, trying on a coy babyish face and she would feel pity, then pain, then resentment, then guilt, then anger – a horrible cycle ending in repulsion and a pressure to push the child away.

Not indeed that Sapphire was that much of a child any more. Even though she acted like a kid, she would be thirteen at the end of this summer. Two years younger than Corrine had been when she took up with Wilson and started her pop career.

'Look, darling,' she said as Sapphire plonked down beside her on the floor of the attic, 'this is me when I was a pop star.'

'Did you know Alfie then?'

You see this is why Sapphire drove her mad. Of course she knew that Corrine couldn't have known Alfie then because it was years beforehand. The child knew that and still she asked. Why? She was pretending to be stupid. Just to annoy Corrine. It was intolerable manipulation. Really it was.

'No, *of course* I didn't, dear. You *know* I didn't. I've told you before.'

'Did you know Wilson then?'

The child was deliberately trying to annoy her now.

'That's not the point, Sapphire. The point is that when these pictures were taken, when I was a big pop star in England, I was only three years older than you are now.'

Her daughter blinked at her blankly.

They had had this conversation before and Sapphire had always seemed to completely miss the point. Corrine didn't want to drum it in, but it was time. The child had to grow up. It was for her own good.

'Look, Sapphire. I know you've said you don't want to go to boarding school, but—'

The doorbell rang.

'It's Aoife Breslin, Mummy. I forgot to tell you!' And Sapphire banged her forehead with the palm of her hand in an uncharacteristically adult gesture. 'I saw her at the shop this morning and she said she was going to call round this afternoon. She says she has something very important to ask you. Will I go down and let her in, Mummy?'

More neighbours. Aoife Breslin, some spotty hick child whose mother owned Breslin's 'fashion' shop where, out of neighbourly pressure, Corrine had felt obliged to buy a couple of dreadful cardigans over the years. Aoife had babysat for her fairly regularly over the years. She was a nice enough girl, but certainly not somebody who would have anything of 'importance' to relay.

Sapphire clambered down the attic ladder and thundered down the stairs ahead of her. Corrine hardly recognized the stunning six-footer who stood in her hall. It couldn't have been more than a few months since she had last seen Aoife, but where she had been a gangly, slightly goofy local girl, she now had the unmistakable languid, confident lounge of the international model. Wearing a Gap vest and a pair of low-slung combats that skimmed her slender hips, Aoife responded elegantly to Sapphire's ebullient hug by placing her hand on the child's head and holding it to her stomach. Corrine hated the way her daughter greeted virtual strangers with such outbursts of affection. It was inappropriate and embarrassing.

'Sapphire!'

The sharp tone in her mother's voice made the girl break away instantly and run into the other room. Aoife's hands flew up as the child fled, and she gave Corrine an odd look. The cheeky little bitch. Six months modelling in Dublin and she thought she was Christy Turlington. That Aoife Breslin was bringing the smell of urban sophistication into her home highlighted to Corinne how starved she was of it and just served to irritate her further.

'Yes, Aoife? Can I help you with something?'

'Well, I hope so. Molly and I are putting on a charity fashion show . . .'

Christ. Not another bloody community project. Apart from Enda the Performing Priest, Corrine was Killa's only 'celebrity' and as such tended to get asked to do everything from opening the school sports day to judging local beauty contests. It was the summer, the silly season when it came to street festivals and 'open days' and excuses to harass a local woman who used to be a pop singer.

'. . . in Donlan's Hotel . . . blah . . . money for Estonian orphans . . . blah . . .'

Really, the sooner she got herself out of this backwater and back to the real life of the city, the better.

'Wonderful cause . . . blah . . . giving something back . . . blah blah . . .'

Whatever it was they wanted her for, she'd fob them off on to Enda. She had too much to deal with to be bothering with all of this.

'. . . friends coming down to model from Dublin . . . blah . . . Molly doing the make-up . . . blah . . . Helen Doherty said I should rope you in . . .'

All of a sudden, Corrine was paying attention.

The Smith Household,
Holland Park, London W11, England

To: mnKa@hotmail.com
From: Hettie@2day.co.uk
Re: Let's get Together

Yo Mon. Gaz at LipSinc said U hadn't been around for a few daze? Really hope UROK. Was hoping to hook up with U & Alf later on for capp'chios and catch ups. Givesa ring, babe.

Hugs! Hettie

8

'I'll have a jar of that aul shtuff ye gev me to try out the last time.'

'The Age-Defying Vitamin-Enhanced Nutriv Serum?'

'That's the one.'

Molly looked at the ravaged visage of Eleanor Jackson and knew for sure that, vitamin enhanced or not, it was going to take more than a nutriv serum to turn back the clock on this one.

'Eleanor, I'll tell you now but the Nutriv Serum is fifty euro, a pot.'

'I don't care. It smells lovely.'

'It's a lot of money, Eleanor.'

'Are ye going to sell me the jar or not, girl? Isn't my money as good as anyone else's? I've the cash here look, and plenty of it!'

Molly peered into the old lady's bent navy plastic purse as she was instructed and saw a five-euro note, a handful of change and a couple of brown blobs which she hoped, most sincerely, were raisins. Her father reckoned Eleanor Jackson, despite (in fact probably because of) the shabby old coat and the worn tea-cosy hat, was rotten with money. Just before the currency changeover to the euro, Eleanor had started anxiously to dispose of large wedges of Irish punts she had been stuffing in her mattress for decades. Her onslaught on the shops of Killa had begun on Molly's day off when she had managed to clean Flynn's of its entire season's stock of YSL colour cosmetics and half the perfume counter. When Molly had enquired of her rather hapless stand-in, Mr Flynn's fifteen-year-old son, and discovered that the 'big spender' was the seventy-something woman least likely to win any meticulously groomed pensioner prizes she went to Eleanor's house. Peering through the front window, Molly could see that she had stocked up on everything she could conceivably lay her hands on; actual usefulness seeming to have got lost in the frenzy to 'get rid' of her money before it turned euro. The parlour walls were banked up with turf briquettes, Cornflakes, boxes of teabags, washing powder, a long line of wellington boots, copious quantities of wool and a large basket of children's footballs. Through the letterbox she could see that the boxes in the hallway contained, amongst other things, a Slendertone breast-firming unit, a yoghurt maker and a juicer. Molly knew better than to tackle the formidable Mrs Jackson on her own. So she went and had a chat with Greg Kelly in the Credit Union, who came down to the house and gently persuaded Eleanor that she could put her money in his bank where he would mind it for her and give it back to her any time she wanted. If she was worried that it wasn't all there at any given time, he promised to take it all out of the vault, in cash, and put it on a table so she could see for herself that he hadn't stolen it. It was an offer he would come to regret as Eleanor Jackson had taken him up on it several times since. She was a difficult old woman to reason with, as Molly knew well. Rarely a week went past when the perky young beauty consultant did not find herself having to dissuade Mrs Jackson from some outrageously expensive or inappropriate purchase. It seemed that, since her exposure to YSL make-up, the old lady had acquired a taste for expensive cosmetics. Quite what she did with them Molly was at a loss to imagine. But she felt it her responsibility as a caring neighbour, not to mention a qualified cosmetition, to monitor and modify Eleanor Jackson's consumption of beauty products.

'Will you not take a pot of the Pond's Cold Cream, Eleanor? It did you grand before.'

'Which one is that now? And it's *Mrs* Jackson.'

'It comes in the pink and white pot, Mrs Jackson.'

Molly came around the counter and out onto the shop floor where she picked a tub of said cream from the 'cheap' shelves.

'Is it any good?'

'Of course it's good. You used it for years.'

And the two of them looked at one another for a few moments, the question of Pond's effectiveness in either improving or maintaining Eleanor Jackson's face hanging in the air between them.

'How much is it?'

'Four ninety-nine.'

'It must be awful rubbish so to be that cheap?'

'Not necessarily.'

'Will you try it out on me?'

Molly's heart sank. She had a lot on today. New stock had just arrived and had to be priced and put out. The Guerlain display needed replenishing and, frankly, a good going over with the wet-wipes. She had a committee meeting later for the fashion show and had promised Aoife that she would put some ideas together for the make-up. Plus she still had to nip out to Fonzie and get her magazines for this week – although things were so busy lately, she didn't know when she was going to get the time to read them. The very last thing she needed now was to be giving a facial to Eleanor Jackson. Even if Molly Walshe had known how to say 'no', which she didn't, it would have been too late. The old lady had already hoisted herself up onto the white leatherette high stool and had the coat off, a protective bib thrown across her ample chest and her head slung back with eyes shut in anticipation of a 'five-minute trial facial' at the hands of her young neighbour.

'I thought I'd drop the mags in to you and see if you fancied popping over to Moran's for lunch?'

Fonzie was in love with Molly Walshe. Evidence of this was his willingness to put himself in the direct firing line of Hag Jackson.

'She's busy!'

Molly ran her cold palms gently across the saggy cheeks and they stretched back easily in a grinning grimace.

'Fonzie, thanks a million – pop them in behind the counter there.'

'Waste of money! I wouldn't give that fool or any belonging to him a penny of my money!'

Eleanor Jackson regarded Fonzie through the haze of unabsorbed skin cream with a look of undisguised loathing. Fonzie's Uncle Dez had sold Eleanor the basket of footballs from outside his shop: 'Had them for years. Last sold one in 1982. I gave her a good price, mind.' He was delighted to be rid of them, and not one single bit delighted when Mrs Jackson arrived in his shop two weeks later with the basket strapped to her back, the balls arranged in various receptacles around her shopping trolley and announced, 'They're all here. You can count 'em. I want my money back.'

A battle of wills ensued, the broad result of which was the defamation of Dezzie Mallarkey and all belonging to him. Which included Fonzie.

'He's a fool!'

Fonzie was in love with Molly Walshe, so he shuffled slightly and said, 'Will you follow me up to Moran's?'

'I can't today, Fonzie. I've mountains to do. I'm sorry. Thanks for bringing those down. You're a dote.'

As if Molly would follow him anywhere.

'Fool! Fool!' Mrs Jackson shouted after him, straining up off her stool until she almost toppling over.

Fonzie was in love with Molly Walshe and Molly Walshe was in love with Alfie Smith. Alfie Smith was an international rock star and Fonzie Mallarkey worked in his uncle's newsagent's shop. On the glamorous job stakes, there was little competition. How and ever, in the looks department, Fonzie could, and there was no doubt about it, hold his own. It was a source of constant admiration and puzzlement to the inhabitants of Killa as to how young Fonzie Mallarkey had inherited his particular brand of handsomeness. For a man round these parts might be blessed with a fine head of hair, or even a fine head of hair and a good physique. To have a fine head of hair, a good physique, a straight set of teeth and a pair of twinkling blue eyes was to have been proffered every advantage possible. At least, that's what one would have thought before Fonzie Mallarkey developed into young adulthood and displayed, to the astonishment of everyone, all of the above plus the added, unprecedented attributes of olive skin and chiselled features. Speculation was rife as to his origins, and a friendship his mother had enjoyed with a visiting Italian priest before he was born. 'They went on that coach trip to the Holy Land.' 'Never mind Holy Land, I heard it was more Holdy Hand between herself and the I-Talian.' Whether he was the offspring of a priest or not, it was generally agreed that this extraordinarily handsome young man was destined for great things. He had the look of a surgeon about him. Or better still, a television actor playing a surgeon. In fact, if you put Alfie Smith and Fonzie Mallarkey side by side and asked which one of these men is a famous rock star and which one works in his uncle's newsagent's shop in a small village in the middle of nowhere, it would have been instant demotion for Mr Smith. It was this very thought, coupled with the fact that Molly Walshe had never met Alfie Smith and in all likelihood, never would, that kept Fonzie's spirits up on the many occasions these days when he found himself being rejected by the bright, friendly blonde he had picked out of the females in Killa to be, eventually, his wife.

Molly was only twenty-three and he was coming up for thirty. She was young, and there was plenty of time for her to get sense. In the meantime, Fonzie would keep supplying her with her weekly dose of celebrity gossip and enjoy the occasional lunchtime soup and sandwich ensemble in Moran's pub.

Molly was itching to get at her magazines. She patted the sides of Eleanor's head to indicate that she was finished, but the old lady resolutely stretched her head further into Molly's breast to indicate that she wanted her to continue.

'That's it now, Mrs Jackson. All finished,' and she whipped the bib off and moved quickly around the chair and back to the professional safety of her behind-the-counter position.

'That was never five minutes.'

'Six and a half, Mrs Jackson. Do you want the Pond's then or not?'

It was unheard of for Molly to be sharp with any of her customers, but there did not seem to be another way to communicate with Eleanor Jackson. Besides, this was the fourth 'trial facial' she had given the old woman this month, and she was beginning to lose patience.

Eleanor gurned into the patch of plastic mirror on the Guerlain display and said, 'Doesn't seem to have made that much of a difference.'

'We'll leave it then so for today,' and correctly assessing

that the old woman was about to pitch for a trial facial of the Age-Defying Nutriv added, 'I'm closing for lunch now, Mrs Jackson. See you later in the week no doubt.'

On her way out, Eleanor helpfully commented, 'That display needs a good wipe. It's filthy.'

⬭

Alfie Smith was married now. It had happened a few weeks ago. In a Scottish Castle. *OK!* magazine had been there. MoniKa and Alfie had been paid over a million, but they had given the money to charity. Molly didn't like to be unfair to MoniKa, she seemed all right, from what Molly knew of her, but she was pretty sure the charity angle was Alfie. That was the kind of guy he had always been. Generous. Even in U&Us, all those years ago when they had both been just kids, Alfie had been the one always talking out about 'serious issues' when the others were just boys in a band. In one of their first interviews in *Smash Hits* (Molly still had it at home), the boys were asked what their hopes were for the future. All the others had said stuff about cars and women and being famous for years to come. Alfie had spoken about eradicating (she thought that was the word) world poverty and using his fame to help the children. Aoife had been really cynical and nasty about it, saying that he only went on like that for the publicity. But Molly had defended him. 'Has it ever dawned on you, Aoife, that maybe he *does* care? That maybe he *is* a genuinely nice person?'

'Hey. He's only a pop singer, Moll. Don't take it so seriously.'

But Molly had been right, because here he was, all these years later, giving his one-million-pound fee from *OK!* magazine to a children's charity. What would Aoife think of that? she wondered. Except, she knew there wasn't any point in saying anything. Aoife thought she was stupid for reading magazines. 'You should be out there doing the real thing.' Molly didn't quite know what she meant, except that she was always nagging her to 'move up to Dublin for a while' and 'give the make-up thing a lash. You can move in with me. I've loads of contacts.' But Molly wasn't interested. She didn't really understand what 'contacts' meant; they were like people you didn't know well enough to call friends, and yet they could do more for you than your friends could. Like get you jobs and introduce you to other 'contacts'. It all sounded very high powered and glamorous, but scary and not really Molly's scene. Was the make-up artist Julian August that she had done the course in Galway with a contact? she wondered.

'Do you have his mobile number?' Aoife asked.

'God, no!' said Molly.

'Then he's no good.' Aoife waved him off.

'He was nice, though,' Molly said. And that counted for something, surely. She might never see Julian again, but she had enjoyed meeting him and he had been nice. Sort of like it was with herself and Alfie. She didn't *know* him *per se*, in the sense of ever having actually met him. But she did sort of 'know' him through listening to his records, and reading about him, and studying photographs of him. Of course, sometimes Alfie would do something that surprised her and Molly would wonder if, despite all her efforts, she really knew him at all. Like marrying MoniKa. Not that we should get her wrong, you understand. MoniKa was fine, as far as models go. Not, indeed, that she had anything against models. Wasn't Aoife, her best friend in the whole world, a model? Off to Paris to do catwalk shows and everything. Might be on fashion TV one of these days yet. Might even *meet* MoniKa. Wouldn't that be something? How special would the big fashion model be then, married to Alfie Smith and hobnobbing with one of Molly's ordinary friends from Killa? Not so high and mighty then, Mrs MoniKa Smith, eh? Because, if truth be known, Molly suspected that MoniKa was only after the status and fame that being married to Alfie gave her. She was, it was true, a very big-name international fashion model. But she wanted to become an actress (didn't they all!), and Molly was convinced, although she had yet to work out quite how, that MoniKa's marriage to Alfie was a cynical ploy to help her do this. Just look at her history. She had been on the celebrity mag circuit for about four years. OK, so she was a model. But mostly what she was famous for was her boyfriends: four film actors, an American millionaire playboy, the famous hair-dresser. And now she was married to Alfie. Of course, Molly had been watching them closely through the year of their courtship, but honestly, she really had not thought it was going to last. The wedding was big and showy. Her idea, of course, not his. Alfie would have gone along with it, smiled for the cameras but only for the whole magazine-fee-for-charity angle. But that type of thing just wasn't his scene. Never had been. The new house in Holland Park would doubtless be in *Hello!* or *2Day* soon, and it would be interesting to see what Mon had done with that. Then, thought Molly, we'll have a proper idea of what is going on. She would be able to tell, instantly, of course, if it was just a show-house or if this woman was going to be able to make a real home for Alfie. Like his mum's house. Sharon had great taste, but then she was a really special woman – Alfie's mum. A single parent. What an amazing person. Raised him, and his brother Sidney and sister Kim, all by herself. It can't have been easy. And she was so glamorous! Molly loved to see her smiling out from the pages of *Woman* and *Woman's Own* the odd time, and, of course, you could see the pride shine out of every pore in her—

'Corn plasters.'

No chance she'd get a sneaky ten seconds to flick through a magazine in this place.

'Last aisle, third shelf down – where they've been for the last five years,' she snapped at Mr Brown.

No need for that kind of unpleasantness, said the shy old man's hurt eyes as he flicked a brief look at the pretty girl he asked for the whereabouts of corn plasters every week.

If Molly felt guilty, it was masked by an ongoing sense of annoyance that Mr Flynn had refused to move her counter from right beside the front door where every passing customer might enquire after their corn plasters and their nappy-rash creams. She was trying to develop his business, and her own skills in the field of cosmetic consultancy, and nobody seemed to be taking her seriously.

'Hiya.' At last someone with a bit of sense. Although Aoife was looking as scruffy as hell. She hadn't a scrap of make-up on. Honestly, Molly wondered sometimes how she got into modelling in the first place with the casual gear and not even bothering with a bit of mascara in the mornings. It took Molly the full hour, between the daily wash and blow dry and the heated eyelash tongs. It was annoying, now, really it was.

'What's eating you?'

Aoife could tell by Molly's face there was something up.

'Nothing.'

Then a little burst.

'Jesus, Aoife! Would you not put a bit of lipstick on yourself in the mornings?'

'Ah, right. Alfie back from honeymoon, then?'

And she leant the top half of her six-foot frame over the counter and strained to see that month's cover of *Hello!*.

'Don't be stupid. I just don't think it's right you should be going around selling tickets for the fashion show looking like *that*.'

'Like what?' Aoife smiled widely. She was wearing her brother's combats, her five-year-old sister's Barbie T-shirt under her dad's fishing jacket, and one of her granny's headscarves. She looked shit-cool and she knew it. It just wasn't Killa's conventional idea of what a model should look like. Aoife came home every weekend from Dublin and stayed around for longer periods if she had a quiet patch between jobs. No one here had any idea how successful she was because most of her work was abroad and her substantial earnings were swallowed up by a small apartment in Dublin's trendy Temple Bar. She had featured in a few ad campaigns in English magazines, but nobody had recognized her and she wasn't the type to go pointing herself out to people. None of the pictures, she thought, looked remotely like herself anyway so somehow that made them not count. In one picture, she had been so heavily airbrushed that Molly, a serious consumer of magazines, had actually pointed the picture out to her and said, 'I think this make-up would really suit you, Aoife.' Molly was always coming up with advice and tips on how her friend could 'sell' herself better as a model. Aoife didn't put her straight. She didn't want to make Molly feel stupid. Because Molly wasn't stupid, she just didn't understand how things ran outside of Killa. Aoife knew the U2 and Godot crowd up in Dublin, had bumped into or boogied with them at the odd fashion show or designer party in Paris. They were no big deal. Molly and her friends down in Killa were as good as any of them, and better than most. That's why Molly's idolizing of celebrities annoyed her. It was like she was putting herself down in placing these false gods on a pedestal. In any case, it wouldn't matter soon as Aoife had plans on that score.

'Anyway, put the mag aside. It's all changed.'

'What's changed?'

'The fashion show.'

'Aoife, I've mountains to do. Can this not wait until the meeting?'

'That's what I'm telling you. It's all changed, and I need your support telling the committee tonight.'

Another one of Aoife's hare-brained ideas and no doubt

Molly was going to have to 'mollify' and smooth things over with the collection of ratchet-faced busybodies who had added the fashion show to a long list of 'committee' memberships that made them the self-appointed fart-police of Killa. Insofar as they were so far into every aspect of town business that nobody in Killa got to fart without their knowledge or consent.

Between Eleanor Jackson's facial, the grubby Guerlain unit, this week's pile of unread magazines, and now possible unpleasantness among the Killa committee members, Molly Walshe felt that life could not possibly get much more stressful.

The Smith Household,
Holland Park, London W11, England

To: mnKa@hotmail.com
From: Hettie@2day.co.uk
Re: RUOK

Gaah girl. Not like U not 2 get back 2 me! Called round to
the house earlier but u weren't in. Have you gone on holi-
daze and not told me? Gaz is being VERY silent which is
NOT like him so am getting teensy but worried. Please just
call and let me know that U and Alfie ROK. Noo GO!SUSHI
just opened round the corner in Camden. *Really* fancy taking
the 2 of U there for a bite tomorrow night? Call to confirm,
babes.

Hugs as per, Hettie

9

Helen was clearing out the office, getting it ready for the personal assistant she had starting work next week. Her accountant had suggested his daughter, a serious-minded but personable kid who had just graduated from Trinity and was looking for something to tide her over until she decided what she wanted to do next. Emily could, at least, be trusted not to get starstruck and Helen really did need help with her mounting 'stuff to do' list. It ranged in length and breadth of importance from raising $400,000 for Afghan orphans to organizing the twins having their teeth cleaned to ordering and arranging delivery of a motorbike which the Godot lads wanted to buy their manager for his birthday. On top of the charity stuff that she chose to do, and the wife/mother stuff that it was her duty to do, Helen had this constant flotsam of favours and promised good deeds floating about on the surface of her life. An acquaintance's daughter wanted to be a charity volunteer – could Helen fix her up? The nice man who delivered her organic vegetables had an older sister who had MS and was a big fan of Wilson. Could Helen fix it up for the pop singer to visit her in the home in Cavan? Failing that, a signed album would be nice. Sim missed her family and Helen had promised to teach her how to use e-mail.

The list was endless and Helen was wrecked. She needed a holiday. They were all supposed to have been going to stay in the beach house in Florida for a month, but then Godot got nominated for some award and the bass player's second marriage broke up and Mal decided that if they started work on the new album it would help him get over it and the twins said that Florida was 'boring' and blah blah blah, between one thing and another it seemed easier to stay at home. Money, Helen knew, was supposed to make one's life easier, but between keeping up the running of their four houses – three of which she had the time neither to visit nor sell – keeping abreast of her own work commitments whilst being attentive and reassuring to her husband, it seemed small comfort sometimes. Then there was the guilt. It was ludicrous, she knew. She gave a lot away, but she certainly wasn't going to give everything away. What would be the point of that? Mal, and in her support of him Helen, had earned it. Nobody was going to argue that Godot deserved their success, and used it to help others. As it was, people thought they were both saints. Last year she'd booked first-class flights to Florida for herself and her entourage and had asked the agent, just out of curiosity, how much the bill was. Nearly twenty thousand euros. She knew how much money that was because every day she'd be getting those pledges in. Four thousand ('keep it anonymous, don't want every fucker coming after me'). Ten thousand in corporate sponsorship – logo good and big so everyone can see what nice guys we are. Two hundred euros a head for that charity dinner? That'll be a table for ten at two grand and make sure it's adjacent to his competitors so the two of them will raise the stakes at the auction. Helen had traded down to business class, which was still astronomical, then donated the difference anonymously to a Miami drugs rehab project. The twins had complained loudly *en route* and for months afterwards about the enforced poverty of business-class transatlantic. Not for the first time, Helen had wondered about the wisdom of not having sent them to military college, or better still borstal when they were eleven instead of indulging them in their parents' wealthy lifestyle. Although in reality the twins were just being honest. Mal and herself could talk the talk, but all that did really was make them a more publicly palatable version of the very, very rich bastards that they were. They'd fly a private jet full of dignitaries over to Croatia to see for themselves the war orphanage their money was building. But by God, the in-flight water better be the right brand, and pre-packed sandwiches? Please! Is there no chef on board?

The upshot being that the twins wouldn't fly business class, and they were turning into such vile materialistic little shits that Helen felt compelled to shatter their smugness by refusing to spend the money upgrading. There was no way she could go herself and leave them at home. Even if she cut off their income supply completely, they would find a way of wreaking havoc. Every drug-dealer, club-owner and lapdancer in Dublin knew that Mummy and Daddy would be good for the credit.

Helen had fought with Mal over it.

'Teach them a lesson, Mal. If we don't pay, they'll have to find a way of paying themselves.'

'What like – get a job in Dunnes stacking shelves at the weekends?'

'Well, why not?'

Helen looked at her husband and got the answer in his carefree open grin. Good-looking, roguish, brimful of testosterone-fuelled confidence. The twins had the same look, except in fifteen-year-old boys who have enjoyed every privilege money can buy and have no particular discernible talent to define them it comes across as arrogant and spoiled.

Helen wanted to be proud of her boys. They were handsome and intelligent and she was proud of them for that, but she wanted to be prouder. Prouder of herself too. Was she naïve to imagine that if she gave enough to charity, it would balance the fluff and the frippery of being a rich rock wife? She had just returned from the Paris couture shows, and found that they got harder to sit through every year. It hadn't always been like that. When she had started going some ten years ago, Helen and her friends Madge and Carmel had had a ball. Rich and raunchy, they sat right up front with the disapproving press and were 'the *awful* Irish women', skittering and giggling and half-cut most of the time. Flying in the face of a fashion etiquette they were barely aware existed, they were just out on a glorified girls' spree. They all three spent money. They knew if they didn't they wouldn't be invited back next year, and if they were wrong regarding candy-striped culottes and pinstriped puff-balls, they were right about that. Every other season the three women gathered their couture invites into their Burberry travel wallets, and headed over to the Costes where they would have pre-booked their suite from the year before. Their profiles as regular show-goers gathered momentum, and they began to settle more sedately into the scene. This was shopping at its highest level. If you were going to spend three grand on a jacket, you had at least to look as if you cared. So they sat, chewing the end of their pens, trying to decide whether to go for the Valentino or the Chloe or both and marking them off on their running orders. They made appointments at the ateliers where they kissed and congratulated the designers and pretended to be honoured that this great talent was going to oversee the sewing of a few sequins on a skirt and charge them several thousand pounds for it. As time went on, the excitement of those early years – the buzz when you realize you are rich and can more or less do all of those things you never thought you would be able to do – had worn off. Paris fashion shows, private planes; the thrill of first mixing with the rich and famous and then realizing you are one of them yourself. They were heady times. Times when you thought you had enough money not to give a shit. Before you realize that actually that amount of money doesn't exist.

Helen's office was a small box room at the front of the house; it had originally been some sort of a waiting room, an extension of the hall where the staff would bring guests before they were admitted to the drawing room. Helen had chosen it as her office because she never imagined that her work would require more than the most meagre of space and attention. In the end, it had turned out to be one of the most used rooms in the house. Whilst the enormous games/recreation room and custom-built gym lay idle most of the time, this tiny space was crammed with boxes of photographs, files, bits of paper, personal and business and both, all waiting to be organized into a filing cabinet or a leather-bound photo album. Helen stuck her hand into a box and absent-mindedly pulled out a picture of the three of them back in the days of the Pink. Bleached fringes and black eyes, posing like the Human League girls. Carmel and Helen had met at boarding school. Carmel's family were second-generation Irish builders and had the biggest construction company in the UK. Carmel 'worked' for the family firm and, from as far back as they could both remember, had charged everything to a bottomless bank account she had never seen a statement for. Madge, like Helen, had started modelling in her late teens, and ended up married to Godot's drummer, Pad. The three women had enjoyed as wild an early twenties as anyone could have imagined: Helen and Madge provided the men, the drugs and the street cred. Carmel – or rather her daddy – provided the cash. The Godot boys weren't famous, but they were cool and they were on the up. Dublin '83 and the Pink Elephant was the only place worth being seen. It was wall-to-wall English rock singers, over in Ireland to write their albums, which would be tax free if completed in this new haven for artists and writers. They mixed it up with a 'colourful' local crowd, sifted and contrived by the club's manager for maximum interest with minimum trouble. Spandau, Frankie, the lads from Leppard – the Pink provided a glossy haven for the bright stars of Thatcher's Britain to hide away from the fame and the fans. A place where they could feel ordinary in the company of fellow extraordinary people. Madge and Helen scored themselves jobs as 'hostesses': glorified waitresses whose model beauty was their calling card to mingle with the stars. During the day, they did the occasional fashion shoot, but their lives were largely played out in the cocooned glamour of nightclub life. They wore fishnet tights as sleeves under tight Lycra catsuits and high leather boots with a dozen wrap-around buckles. They backcombed their hair into elegant quiffs and carved black worried-looking eyes out for themselves with kohl and shadow. They tried to create personalities that were as intense and disturbing as their clothes and make-up made them look, but they were too damn pretty and too damn happy for it to work. Looking back now, there was a comic innocence in their trying to wring some seriousness out of the relentless fun they were having. Fun was something Helen needed to contrive these days. Madge would talk her into the couture shows with the threat of it every year: 'Helen, it'll be fun!' But the reality was, it had been a good few years since the three women had had fun together.

Madge had been divorced from Pad for five years, and was bitter. She believed she had been traded in for a younger model, but even Helen, who was one of her closest friends, could see that Madge would be a difficult, high-maintenance wife. The happy-go-lucky, funny, tarty teenager Helen was holding in her hand was well and truly gone. No kids (her choice) had meant that her settlement after nine years had been considerably less than it might have been. The 'hairy little bitch' Pad had 'dumped' her for had produced three kids in two years and while she had dated profusely over the time they had been apart, she had yet to get anyone to marry her again. Madge complained about not having had any children. She complained about not having enough money. She complained about the towels in the hotel suite, the blandness of this season's fashions, the fizziness of the mineral water in Paris bars. She had complained so much in Paris that Helen had thought she was going to explode and had resolved that this was the very last year she was going to the shows.

At least this time, she had achieved something. Back-stage at Peter O'Brien's show she had been introduced to the sweetest young model, Aoife Breslin. The kid was from Killa in Co. Mayo, close to the old convent they had bought years ago. That hadn't worked out: Mal had stayed there for a couple of months working, then announced he thought they should sell. Helen had loved the area, and had been looking forward to doing the convent up and perhaps basing herself and the kids down there full time. There had been something about the place, some rugged beauty that had made her feel she could escape there, melt herself and her family into the landscape. Anyway, it hadn't happened, but she was always interested if the subject of Killa came up, which it rarely did. Aoife had been asking

Helen's advice about some charity fashion show she was putting on down there and then the strangest thing happened. This old pop song from the Eighties came on the radio: a boppy number by the singer Sapphire. And quite out of the blue, Helen remembered having met Corrine and that she had done that great interview with Mal, and that she had met her in Dublin and maybe heard something, seen some snippet in the *Sunday Indo*, about her moving down to the west. Then Aoife was complaining that the people in Killa had no sense of style and that she was the only one who had a clue about fashion and that there was only one other woman, a writer who lived in the area, who knew anything at all about how to dress properly and Helen found herself blurting out, 'That would be Corrine.'

'Oh, you know her.'

'Well, kind of.'

And perhaps it was the awfulness of Madge that week, or the presence of this girl reminding her that there was a place that wasn't Paris or London or New York, where real people, ordinary people, led real, ordinary lives and this person Corrine, who used to be a singer and was now a writer, this person whom she knew little more about than just that, seemed to epitomize something that Helen, in that moment, craved and she said, 'We lost touch, but you should rope her in with the show. Tell her I was asking after her. I just may come down for it myself.'

Now, surrounded by the paperwork mountain of her last ten years in this house, Helen thought absent-mindedly of her conversation with the young model and perhaps making good her promise to revisit Killa, using the fashion show as an excuse.

She was pondering this very thought when there was a persistent, almost aggressive, ringing on her doorbell. It being Sim's day off, Helen went to answer it herself.

The Smith Household,
Holland Park, London W11, England

To: mnKa@hotmail.com
From: Gary@LipsInc.co.uk
Re: Mon's great escape

If you want to disappear for a bit, sweets, your best bet is
the *Vogue* shoot in Tangier. They've already got a first
option on you, but I was holding out in case the L'Oreal ad
came through. They were just on asking about confirmation
so I said it was looking good. No money – as per usual – but
they leave tomorrow and, once you can keep that fucker
McIvor quiet, your lovely reliable model agent (I don't know
why you need a press agent when you've got me, darling!)
won't be telling where you are. It's a five-day booking but
may run over. I'll mail the details later.

Kisses, Gary

PS Hettie dropped in. Says will you give her a ring.

10

'Have you ever seen anything more *adorable* in your life?'

Six-year-old Malaga Battersby was gazing up at Stephen with batting blue-shadowed eyes flanked by her shaking, star-struck parents, Kylie and Jason.

'You've gone too fucking far this time,' Wilson hissed in his partner's ear before turning a forced smile back on to the Battersbys and saying, 'Malaga? That's an unusual name.'

'We was on 'oliday when she was ... um ... congealed,' Kylie offered while Jason shuffled and added as explanation.

'Like the Beckhams, you know? Brooklyn an' all that.'

'Only we fought of it first.'

'Yeah, 'cept it weren't really Malaga.'

'We was in Magaloof.'

'Yeah, but we didn't fink that would saand as good.'

'Specially not wiv a girl.'

'Magaloof. Don't saand right, does it?'

⬭

'Magaloof!'

'Malaga. And she *was* adorable.'

'She was a monstrosity!'

'She was only six.'

'I don't *care*! She was *vile*. They were *all* vile! The things you put me through, Stephen. I know you think it's important to stay sweet with the locals, and I agree, it's a nice idea to let the serfs have the grounds for the Summer Fete, but a beauty pageant for the under-tens? No way! Fucking forget it!'

Stephen had lied to Wilson by telling him that he was going to be judging the fete's cake-making competition and that a group of local women were coming in with a selection of fayre for him to taste. Wilson considered himself something of an expert when it came to home-made fruitcake and its like. He longed to have a Mrs Bridges type of old-fashioned housekeeper knocking out traditional English pies and puddings for him. But even if such a person were to make themselves available, they would never get past Stephen's cholesterol patrol. That was why he went willingly to the community centre in their local village of Browsling in the mistaken belief that this rare foray into the ordinary world of mere mortals would involve an afternoon spent munching his way through copious volumes of home-cooked goodies. Arguing the merits of a simple farmhouse brack, say, against the complex glamour of a coffee cream. 'I'll have another slither – just to be sure.' Perhaps, he thought, whilst forgoing his elevenses to prepare for the onslaught, he might even make contact with some kindly middle-aged frau from the church who would sneak him the odd jam sponge when Stephen wasn't looking.

When the first person to enter the judging suite was not a grey-haired woman in a tabard laden down with a tray of apple slices, but a couple of cheaply attired youngsters and their pink-clad, ponytailed six-year-old who proceeded to perform a song-and-dance routine of 'Come on Baby, Light My Fire', Wilson was underwhelmed, to say the least. To say that the afternoon did not improve after that would also be an understatement. After a two-hour 'lie down' with a cold compress one end and a hot-water bottle at the other, Stephen thought Wilson would have calmed down. At least sufficiently calmed for him to say: 'Calm down, Wilson. You were all right when you thought it was cake tasting.'

'Calm down! Calm down! You *lied* to me, Stephen. You *lied*!'

Stephen could see the heat rising in his partner. There was a turbo tantrum coming on. He wasn't afraid. He could front this out, no problem.

'Well, I knew you'd roll over once there was food involved. Food is more important to you than people.'

'That is an *unbelievable* thing to say. I cannot *believe* you just said that.'

'You'd have no problem if it was dogs, would you? Remember last year when . . .'

'Oh, shut up, Stephen. Shut the *fuck* up. This is not dogs we are talking about here, or people, this is children.

117

Children, Stephen, parading around in front of us in their little leotards or gymslips or whatever. Have you not thought about how that *looks*?'

'How do you mean?'

'You know what I mean. Two old queens hosting a day out for little kids. It looks bad.'

'Oh, now you are really being disgusting. You have a filthy, disgusting mind to even think such a thing.'

'To think what? Grow up, Stephen. You know what I'm talking about. It looks unnatural and weird, two grown gay men hanging about with kids. It *is* unnatural and weird.'

Stephen flinched and, for a split second, Wilson felt bad. For a split second, mind. It's not very long.

'And while we are on the subject of your bullying the shit out of me, I am fed up with it. Do you think I like being so beaten down that I get over-excited at the thought of judging a cake competition?'

'You were fat when I met you.'

'And happy.'

They both knew that was a lie, but Stephen was hurting now. And Wilson was hurting too, in his own way. Which wasn't always easily diagnosed.

'I'll tell you something, Stephen: I am not, and I mean it, going to take any more of this nonsense from you. No, Missy Mr Man, things are going to start changing around here and that's for sure . . .' He was on a roll now, believing his own PR, and that his silent partner was actually drinking in every word.

'Yessir, Chez Wilson is a-changin'. There will be cakes,

and there will be slippers and there will be no more, I repeat, no more talk of children, other people's or adopted or otherwise. No more.'

There. He had said it. Months of skirting around the issue had finally ended. The awkward silences, the wincing and mincing around the elephant in the room that neither of them felt prepared to confront. There had been that first conversation when Stephen brought it up. It had been short and apparently 'throwaway'. A 'thought' after seeing an article about gay parents in a Sunday supplement. 'Might be something to think about?' he had said. But the way he had laid the article carefully over Wilson's cocoa and something in the way he said it – a bright inflection over the last word – let Wilson know there was more to it than that. Stephen's voice had only ever held that tone once before, with regard to the walls of their downstairs 'den'. 'Zebra print might work?' To this day Wilson was not quite sure how the incessant stylishness of his home became vandalized but there was, indeed, a faux zebra-skin finish to his downstairs den walls.

The children thing, however, was an altogether more serious matter.

Stephen loved children. He had two nephews whom he adored, and Wilson had often watched his partner in the rough and tumble of wrestling them, and thought that he was only an appropriate sweater away from looking like the perfect father. His tanned perfection turned from fashionista sexy to clean and wholesome when there were children around. His love of kids and his genuine propensity for fatherhood was, until that point, just something that Wilson had noticed. In that way that he loved Stephen, and would therefore notice things about him without thinking them good or bad. Just different angles from which to view him. Blond, bloated, dragged up, dressed down, they were just different pictures of the same thing. His man. His love. Even after ten years, Wilson could hardly contain his love for Stephen. How much he craved his affection, his attention and how much he wanted to give him in return. For Wilson, that was the deal. Stephen gave him love; Wilson gave him gifts. That was the way it worked. Stephen gave good love, and Wilson didn't really know how that worked. He wrote about love, and that made him money, and he spent that money buying things for Stephen. He would give Stephen anything, *anything* he asked for. The thing is, Stephen didn't really ask for that much. And when he did it was big. Like zebra-print walls. Or a child.

Wilson conceded the den walls, but he could not afford to give in on this one. Stephen had loved him for ten years. Give him a child and that love was history. Who're you gonna love? A porky, cranky, middle-aged queer or a cute little innocent kid? Wilson was no fool. He'd done the maths.

Thankfully the argument against children for a gay couple was more substantial than the argument against zebra-print walls.

Once he had broken the taboo, Wilson made the common mistake of believing he could safely expand on the subject.

'I don't mind your nephews coming down, Stephen,

they are great kids, you know I like them. But I simply will not entertain the children of the village in some sort of revolting beauty pageant just to satisfy your bizarre desire to be a parent. Gay parents, well, I just don't believe in them and that's that. I will not have this relationship turned into an emotional freak show. You're either gay, Stephen, or you're not. If you want kids, you are just going to have to find yourself a woman. That's the way it works. I was "Britain's first famous gay". I am not going to be "Britain's first famous gay parent". Won't do it, Stephen. Won't put myself, won't put *us*, through it – and then there's the poor child to think of.'

It was a mistake of course. All of it. The patronizing way he graciously 'permitted' Stephen's nephews to visit, the word 'freak'. The whole 'get yourself a woman' thing. All. Very. Bad.

Stephen was shocked. Not so much at the contents of Wilson's speech, but more at the fact that Wilson had been blasé enough to believe he could say it without apparent consequence.

'I don't need this,' was all that Stephen said.

Wilson was suddenly shocked himself by the almost macho shrug that Stephen gave as he grabbed his coat and began to march determinedly towards the door.

'I didn't mean it! I'm sorry!' he shouted helplessly after his younger lover as he made the three-corridor journey to the front door. 'Please, Stephen. Don't go! I'm sorry!' But Stephen was having none of it and out he went.

Three hours later, Wilson was still beside himself. Housekeeper Carol had tried to comfort him with tea and sympathy and had even had a stab at a few chocolate fairy cakes. They were from a mix, but they seemed to upset Wilson more for some reason. Cakes! That's what was behind all of this. He'd never touch another cake again. If he hadn't been promised then denied cake, he would never have said such horrible things. Not that he had said anything horrible, really. In fact, not at all, now that he thought back on it. Actually, he had been rather reasonable and nice and Stephen had completely overreacted. The prissy little poof. He was lucky to be shot of him. He was Wilson. WILSON! A world-renowned international everything. No need to be wasting himself on some preening vain queer when he could have his pick of anyone – *anyone* – he wanted. Except . . . Stephen was the only one he wanted and he had let him go. What an idiot – *a fucking idiot* – he was. Stephen was right, he cared more about cake than he did about people. Cake. Chocolate buns. Staring at him. Confronting him with his own greed. His own stupidity. He couldn't bear to look at them.

'Carol! Carol! Come and take these fucking cakes out of my sight!'

She came in carrying the phone handset.

'It's MoniKa. She say's Alfie left her.'

Carol was an official member of the Wilson household's inner sanctum, and as such was trusted and treated to all information therein.

Wilson snatched the phone, eager to share his misery with someone who wasn't going to punish him with cake.

MoniKa was v. upset. Wilson liked MoniKa, and Alfie was his boy and he hated to think of either of them being in trouble, separately or as a couple. But fair's fair – he had his own trauma today and the last thing he needed was to share in somebody else's drama. However, Wilson was the Godfather of the young and famous, and it was his duty to come up with answers. As luck would have it, he came up with one that suited both his supermodel charge and himself.

Stephen was about to settle into his sister's second bedroom in Kingsbury. It had taken him two hours to get there, by the time he found a landmark that would not identify him as an escapee from Wilson's estate, from where he could call a mini-cab driver who would not identify him as Britain's Most Famous Gay Lover. He had left the house with no money and Andy, his brother-in-law, was none too impressed at having to settle the cab fare. At least as not impressed as Stephen was on learning that, thanks to the conversion of the box room into a home office, he had to bunk in with the boys. 'Bunk' being the operative word, as one of them had already commandeered the put-you-up. As he pulled the Man. United duvet cover up over his head, and pushed it quickly down again as the unmistakable stench of pubescent boy hit him, the awfulness of the situation finally hit him. What had he been thinking of? Firstly there was the right here and right now. The crispy duvet, the temporary loss of his skincare regime, the having to be grateful for the hospitality of his poor sister when it was so very below par compared to what he had become used to. Because, say what you like about money not being important, there was no en suite, no gym, no zebra-print den with built-in plasma screen in their three-bed semi in Kingsbury. Beyond that was the future, which really did not bear thinking about. He'd have to earn a living again. Work. Which one of their friends would stick by Wilson instead of him? He'd have to go back and pick up his stuff. Except there was mountains of it, and there'd be nowhere to put it, and was it really his stuff now seeing as how all of it, bar a few sentimental bits and pieces, had been bought for him by Wilson? Was this worth it, leaving on a point of principle like that? How important was it to him, this children thing? Important enough to forgo your choice of twelve en suites? He should have just banished himself out of the bedroom for a couple of nights. That would have been sufficient punishment surely. Yes, this was definitely a step too far. But he couldn't go back. Not now. Not after making a big show of walking out the way he did.

His sister stuck her head in the door.

'Stephen – Wilson's on the phone.'

Thank God! He took the stairs three at a time, grabbed the phone, then took a moment to pitch his voice at 'aloof'.

'Wilson.'

'Stephen.'

And there it was. That feeling. Was it love or just familiarity? Stephen didn't know. But it was like a piece of music that pulls at you, and no matter how schmaltzy or unfashionable it is, you just can't help yourself but be moved. Wilson was old and he was small and when

Stephen had first met him he had not been interested in him as anything other than one of his musical heroes. Now he loved this man like a father, a child, brother, lover, friend. There was no emotion he had not felt towards him. Protective – as the performer's tiny frame and frail ego stepped out in front of a crowd of thousands and in the awe of the audience they would be reminded of Wilson's enormity in the world. Compassion at unexpected times, like when he would still try to hide his body getting out of the bath. Pride when they were all dressed up to go out and the much shorter man would take his arm with an air of propriety and Stephen would feel like the luckiest girl in the world. He had invested so much of who he was in this person that without him he just wasn't complete any more.

'Is the apartment in Tangier open?'

So that's how the old bastard was going to play it. All business. Stephen was in charge of running their various homes around the world. The apartment in Tangier was a ludicrous indulgence, used only for shopping trips from their Riyadh in Marrakesh. Stephen was supposed to have organized the selling of it last year, which he hadn't got around to.

'No. Why?'

'MoniKa just rang. Alfie has left her and I was wondering if he might have been in touch with you.'

'And that I might have sent him over to Tangier?'

'Yes.'

'As it's the most low-key place we have?'

'Yes.'

'Without telling you?'

'Yes.'

'But I tell you everything.'

'Do you?'

'You know I do. That's the problem.'

Wilson knew that was true. Stephen need never have said anything about the children thing. He had taken a chance, and it hadn't paid off. Worse, Wilson had used it to humiliate and hurt him. However, Wilson was old-school. He was reared in the lower-middle-class tradition of never admitting anything was wrong. Especially if it was your fault.

'You left your toothbrush behind.'

'I know.'

'And your cleanser.'

'Something else too.'

'What?'

'You.'

There was a lovely little silence then and Stephen could totally tell that Wilson was totally chuffed.

'Are you coming home, then?'

'Yes, please.'

'Want me to send the car?'

'Yes, please.'

The break-up had lasted a mere four hours.

'Nearly as long as Alfie's marriage,' Stephen had joked later. Although he knew Wilson was way too fond of the boy to leave it at that.

11

'Ooooooooooooooooooooo, how d'ya like your love?'

They do say that the most important sexual organ is the brain. And for 'Father' Enda Devlin that had certainly proved to be true. Because this recently resigned priest had spent the best part of his forty-five years with his sex life confined to that area. Although not, of course, entirely. For every man, no matter how devoted he is to the Divine Entity of the Church, is bound, if for no other reason than mere physical necessity, to empty his own casket from time to time. Being unable to engage in 'the marriage act', a devout priest must therefore find ways to make 'going it alone' if not a spiritually satisfying experience, then at least a physically successful one. There had been schools of thought in the seminary on this matter, and the young Enda had been enormously grateful to find a pragmatic elder priest to talk to frankly about male masturbation. He had conceded to the temptation of self-abuse on and off since puberty and considered the fact that he had not been struck blind or deaf as nothing short of the miracle of

God's devotion to him and therefore a reason to further strengthen his vocation.

The mentor priest had discussed it with him during a long confession and had said that whilst self-relief would always, in itself, be an occasion of sin, there were ways to minimize the penance, provided you respected certain boundaries and didn't go over the top. Father O'Donnell shied away from specifics but the septuagenarian none the less gave Enda enough information to be getting along with.

'Magazines are used, but they are generally frowned upon. They hang around and can be found by housekeepers and the like. And their presence might tempt one into indulging more often than is absolutely necessary.'

Enda had loved having that conversation. It was such a *relief* (pardon the pun) to be able to get some details on what he should and should not be doing. He knew that, despite his mother's dark cryptic warnings to the contrary, this was an act in which he simply had to indulge if he was to retain his vows of chastity *and* his sanity. And if he was going to have to do it, then he had at least wanted to be sure he was doing it with the utmost respect to Our Lord's calling.

'What about music, Father?'

'How do you mean?'

'Sexy music. You know, like pop music. Disco.'

'Can't stand the stuff myself.'

'I mean, is it all right to relieve oneself to music?'

'In a disco, you mean? Well public displays are usually

frowned upon, but I suppose if you confine yourself to the toilets.'

He wasn't getting where Enda was coming from at all.

Enda had been given a transistor radio for his thirteenth birthday, and this small box had provided temporary liberation from the confines of his mother's cloying Catholicism, as well as almost causing his undoing. Through it he had first learned the nature of true sin. Not just the childish sins of backchat to your parents, the accidental breaking of a good piece of china, the surreptitious dropping of a Hail Mary off that last private decade, but the deliberate seeking-out of vice. The listening to pop music on Radio Caroline after he was supposed to be asleep was, of course, a sin. It was not listed in any of the official pamphlets that were lying about the house, but young Enda had calculated it around the venial mark. Mortal sin came in the guise of a one-hit-wonder diva by the name of Andrea True Connection, who cooed and moaned her way through a disco hit entitled 'More More More'. The basic thrust of the lyric was an enquiry as to how the listener would like their 'love'. As in: 'Ooooooooooooooooooooo, how d'ya like your love?' Followed by the assurance that whatever the listener's preference was, the singer was assuming there was an endless supply of it available in her pleas for 'More! More! More!' The bread and butter, so to speak, the specifics of the matter were, in the interests of public propriety, missing. But a generation of teenage boys found that the enquiry alone was delivered in such a suggestive manner that it was enough to cause, enable and effect a conclusion to the matter in hand. The song was in the English hit parade for a number of weeks, and during that time the thirteen-year-old Enda found that life became a little unpredictable. Such was the power of this song that any time it came on the radio a chain of events almost beyond his control kicked into action. That was fine if he was under his covers at night waiting for the song to come on. But if he was, say, down in Connelly's corner shop picking up messages for his mother, or at a Legion of Mary meeting in the church hall and the window cleaners had their transistor disrespectfully blaring outside, it got tricky. When the popularity of 'More More More' began to wane, Enda panicked and in an unprecedented moment of sin, stole 79 Irish pence from his mother's purse to buy a 45 single of the song in Stan's record shop.

He was to wait another five months for his fourteenth birthday before he got a record player on which to play it. His parents had been confounded by their unworldly son's request of such an extravagant gift, but had concluded that he was such a good boy, they could not refuse. As further reward for her son's piety, Enda's mother had taken him to Stan's record shop and bought him 'I'd Like To Teach the World To Sing' by the New Seekers. Enda was blushing wildly, but Stan hadn't said anything. Andrea, and her 'True Connection' with the teenage boys of Killa, was history now. He had a black market going in copies of 'You Sexy Thing' by Hot Chocolate, which had given its profane content away to watchful parents with its open use of the word 'sexy'.

The secret playing of 'More More More' in record

format proved to be something of a challenge. In his efforts to get everyone out of the house, carry the record player upstairs to his room from the living room where his mother had kept it 'for the whole family to enjoy', rig it up, take Andrea out of her hiding place under a slither of carpet beneath his wardrobe that the Hoover wouldn't reach, then allow it to fulfil its special purpose with the constant threat that his parents might come back home at any minute, get it back downstairs and settled into exactly the same position and get Andrea back under her patch of carpet again, Enda had forgotten to play along with the pretence that he had been longing for a record player so that he could play 'I'd Like To Teach the World To Sing'. So when he requested a small portable tape recorder, a new-fangled and quite expensive contraption for his fifteenth birthday, his parents were, understandably, confused as to why he needed another piece of electronic sound equipment when he hardly touched the record player at all. Enda (and this really was a sin which to this day he was certain he would pay for in purgatory), when refused his request, broke down in front of his mother and told her that he wanted the tape recorder so that he could record his nightly devotions to the Blessed Virgin Mary then play them back to her, thus worshipping her in his sleep. His mother assured him that the BVM didn't expect such extreme measures, but while she protested her son was overly devout, secretly she was delighted and the recorder was forthcoming. On more than one occasion Enda's coitus was interrupted by inappropriate visions of the Lord's Mother dancing alongside Andrea TC. This should have been enough to put young Enda off his stride, but then another song came on the scene that sent the arrow on his sin barometer spinning. Enda did not know its name, or the artist 'performing'. He only heard it on the radio a few times, but the impact the Orgasm Song made on him was so deep, so abiding, that Enda knew if he allowed this record into his possession it would surely go into direct competition with his commitment to the Catholic Church in general and his devotion to the Virgin Mary in particular. Andrea's True Connection was bad. She was sinful. But the Orgasm Song could, if it were allowed to take hold, put his very vocation in jeopardy. Basically it was about a man and a woman engaged in what can only be described as conjugal relations. This was the mid-seventies and young Enda was not stupid. He wasn't naïve. Part of having a vocation to priesthood was knowing what you were up against and there was sex going off all over the place. He had seen it himself – young people his age kissing in discos, not to mention the nudie magazines going around the hurling team – and he knew for a fact that there were people living in a state of sin in his very own village. But even with all he knew of the world, the Orgasm Song took the biscuit. It featured the voice, half-speaking half-singing, of a gentleman of, Enda presumed more than knew, African-American origin. Throughout the three or so minutes of the song he was instructing and encouraging his female partner (one would have hoped his wife, although anyone listening to them would have realized that that wasn't really the point) in the art of lovemaking. This chap seemed to consider himself something of an expert in that field, and his determination to elicit the most enjoyable possible conclusion for his ladyfriend (wife) during their joint endeavour was nothing short of admirable.

Enda's problem was not the sexual arousal that he got from the Orgasm Song but the longing that it inspired in him to make love to a woman. Once he started down that road, he was finished. The rules were largely unspoken, but they were clear. In order of sexual partners to be most avoided, women were at the top of the list because they could get pregnant, they might tell, and they would almost certainly fall in love with you if they were Irish and you were a priest. Nuns, in particular, were a disaster, as they tended to bring God into the whole thing and shatter vocations before and behind them. Next were adult males, who were, on the whole, more trustworthy than women, but still had the capacity if not the inclination to tell. Farm animals were hard to access and not to everybody's taste, but they tended to be favoured, in theory at least, by old-school rustic-reared clergy.

A virgin at forty-one, committed to the Catholic Church and bound by its rules, Enda had never engaged in any sexual act with another human being. He was tactile – a voracious and enthusiastic hugger. He wasn't a fuddy-duddy stick-in-the-mud. He wore regular clothes sometimes – he even had a sweatshirt with FCUK branded across his chest that he got given by the Flannery kids after he married them last year. He knew how to party – ask any of the kids down at the local youth club and they'd tell you Father Enda was 'sound'. When the child-abuse scandals started to break, Enda stood firm in his belief that these were the isolated actions of disturbed men who happened to be priests. He didn't run scared. He told his flock that the Church needed, more than ever, the good people like them to stay and fight these evils from within. The Church had given so much to the community that was good and wholesome and worthy, and now it needed the community to give back. The people stayed, in his parish at least – but the younger ones didn't believe in the Church any more. They believed in Enda. The baby-boomer generation of middle-aged women in particular were enraged by their Church's betrayal of them. They had spent the Swinging Sixties in small-town Ireland where they weren't allowed to use contraception and stayed with husbands they loathed for fear of purgatory and divine retribution. These self-same priests that had subjected them to moral terrorism as children and told them to carry on having children they didn't want in preference to taking the pill or – worse – denying their husbands, it now turned out had been either abusing little kids themselves or covering up for others who had. For these women, the supposed backbone of Killa's Catholic community, the open kindness of Father Enda was all that kept them coming to mass.

Then one day Enda was having a chat with the Bishop. It was a small thing really that set him off. A lie. Not a big one, and not the first one by any means, but whatever it was about the timing or the day, it made an impact on him. Bishop Dunne was on about money, as usual. Contributions had fallen off in Killa and he was 'disappointed'. Could Enda try and organize a fundraiser to make up lost ground before the end of the year? The Vatican was putting pressure on Ireland. There was a fortune being paid out in compensation claims and lawyers' fees, and every parish, no matter how small, had to do its bit.

The Catholic Church, it seemed, was *very* short of money.

Enda looked around the study in the Bishop's palace: opulent red with mahogany shelves groaning with leather-bound books and first editions. It was a square ugly building, constructed in the 1950s to look like a 'palace' with turrets and balconies and bay windows. There was at least an acre of landscaped gardens and twelve bedrooms. Twelve bedrooms and only one Bishop. It made sense. Enda looked at Bishop Dunne and he just blurted it out.

'You could sell this place.'

The Bishop looked at him incredulously, and when Enda didn't indicate that he was joking, the old boy became incandescent with rage.

'How dare you! I have never been spoken to in such a way in my entire career.'

'I'm sorry, I just thought that if we were short of money the palace would probably be worth at least a million euros.'

Bishop Dunne would have ejected him with a sharply administered boot to the backside if he had been a younger man and didn't believe that Father Enda wasn't just a bit of a simpleton. Or if he could find another priest from the fast-dwindling supplies of young men who were prepared to take up a career that had come to carry the automatic stigma of 'child molester'.

'It's not mine to sell, Enda. It belongs to the parishioners of this Church.'

Lie One.

'Yes, but ultimately it belongs to the Vatican, Bishop.'

'Who are managing it for the parishioners of this area who choose to use it to house their highest-ranking religious. Their bishop. Me.'

Lie Two.

Enda decided that enough was enough. He had defended the Church as a whole and this wretched Bishop in particular for long enough. He had been denied everything he had ever asked for by both. Request for transfer to the missions? Denied. Request for self-financing sabbatical in the missions? Denied. Request for diocese donation for improvements to Killa community centre? Denied. Numerous dispensations to perform weddings on Sundays, marry a non-R.C. to a parishioner, spice up mass with a visiting lay speaker – denied, denied, denied. Enda decided to fight back. That Sunday he informed his congregation that the Bishop's palace on the outskirts of Killa village belonged to them, and that the powers that 'managed' the building for them would like to know how they thought it could best be used to serve the interests of the community. Did they want it to continue to house their highest-ranking religious, or could they think of any other use for it? The following Sunday the suggestion box was overflowing, and Enda livened proceedings up by picking a few out and reading them aloud from the pulpit during his sermon. Overwhelmingly, the people of Killa wanted to evict Bishop Dunne (several of them suggesting considerably less salubrious housing alternatives, like a caravan), in favour of a local theatre, museum, various co-operative commercial ideas including a small hotel, a retreat for battered wives and a holiday camp for disabled children – the list was creative, interesting and endless. Aside from one or two die-hards, bishops did not feature in the people's plans for the people's palace.

The Bishop was not, naturally enough, impressed. Not being much of a mass-goer himself, his spies had sent word back. Dunne had to sit on the horror of it for a few days before he could safely bring the errant priest in for a telling-off without risk of his falling into an apoplectic coma.

The housekeeper kept Enda standing in the hall for twenty minutes before allowing him into the drawing room where Bishop Dunne was sitting in a leather chair by the fire, the very picture of devout, aged dignity. He was going to take this chat handy. No histrionics, no raised voices – just quiet, mannered conversation. Bishop Dunne believed in the 'less is more' tactic of threat delivery. Say your piece then let it sink into the silence and watch 'em sweat.

'This is a very serious matter, Enda. Very serious. There has been talk of your resigning.'

The Bishop cracked the finger of a KitKat into the dusty silence and dipped it in his tea before lashing it in for his dentures to handle. Now. Let him chew that one over. Sit back and watch the misguided idiot realize that you can't go about casting aspers—

'Fine. I resign, then.'

Dunne choked on his chocolate, and by the time he recovered, Enda was already out the door. Bishop Dunne, having upset the last committed priest in the county – possibly the country – was back saying mass again.

Enda was shocked himself. The decision to become a priest was one which had gradually dawned on him throughout his childhood until, by the time he was eighteen, he had found it had gripped him so totally that there was nothing else he could possibly do. The decision to leave had leapt on him in the time it took to say the words 'I resign'. Over the coming days, he began to regret the rashness of his actions. What would he do now? Where would he live? Who was he if he wasn't 'Father Enda'?

He was considering ways to approach the Bishop and beg for his job back when he met Corrine and everything began to change.

PART TWO

NOSEY PARKER

'I'M JUST HONEST – THAT'S ALL'

GIVE 'EM A BREAK, RON!

Yes, it's true. Honest Ron is going soft on ya. What about that s***head Alfie Smith walking out on his wife after less than two weeks? Course, it's not official. In fact, that w*** mag *Hello!* has a big story this week featuring Sharon Smith and MoniKa looking all cosy at the 'love nest' in Holland Park, but no sign of our Alf. What Nosey Parker wants to know is where is the man that's supposed to be doing the loving? Tell you something, if Ron had a cracker like that at home, he'd have her chained to the bedposts. (And the mum and all! What a tight-looking bit of stuff – stop it, you randy bastard!)

They say: 'He's away on tour.' *We say:* 'What tour? He's just not man enough to perform "off camera".' *What do you think?*

Is Alfie gay? Phone 080027821 if you think Britain's top pop idol is a shirt lifter, 080027822 if you think he isn't and 080027823 if you're Not Sure.

(Calls charged at a rate of £5 per minute.)

141

12

There are things that you know, that you don't know that you know until you need to know them. For instance, Alfie wasn't aware that he knew the name of the celebrity Costa del Dublin until he found himself saying to the taxi driver, 'Killy-ney?'

'Killiney?'

'Yeah. Thanks.'

He must have picked it up in the same way that Greek scholars discover that they know who Halle Berry is even though they haven't the remotest interest in the Oscars. It's an age when celebrity gossip is so prevalent that even the celebrities fall victim to it. And as for taxi drivers?

'Some beautiful houses out there. Be-eauti-ful. Yer man Eddie Irving lives up there, so does Neil Jordan and Bono, and Mal Doherty, I know them all. Had them all in the car . . .'

'That's where I'm going. Mal Doherty's house.'

'No!' he said with a star-struck enthusiasm that suggested he might have been exaggerating.

Alfie kept the cap down and spun some story about

how he was a gardening expert being called in to have a look at Mal's trees. Why, he thought to himself later, do we always choose lies around things we know *nothing* about? Like from thin air. Trees! Needless to say the driver was an amateur horticulturalist with a special interest in tree surgery.

The sweat was already pouring off Alfie by the time he got to Mal's front door. Then he had to go through the mortification of introducing himself to the wife of a man he had met once, briefly, in one of those mortifying 'I'm only here because my publicist *made* me' moments, backstage at *Top Of The Pops*. Mal had been friendly in that we're-all-part-of-the-same-rock-brotherhood way, but Alfie knew he was just being polite. Once a boy-band teeny, always a boy-band teeny, and while Alfie secretly believed that he was as good as the slim-trousered, sneering, pointy-featured indie love-prince, he wasn't expecting the warmest of welcomes. He would surely think Alfie was a freak showing up on his doorstep like that, but to be honest, Alfie didn't know what else to do. Aside from that one piece of information that he didn't know that he knew, his mind had gone completely blank.

As it happened, Mal's wife Helen was a peach. What he had been brought up to describe as 'a real lady'. Younger of course (but probably not too much) than his own mum, but every bit as nice. He didn't even have to explain himself. She got 'it' straight away and said she would do everything she could to help. She made him ring his manager. Karl could get on to MoniKa and Sharon, if Alfie couldn't face talking to them himself, but Helen insisted he let his nearest and dearest know that he wasn't dead. That was only fair. The set-up at Doherty's was really cool. All the phones had these security attachments which meant the numbers couldn't be traced to the country of origin. Even Wilson – and he had everything – didn't have a phone system like that.

'Wilson doesn't have a million German nutters trying to get hold of his phone number,' Helen explained.

It was no use pretending that Mal was a genial host, because he wasn't. He seemed to be making a point of keeping out of his new house guest's way. Giving the briefest of 'hey, man' greetings before scuttling off with his beer to his 'studio' at the back of the house. None of the friendly 'come and join me for a jam' stuff. Alfie suspected that he didn't want him there, but Helen was reassuring, putting Mal's grunts down to 'stress' and 'artistic temperament'. Alfie thought he might have picked up a hint of irony in her voice when she said that, but he hoped he hadn't. That really was the coolest thing ever. A wife who puts her husband's moods down to an 'artistic temperament'. That was the sort of wife he wanted. Alfie thought Mal was shit cool anyway, but having a nice normal wife like Helen? That was the business. None of your trophy wife supermodel shit. Helen was a 'real' woman.

Those first forty-eight hours away from his life, Alfie felt like he was on a rollercoaster. High. But not high happy. High as in manic. But not in a crazy way. Unless you counted the fact that what he had done was sort of crazy. He felt elated when he thought about it, then not. Sad at having let his mum down – leaving MoniKa like that. Then immediately angry at how people expected him to be a certain way, and certain that he had done the right thing. Then sad again because he knew that they loved him, and not so sure of himself. In all honesty, it was a buzz being away from it all, but at the same time it was a grade-one headfuck.

He had only intended to stay for a few hours, until he got his head around where was a safe and anonymous place for him to go. But once he got there, he didn't really feel much like moving. It reminded him of the few months he spent living with Wilson and Stephen. Like being in a really fantastic hotel, except he could wander into the kitchen any time he wanted. He felt like part of the family, but without the expectations and the emotional clutter. This was the type of home that he wanted. Secluded and private and classy. Like Helen. MoniKa looked classy, but she was bossy and she had arranged for *2Day* magazine to come around to the house without consulting him. Actually, she had consulted him and he had said 'yes' (as long as they could give the money to charity), but that wasn't really the point. The point was that she didn't really mind about *2Day* magazine coming around and he did. He only did it because they could give the money to charity, but he suspected that MoniKa wouldn't have cared if they had kept the fee themselves. In fact, he thought, maybe, just maybe, MoniKa was the sort of person who might have done it for nothing. That she *liked* being a celebrity. It was all right to love your job, and it was all right, even, to like the money. But liking being a *celebrity*? Actually *enjoying* the attention? Well, that was just pure naff, wasn't it? I mean, who'd want to be married to a woman like that? He was telling all of this to Helen in the kitchen on day three – making himself useful by entertaining Helen with a bit of chat while she was cooking the dinner. He offered to help, but Helen was one of those women who didn't want other people flustering about in her kitchen. A lady who liked to be in control. Like Mon. But not like Mon. MoniKa didn't cook. It didn't matter. Or did it really? It must do if here he was, quite happily living in the house of a complete stranger rather than going back to his wife in Holland Park. His brain was starting to sizzle and Alfie was glad when Helen gave him the opportunity to think about something else.

'You'd better start thinking about what you want to do, Alfie. I've to go down to Mayo to do this charity show I've been arranging. You know you're welcome to stay here in the house.'

Alfie was no fool. Helen was very politely telling him it was time for him to fuck off. But he just couldn't go back. Not now. Perhaps never. He didn't know. All he knew at that moment was that he wanted to feel safe, and he felt safe with this woman. She wasn't the type to dump him. The fact that she had taken him in at all told him that.

'I'll come with you, if that's OK. I've always wanted to go to . . . em . . .'

'Mayo?'

'That's right.'

There was a weary look in this woman's eyes that told Alfie she did not want him to go with her. That she had had enough. Not just of him, but of everything.

146

Fuck it – he said to himself, as long as she said 'yes', he'd leave her alone once he felt able. He was good company. He was no hassle. It'd be fine. They'd have a nice big house he could hide in until—

'Well,' Helen said, 'you'd better think of a story, Alfie, because we don't have a house down there for you to hide in. You'll be roughing it out in public like the rest of us.'

'Shit, really?'

'Shit really.'

'We'll be in a hotel, then?'

'No.'

'Private house?'

Maybe they were staying in the country home of some big Hollywood name. Didn't Sting and Trudi have a castle in . . .

'B&B.'

. . . Scotland, obviously. A bed and bloody breakfast?

'The only decent hotel in town is all booked up for the models and special guests. The rest of us have to make do with what's left.'

Alfie tried to let it all sink in. This was do-or-die time. Invent a new identity or go back to the old one right away.

'You can be a roadie if you like? If you know anything about rigging, I can put you in with the road manager. She's a mate. Won't ask any questions.'

'I've a bad back.'

God, he sounded like a right precious little poof. The truth was, he had a fear of heights. Supposing they tried to send him up a ladder? Helen was laying the table now.

Alfie could tell from her precise movements that she was losing patience with him.

'Well, you have to do something, Alfie. I can't just drag you along for no reason, or hide you in a barn.'

Alfie felt a shot of panic rise through him that he was in danger of blowing himself out of this.

'I can DJ.'

'We have a DJ.'

'I'm better.'

Yeah right. He'd heard Helen put together this show. She had every shit-hot designer, DJ, supermodel, stylist, make-up artist in Europe flying in for this gig. Dragging them all down to the arse end of this tiny island to work for nothing. For charity, of course, but ultimately – for her. Helen Doherty. She was some player. Then there were the punters who were paying two grand a skull to sit in a tent in the middle of a field to see a few frocks they'd doubtless already seen in the comfort of Paris five months ago, having to finance their own transport into the bargain. Fuck's sake, she'd been on to some of them looking for lifts! 'Paddy – any chance you could divert to Milan on the way across and pick up Julian August? The make-up artist. You're a saint, darling. It's for the children. *Of course* he'll do Charlene's face on the way over. She *loves* him!'

Alfie knew he wasn't better than the DJ Helen had arranged for the show. And so did she. But they both knew that Alfie had talent, and she knew something that Alfie didn't know that he knew. That he was an egotistical, self-important, 'artistically' tempered shit-head – just like her husband Mal. In that sense, she had neither the inclination nor the energy to fight.

She waved Alfie out of the room.

'Mal has decks and records and stuff – clear it with him. I'll set up a meeting with the production people down there so you won't have much time. You'd better not let me down.'

Alfie had to go and kiss Mal Doherty's arse to get what he needed. It had been a long time since Alfie had had to ask anyone for anything they didn't want to give him. In a funny sort of way, he kind of enjoyed it.

Vogue Suite, The Hilton Hotel, Tangier, Morocco

To: mnKa@hotmail.com
From: Justin@McIvorManagement.co.uk
Re: Firefighting

This is a fucking mess, MoniKa. Alfie not turning up on the *2Day* shoot is bad fucking form. I know we still get to keep the money, but it makes me look unprofessional when I don't deliver on my promises. People will start to think I'm dishonest, and dishonesty is a big no-no in this game. Anyway, we'll just have to do what we can. Don't get all fucked up over Ron – I've got him sorted and for God's sake, MoniKa, give the *2Day* bimbo a wide birth for the time being until I can figure out just where we are. If we play this right, Alfie disappearing might not turn out to be such a bad thing for your career.

You just keep your head down like a good girl, and leave it up to Uncle Justin.

PS Still fighting for the pink Beetle. I think you may have to let that one go, babe.

13

Corrine would be lying if she said she hadn't enjoyed feeling a part of something again. Originally the fashion show had been planned as a low-key local affair. Aoife and a few of her little chums coming down from Dublin to model some dreadful clothes for her mother's shop. Five euros a head and a makeshift catwalk in Donlan's Hotel. Then the disco, a few chips on the way home – a great night had by all and a few bob eventually filtered through to some Estonian orphans, or whatever. Ghastly. A waste of time.

Corrine persuaded Aoife that they could do an awful lot better than that. Why not put on something really high-profile, *really* glamorous – raise tonnes of money and put Killa on the map? They had the support of Helen Doherty and as the older woman confided: 'Trust me, Aoife – *she'll* be expecting a lot more than a handful of grubby fivers in a Dunnes bag.'

'Really? She hadn't seemed that way,' Aoife replied, then, 'She said to say she was asking after you.'

I bet she did, Corrine thought. I bet she fucking did.

She felt annoyed that this woman had the power to cause a conversation about herself on the other side of the country just because she was the wife of somebody famous. It seemed unfair. Who the hell was Helen, after all? What had she done in her own right? Retired from being a pop star in her twenties, written a book and reared a child on her own? I don't think so. A bit of charity work, for fuck's sake. Organized a couple of parties. Big deal. So Corrine decided to have a go herself. Somewhere in her subconscious, of course, the possibilities were there. But she could never have imagined the doors that charity would reopen up for her. She dug out an old address book and began to go through it. Corrine had never had friends so much as contacts. People who knew people. Everyone was friendly; they might even describe themselves as 'friends' but you didn't call unless you had a reason. You certainly didn't call and say, 'Hi, remember me? I used to be famous and now I'm a nobody. Please will you help me get back in the scene?' But call and say, 'I am calling on behalf of Estonian orphans,' and it's all, 'Aren't you Corrine the singer/journalist/novelist? Darling, where've you *been*?'

Her phone bill was going to be horrendous but she didn't care. Corrine felt like she was at the centre of something again. Old record company bosses in America? She tracked them down. Young singers she had started out with who were now established rock royalty? They called her back. When she ran out of names, she went through Aoife's contact book, which was full of model agents and mobiles for funky chart-topping DJs and their managers.

Aoife had said she would put the calls in herself but Corrine insisted she had 'Too much else to organize. Have you got in touch with the marquee people yet?'

Ten days before the show, Aoife came around and said that she had been doing some sums. If all of the ticket sales came in as Corrine had estimated, by the time they had paid for the marquee, stage and seat rigging, lights, music, backstage construction, canapés and champagne for five hundred guests, flights from Dublin, transfers to and from Knock airport, accommodation, hair and make-up, they were going to have 15,000 euros . . .

'That's not bad . . .' said Corrine.

'. . . worth of debt,' said Aoife.

'Oh.'

Aoife had suggested they should call Helen to see if she could help. Corrine had said no. This is my gig – *our* gig.

Then she had thought about it. What was the big deal? She had nothing to prove. Her part of the mission was accomplished. She had raised the money – well, most of it, and if she was going to give her hard-won thousands to Helen to dole out to orphans, she may as well get her to work for some of that glory.

So she rang her.

'Corrine! I'm *delighted* you called. So *good* to hear from you.'

Patronizing shit or genuine niceness? Corrine had given out and taken in so much insincerity in the last few weeks, she neither knew nor cared any more.

Helen was sympathetic to the fact that 'costs had got a little out of control'.

'Ugh, tell me about it. Don't worry a bit, Corrine. I've been there a million times – you just tell me where things are at and I'll put it all together. It will be an excuse for me to get out of town for a few days.'

Just like that. *Get out of town for a few days.* Like – to the middle of nowhere where sad has-beens like you live, Corrine. *I've done this a million times.* Yeah, but have you ever written a fucking book? Recorded any best-selling albums?

'Mal might come down – you never know. I'm sure he'd love to see you again.'

Corrine's stomach spun over when Helen said that. Mal would know she was going to be there because Helen would tell him. And if he came – *if* he came – it would be a statement. Did she give a shit any more? If she did she certainly wasn't going to go there in her own mind. Not again. Not after he abandoned her the last time. She had enough to do planning her glorious social comeback at this show.

Enda, of course, was semi-hysterical with excitement and encouragement. If God needed a model from which to clone do-gooding hippie types for his second coming, Enda was it.

'Is there *anything* I can do to help?' he kept asking. 'Anything? *Anything* at all?'

She made him take Sapphire off her hands for a few days. Got the two of them away from the house and out from under her feet. And there was one other thing she asked him to do for her.

'Enda – do you think you could just leave me alone for

a while? I'm very stressed with this fashion show thing. Just stay over at yours for the time being.'

He had been mortified. But fuck it. If he was that mortified at her mentioning sex, then he shouldn't be harassing her for it all the time. It wasn't even the sex she minded so much. It was all that physical contact, invasive 'touching'. Like she was a fucking cat. Stroking her: 'you're so beautiful, you're so marvellous, you're such a good person, Corrine.' It made her want to puke. On and on, stroking her and cooing over her until she wanted to fucking scream. Then there was just the fact that he was there. With his brave attempt at a ponytail and his drain-pipe 'denims' and that little scrap of plaited fabric he had started to wear around his wrist.

'What is that *thing*?' she had eventually said to him, after days of keeping her irritation in check.

'It's a peace bracelet. Sapphire bought it for me in the chemist's.'

And that was another thing. Sapphire and Enda, all wrapped up in each other. She didn't want the child to get hurt.

If she had never been that keen on Enda, Corrine was now finding him insufferable. Organizing this show had put things into perspective for her. Getting back in touch with people she used to know – the agents, the names, the publishers. These were the real people in her life. Her people. The people who had been around when she had been doing things. And now, here she was 'doing' something again, and they were helping her make it happen. Enda was offering but what could he do? He was powerless. Useless. Just like everybody else in this shitty little town. So she'd be having a chat and a laugh with, say, Zac at her old management agency in New York and she'd feel like she was just around the corner from him in some fabulous loft and she thought that probably he felt like that too. Then she'd look up and Enda would be standing there in a bad jumper with a sad look on his face like he was jealous or something and she would be reminded that she wasn't in New York, or Paris, or even Notting Hill, London. She was in this tiny rural backwater fucking a complete nobody for the want of anybody else being available. It was pathetic – the whole thing. He was pathetic and that made her pathetic for being with him. It was wrong. So wrong. It was not what she was all about. Not Corrine. She was better than this. She would hook up with all her old friends at the show – make appointments for meetings with publishers over the coming weeks. Then it would be Sapphire to boarding school next term, sell Killa, back over to the flat in London and – boom! – fab new life. In the meantime there was no point in upsetting the people around her. She couldn't handle the whole weepy 'but I love you' drama that was sure to ensue if she ditched Enda. She had too much other stuff to be doing. In any case, she needed him on side for babysitting gigs now she was going to be backwards and forwards to London all the time.

Vogue Suite, The Hilton Hotel,
Tangier, Morocco

To: mnKa@hotmail.com
From: Justin@McIvorManagement.co.uk
Re: Sorry, sorry, sorry

Yeah – sorry sorry sorry, babe. Of course you didn't marry
Alfie for career purposes. Of course you love him. I didn't
mean to suggest for one second that you are not devastated
at his disappearance and genuinely worried for him. Jesus
Mon, what kind of an arsehole do you think I am? No babe. All
I was saying was that we have to make the best of this
situation. I know you are a sensitive artistic person and that
you get very upset by Honest Ron and his like slagging you
off. I know that about you, sweetheart. That's why I am your
press agent, remember? Because I understand how hurt and
affected you are by bad publicity. This is as much about
keeping people off your back, babe, as it is about the money. I
know that better than anyone. All I am saying is – you leave
me to deal with Ron and the tabloids. As for Hettie, I know
she's your friend, but at the end of the day she is acting for
her employers and they'll be looking for cash-back.
Sometimes you just move on from people you know?

Bit surprised to hear you had gone to Tangier, but I suppose
it's only for a week – although a lot can happen in that time.

Take it easy and *don't worry*! Justin's in control.

PS No – there's no word on the car yet. Do you really think it's worth the hassle?

14

When Aoife had said 'things had changed' *vis-à-vis* the fashion show, she was not joking.

'One *hundred* euros a ticket?'

'One thousand.'

'One *thousand* euros a ticket? Are you *MAD*?'

'Corrine says they'll pay it. Helen and Corrine reckon the more you charge, the better they like it.'

'Not round here they don't.'

'Well then, we'll just have to ship the audience in. Helen and Corrine have loads of rich friends.'

'You'll never get it past the committee.'

'Fuck the committee.'

It was an interesting concept, and not one that Molly had ever considered before. She was not rebellious by nature, and there was always the small-town element to consider. If you upset people, you could never be certain what the consequences were going to be, but you could be sure that there would be no way of escaping them.

'It's all right for you. You can come and go as you please. I have to live here.'

'No, you don't.'

Gaaah. And that's the way it always was with Aoife. No matter what Molly reasoned, she always turned it into a challenge.

'But I like it here.'

'So do I. Except how do *you* know how much you like it if you've nothing to compare it to?'

What Aoife failed to understand was that Molly was not her. Aoife had always been adventurous and interested in things outside of Killa—

'Bullshit. Sure look at you swallowing that celebrity mag crap. You love it! All I'm saying is – get out there and experience some of it for yourself instead of just sitting around looking at pictures.'

Under the weight of Aoife's nagging, Molly had been up to Dublin a couple of times to stay with her overnight, but she hadn't liked it. Aoife's friends all dressed in 'odd' clothes, and were beautiful in a thin and serious way that sort of scared her.

They went to a nightclub where they didn't have to pay to get in and were ushered upstairs to a 'private' room where there was no dancefloor and waitresses brought their drinks over to them. Before she got the bus home the next day, Aoife had taken her shopping on Grafton Street. While she was getting some cash out, Aoife had stopped to talk to a small pretty woman dressed in black. She had looked like a nice ordinary person, then Aoife had come back and said, 'That was Ali – Bono's wife.' Molly had felt embarrassed and weird when she said that, like maybe Aoife was lying: Aoife was always hinting that she knew famous people, but when Molly asked her for 'the gossip', she never had any. Surely, if she knew all these people, she would be full of stories? So then maybe Aoife didn't know any and was just showing off in a sly, sideways kind of a way. Either way, Molly felt uncomfortable when Aoife talked about Dublin and her travels. It seemed so far away from their life in Killa – but now Aoife was bringing it all into their home town with this mad expensive fashion show. Who, in the name of God, had a thousand – one *thousand* euros! – to spend on a ticket for a fashion show? Modelling Breslin's Spring/Summer Ladieswear at that!

'That's the other thing. We're flying the clothes in from Paris and London. You have to help me tell Mum.'

Well, it just got better and better and more and more bizarre after that.

First, clothes being flown in from other countries without (a) the models even trying the stuff on and (b) when there was loads of perfectly good gear, if not in Killa or neighbouring Gorrib, well then – Galway, for crying out loud!

'What happens if the model is a size twelve and the dress is a ten?'

'We'll have a fitting on the afternoon of the show, and there is no such thing as a size-twelve model.'

Molly screwed her face up and sneered back jokily, 'Dere'snosuch ding azza zize-dwelve model. God, you should hear yourself!'

'Can I help it if I'm a gorgeous size-eight supermodel?'

'You're a bloody aul tramp – look at the state of you.'

Aoife was wearing an eight- to nine-year-old's Bob the

Builder pyjama top, with a pair of outsized plastic pound-shop sunglasses perched on her head. They were in the Walshes' B&B, getting the place ready for the incoming guests.

'And they,' Molly groaned, swiping at the glasses, 'are disgusting.'

'They're ironic.'

Molly didn't know what that meant, so she just said, 'Sure they are,' in as sarcastic a voice as she could muster then, 'Run downstairs and tell Mam we need some more Coffeemate sachets.'

Molly had taken the week off because the show was completely taking over both their lives and they only had a couple more days to go. Things had got a lot calmer since this woman Helen (who Aoife said was married to Mal Doherty from Godot. Right.) had taken things over in Dublin, but herself and Aoife were still 'the ground forces' as far as Killa was concerned. Corrine wasn't really doing so much except making sure that the towels and furnishings were up to scratch in the hotel rooms she had booked for her 'rich' friends. Dolan's Hotel had three stars, and was good enough for anyone, Molly secretly thought, but sure it was best not to say anything. As for the B&B, it was fully booked. Aside from the big hotel, most visitors to Killa stayed in either the rented mobile homes behind the sand dunes on the beach or in one of the many B&Bs that stood along the main road of the town. Of them, Walshe's was the largest and the grandest and had the best reputation. The fact that they were fully booked from May to September, with many regulars choosing to come off-season, paid testament to that. And why wouldn't they come? the Walshe family thought smugly to themselves. Mary, Molly's mum, kept a spotless house and Jack was an amateur chef so there was a choice on the breakfast menu. Oh yes. Eggs Benedict *or* Smoked Salmon Potato Cakes *or* Big Irish (fry) *or* Continental *with* (for the judicious slimmer) Muesli and Fruit. Many of the rooms were en suite and regardless of whether you got a 'premium with en suite' or not, every one of them had a television and, crucially, full tea- and coffee-making facilities. That meant Coffeemate sachets for the Nescafé and little tubs of long-life milk for the tea. No skimping. There must be two of everything in every room every day. Molly earned her keep by checking the tea- and coffee-making facilities were up to scratch every morning. Aside from that, she might hang out a few sheets from time to time, or keep an eye on the occasional pan full of sausages while her father nipped out to serve an early guest, but generally her parents left her alone.

'You've the easiest life.'

Molly hated when Aoife talked to her like that. Patronizing her. Aoife made out she was jealous of Molly sometimes, but she was only being polite. They both knew neither would want to trade places with the other.

'Oooh – nearly forgot. What was the name of that make-up artist you did that course with in Galway?'

'Julian August.'

'That's him. Well, he's flying over to do the show.'

Molly almost dropped the half-dozen teabags she was stuffing into their plastic basket.

'You're joking!'

'Am not. I've booked him in here.'

'You're joking!'

'God's honest truth.'

'Julian August?'

'Himself.'

'Coming here?'

'That's it.'

'To this house?'

'Walshe's B&B.'

'You're joking!'

'He's bringing a team from Dublin up with him, but I've booked you in as his special assistant for the night.'

'I don't believe it!'

When Molly had heard she wasn't going to be doing all the make-up herself, she was slightly put out. Until she realized what a huge affair it was going to be, and then she was relieved. Twenty-five of those skinny, smoking, weirdo friends of Aoife's to do in a couple of hours and the whole of Killa and God knows who else in watching? No thanks. But assisting Julian August – and the fact that she knew him – well she had *met* him – it was just too brilliant. And he'd be coming to the house. Staying there. With her and the family! Would he remember her, Molly wondered.

'Will he remember me, do you think?' Molly asked.

'Well, I don't know,' Aoife said, then not wishing to put a downer on Molly's excitement, 'I'm sure he'll know you when he sees you.'

'Maybe he will.'

Ultimately, Molly didn't really mind. Between the glamour of the show, the buzz of getting it all ready, and now her doing the make-up with Mr August himself, Molly Walshe felt that life could not possibly get much more exciting.

15

They had had this big row just before Helen left for Killa.

'If you walk out on me now, don't bother coming back.'

Big dramatic threats. Right at the last minute when it's too late to do anything about it. Typical. What the fuck did Mal expect her to do? Drop the show in Killa and let all those people down? Apparently yes.

'You always put everyone else before us,' Mal complained. 'I don't mind you doing charity stuff, but you just take everything on and *we're* suffering.'

Helen knew that Alfie had been the last straw for Mal. He had kind of been the last straw for her too, but what could she have done? The poor lad needed to hide out somewhere, and it's not like he'd given her much of a choice arriving up on the doorstep like that. The kid was no trouble really. He'd be out of their hair soon enough. Besides, when she was loading the car and waiting for the driver and Alfie to finish their breakfast was not the time to be discussing this. The time was a few days ago, when Alfie arrived or on any one of the endless number of nights over the past five years when they lay in bed next to each other, not touching, and pretending to be asleep. This passionate outburst was vintage Mal. No comment for months on end, just quietly moody. Maybe there is something wrong and maybe there isn't. No way of telling and then suddenly – bam! – 'you don't love me any more'; 'we never have sex'; 'you're abandoning me'; 'you're not taking this marriage seriously'.

Helen loved that one. *Not taking this marriage seriously*. Leaving him, for the first time ever, to spend quality time with his two grown sons and his mother – *his* mother – while Helen – what? Did a 'promotional' photo shoot for *Vogue* on the back of a yacht with a bunch of naked supermodels? Stayed on between shows in Rome for a 'wild weekend of rock 'n' roll raunchy sex' story for a couple of groupies to sell to an English newspaper? Fell in love with some fucking mystery slag that everyone knows about expect his own wife who then has to take a year out of her life to follow him around the world like a fucking lapdog to protect Mal Doherty from his own passions? No. While she takes a few days out to oversee a charity fashion show she had given her word to be at, and maybe – gasp at the betrayal of it! – take a couple of days' holiday at the other end to stay with a new (female) friend.

As for *we never have sex*, that was as much his remit as it was hers. *Abandoning* him? Please. It was doorstep hyperbole designed to elicit a lavish emotional response he knew full well, if he knew Helen at all, he was not going to get. His way of making her feel not only guilty, but to highlight her dispassion. Remind her that she was a cold bitch, as well as a bad wife and, probably, mother. She was neither and she knew it. This was all attention-seeking bollocks. Teenage shit.

In the next forty-eight hours Helen was going to have to oversee the erection and decoration of a marquee, and catering for the five hundred guests who had paid big bucks for this event, and the fifty or so 'guests' who were giving their services for nothing. Their transport and their expensively constructed and dressed bodies would also have to be suitably accommodated along with their egos. All this had to be done without upsetting the natives who, hopefully, Corrine would have under control. There were flowers to be arranged, choreographers to be cooed at, champagne glasses to be counted, goody bags to be filled and put under each chair. Every stylish item from canapés to clothing had to be shipped from London/Dublin/Paris to tiny Killa. Originally the show's location had been an unfortunate coincidence, and once the show grew in size, it would have made sense to relocate to a bigger city. But, as with all things 'fashion', by that time Killa's 'outpost' tag had become a positive and it was too late.

'Darling – off to the middle-of-nowheres-ville this weekend for little Aoife's show.'

'R-land is *so* cool.'

'Oh, but Dublin's pass–*say*. It has to be the country, darling. The *cunt*ry.'

'Scenery – scenery! I need scenery.'

Several high-profile fashionistas had arranged to stay on at various 'shabby-chic' and 'tacky-trendy' locations around the country, and they were all the type of impractical halfwits who would need to have the hire cars delivered to their doors and maps highlighted in pink marker.

Helen was the only person involved who knew how to put a show together in this detail. Aoife knew about make-up and hair and backstage histrionics, but she didn't know how to calm down a supermodel when her arch rival is not only on stage before her, but has nabbed the Manolo mules she had earmarked. Helen knew how to set her voice at just the right tone to convey that their choice of shoe for a three-minute catwalk and the plight of the starving Ethiopian was of equal importance to her – and then let them work it out for themselves. Aoife and Corrine might think they could put this show on without her, but Helen knew that they couldn't. But they could not possibly know that until after the event. If she rang them now and said that she had to stay home, made some excuse, they would be OK with it. But Helen was damned if she was going to do that. The bottom line was that she had been looking forward to getting away for a few days on her own. If she engaged with Mal in this charade of a fight – in this teenage ranting – all he would get himself was a grudging wife for the next couple of weeks. Plus he would have won. He had won enough, Helen decided.

Artistic temperament, she said to herself, and walked calmly down the steps, loading her bag into the boot. Sometimes, when she was really mad, Helen used that one to her own advantage. Only when he was being a complete wanker. Which seemed like more and more these days. Or perhaps he had always been a complete wanker and it was only now she was starting to see it. What-fucking-ever.

'You don't love me any more,' he shouted after her, as she was getting into the car. For a second Helen froze, thinking about turning around. But she saw him instead in her mind's eye. On the steps of their magnificent house, crumpled and bony, blazing blue eyes all fired up. Pleading with her; limbs crossing over each other like an uncontained schoolboy. He would look pained and passionate – just like he did in one of his own grainy MTV videos. He was loved by a million women, and they only ever saw him pretending to look the way she knew he was looking at her now. What each and every one of those million women would not give to be in her position. How could she not love Mal Doherty? How could she have him and not love him? The idea was ludicrous. To the world, and probably, no definitely, she decided, to him. He was putting it on, being spoiled and teenage and he could fuck off. If it was drama he wanted, then it was drama she was going to give him. She slid silently into the back seat of the limo.

Right on cue, Alfie skipped down the steps and into the car, giving Mal a chummy punch on the arm and a 'thanks, mate' before hopping into the front.

As they drove off, Helen looked back through the tinted window, and saw Mal's stunned face. She felt bad. But then, after a few seconds it faded. They bought crap coffee and scary meat pasties when they stopped for petrol on the N5, and later Alfie and Frank the driver had a singsong to one of his own CDs. It was a laugh, and Helen felt briefly guilty that she didn't feel worse about leaving Mal the way she did.

To: mnKa@hotmail.com
From: Justin@McIvorManagement.co.uk
Re: Deal is done!

Problem over – Ron Parker is on side. The deal is his paper
will throw their resources into helping us find Alfie, once you
give Ron the exclusive on the happy reunion. I know
everyone thinks Ron is a bit of a prick, but he's all right
really.

Job done – Justin

To: mnKa@hotmail.com
From: Justin@McIvorManagement.co.uk
Re: Deal is done!

Yeah – chill out, sweetheart, I know what I'm doing. Let's
find Alfie first, then worry about brokering a deal re the
reunion piece. Jesus, Mon, it doesn't pay to look too greedy
upfront. You just leave the negotiations to me.

Relax – Justin

To: mnKa@hotmail.com
From: Justin@McIvorManagement.co.uk
Re: Deal is done!

No, babe. I did *not* say you were greedy. All I'm saying is that the papers are not the soft touch that they used to be, and that you have to be politic about these things. Nobody wants to see you prostitute yourself for nothing but at the same time we have to string Ron along if we want him to help find Alfie.

All under control – Justin

To: mnKa@hotmail.com
From: Justin@McIvorManagement.co.uk
Re: Deal is done!

MoniKa love – I did *not* say you were a prostitute. All I said was . . . do you know what, babe? Forget it. Under the terms of my contract with you I am just going to go ahead and sort this mess out. You just look pretty in front of the camera and we'll talk when you get back.

Sorted – Justin.

16

'Where's Bill?'

'Which Bill?'

'Which Bill? Which Bill? What do you mean "which Bill?" Driver Bill – who the fuck do you think I mean?'

Bill was, as Wilson so succinctly put it, Wilson's driver. What that meant in real terms was that everywhere Wilson went that required a car and a person to drive that car, Bill went too. When Wilson stepped off the plane in Los Angeles airport, for instance, Bill would have flown ahead of him (business class) and would be there to greet him. When needs be, Bill would act as security and/or personal assistant, securing him swift passage through the airport away from the pesky public. Except when Stephen was there, then that was a role he would fulfil. But travelling with or without his partner, work or recreation – winter, spring, summer or fall, Bill was the first person that Wilson would see on entering a new country. Now, here they were in a new country, in a field. A wet and rather miserable field. Somewhere in the distance was a shack passing itself off as an airport terminal, a fact which was of no importance to these two, as they had flown in on a private plane which, at this very moment, was turning around to head back to its Hertfordshire base. There was a large amount of what the West of Ireland had on offer to them right there. There was rain, and a westerly wind with which to blow it. There was a great deal of boggy wet grass under foot. From a neighbouring field, the two dapperly turned-out gentlemen were being watched carefully by a herd of curious cows. If they could but see the 'shack' beyond the ground fog that was rising around them, they might have noticed a number of elderly locals doing much the same, except over an afternoon pint in the luxurious glamour of Co. Mayo's (only) airport 'lounge'.

'Oh, *driver* Bill. He's in Spain, I think. Anyway – I gave him the week off.'

A joke. Wilson had neither the patience nor, currently at least, the wardrobe to be dealing with this. He was wearing English country gentleman weekend wear. An ensemble in tartan and tweed kindly put together for him by Ralph (Lauren) for a polo weekend, and designed to attract the attention of young Argentinian horsemen rather than keep out 'the weather'. There were no wellington boots and there was no rainproof hoodie. A waxed leather cuff trim and collar weren't going to do much to assuage the assault course on which they had just landed.

'Don't fuck about, Stephen, I'm not in the mood.' Then the horror of it occurred to him. 'Oh, *don't* tell me we have to walk over there . . .' he said, flinging his arm in the direction of the airport terminal. 'Jesus, Stephen, I ask you to do one thing, *one* thing . . .'

Wilson was fond of saying that, except he asked Stephen to do millions of things and, as it happened, he had not specifically requested that Bill meet them directly off the plane as opposed to the nearby airport terminal. Not, indeed that that mattered under the circumstances.

'No, I mean it. He's on holiday.'

A fat drop of freezing rain slid down the inside of Wilson's leather collar and worked its way with speed down his naked back. It was the last straw in discomfort.

'This is not funny, Stephen . . .'

'Look. You know how you are always saying that you don't need anything if you've got love.'

Wilson listened because he knew by the tone of Stephen's voice that he thought what he was saying was important. It wasn't, natch. But Wilson couldn't risk a tantrum that left him alone, even (possibly) Bill-less in a field.

'Ye-es.'

'And you know how you are always saying that we should down-shift a little from time to time? Stay in touch with the "real" world?'

Wilson did not remember ever having expressed such a sentiment.

'Ye-es.'

'Well – da-daaaaaa!'

Stephen flung his arms out and presented Wilson with the boggy foggy field and its attachments of neighbouring cows and shack-like outhouses.

'And so all right – what are you talking about?'

'This is *it*, Wilson. One whole week of *normality*, darling. Bonding with the common man. No Bill. No limo. No posh hotel phoned ahead to make sure the lilies are fresh and the candles Dyptique. Plus – *plus!* – Alfie will feel *a lot* more comfortable with us blending in with the locals. The last thing *he* needs right now is a big poof fanfare swooping down on him.'

Oh right yeah. Alfie. That's what this was all about. Always about somebody else, never Wilson. Pleurisy. That's what the specialist had told him. You keep that chest dry, Wilson – no damp weather. Antibes, by doctor's orders from September to May or you'll be breathing through a machine within five years. Do they care? Stephen? Bill? The others? No. But one whinge out of Alfie and it's action stations. That's what happens when you get past fifty. Nobody cares. The young get all the attention. All the rewards.

This is what happened. MoniKa rings Wilson all upset and says that Alfie has gone missing. Karl at KLM had rung her and said Alfie was OK, but he won't tell Mon where he is and she's worried. What should she do? Wilson rang Stephen to check was Alfie in Tangier, which he knew himself he wouldn't be, but it had given him an excuse to ring Stephen and bring him back which was a good thing. When Stephen got home neither could bear to talk about the 'other thing', so it was all gossip about Alfie and Mon, and what did he think he was up to and perhaps he should never have married her in the first place and was that Wilson's fault as best man, etc.? Next day, Wilson got on the phone to Karl, who was beside himself. 'Has the little shit any idea the chaos he's caused?' 'Hey! He's just back from honeymoon. I thought he was on holiday anyway?' Wilson said in the boy's defence, but he knew it was bullshit. 'Holiday? Holiday? Fuck's sake, Wilson, you know more than anyone there's no such thing in this game.'

That was true. It was only a couple of days and the press hadn't caught up yet, but by Christ when they did. *2Day* magazine might have suspected something was up, but they were hardly to be feared like the tabloids and in any case seemingly Mon had carried the whole fiasco off a treat. Called in glam Sharon to do a whole 'my new daughter' bit, then played the ditzy model saying she hadn't realized that Alfie was supposed to be there at all.

'Sorry. I've no idea where he is or what time he'll be back.'

That, at least, was true.

Late that night Karl had got a call from his errant client saying he was 'lying low' for a while.

'Wouldn't tell me where he was.'

'Any guesses?'

'Don't ask me, Wilson. You're the big buddy that he hangs out with.'

'When you haven't got him screwed down to some ball-breaking schedule.'

'Hey, don't fucking go blaming this on me. I don't make the kid do anything he doesn't want to do.'

'Like twenty cities in twenty nights?'

'Then time off!'

'Yeah like: Hello, Mum, do you fancy nipping over to – where am I? – oh right, Paris for twenty-four hours? Then whoops – off we go again.'

'Gimme a break, Will. You've been there. You know how hard it is to keep ahead?'

Wilson did. And nobody knew that better than Karl. If Stephen hadn't forced him into cutting back on the tours, he'd still be working six nights out of seven. His fan base seemed like this huge hungry whale that he was never done feeding. There wasn't a stadium in any city in the world big enough to hold a fraction of them. He kept doing one more date; then every one sold out within hours. Individually and en masse he had everything to thank them for. They listened to him and he felt like he owed them his very life. But then underneath it, he knew he could give them every hour of every day for the rest of his life, and still they'd be looking for an encore. All his adult life it had been the audience applause that had fed him. That massive love of so many thousands in one place baying for him, and yet it had been one man who had given him enough that he could start to sit back and let go of them.

'Sure, Karl – just saying I know where he's coming from as well. So if he's not in any of my gaffs, where is he then?'

'Like I said, he wouldn't fucking say.'

'Not even to you?'

'Nope.'

'Cheeky little shit.'

There was a little silence while Karl acknowledged Wilson's sympathy, then the manager said, 'I reckon he's in Ireland.'

The idea seemed rather foolish to Wilson. If he could go anywhere in the whole world, why would he go there? Not that Wilson had anything against Ireland, it was just that it was Wales only further away. Nice scenery, shit weather – why?

Karl second guessed his line of thinking.

'It's near, and he rang within less than a day of going.'

'So – there are loads of places near by. And Karl? Maybe he went by plane?'

'All right then, who does he know in Paris?'

'No one.'

'Rome?'

'Nope.'

'Madrid.'

'No one . . . ayayai! . . . Marbella!'

'Rang round. Nobody has seen or heard from him. I just have this hunch, Will. Dublin, you know? All those shit-cool rock types. Alfie loves all that. U2, Godot. Fancies himself as a lad that way. Plus once you get in with that crowd, they're as tight as a cat's cunt. The press over there are still pretty loose. Tell you what, if I wanted to disappear – that's where I'd go.'

So Karl rang some management chums and sure enough, they found out that Alfie had been hanging out at Mal Doherty's gaff and had gone hide-about in the West with Mal's missus.

Karl could have gone after him but thought that 'Alfie would flip'. Plus he was needed in the office to make excuses.

Stephen booked the whole thing. Or rather, as was beginning to dawn on the stunned, soggy Wilson, didn't book anything.

'You . . . I . . . you . . . fff . . .'

By the time he had computed what he wanted to say, Wilson was so ferociously angry that he could not actually speak. This was the pine chest all over again. Wilson detested pine and Stephen loved it. So for his birthday what did Stephen get him? An antique pine blanket box engraved with Wilson's family crest. Wilson hadn't wanted the chest, but he had to be nice about it because it was a gift. Stephen wanted the chest. He bought the chest for himself and pretended it was for Wilson. Now he was pretending Wilson wanted to 'bond with common man', a concept which, with the notable exception of a rough young window cleaner a number of years ago, was alien to everything Wilson was about. Stephen wanted to play at being 'ordinary' again, and he was manipulating Wilson into going along with him.

In the instant that Wilson reacted, and, in fact, in just hearing his voice saying the words out loud, Stephen realized that he had made a very grave error of judgement. 'Sorry', however, seemed to be in that moment the hardest word. The only possible course of action open to him was to front it out, and make good as soon as was possible. How he was going to do that was another story. Never one to do things by halves, Stephen had taken the precaution of ensuring their week's 'ordinariness' would not be disturbed by leaving mobile phones and modern methods of payment back home in Herts.

'You are fucking mad. He'll kill you,' Carol had said. And as he felt the heels of his Gucci boots sink into the oncoming mud, he realized how right she was.

Wilson followed him because he had no other choice. Beyond shouting, beyond speech, he trudged silently to the airport terminal. Silently he stood behind his misguided partner as he walked up to the car rental desk and got the keys of the car he had ordered for them. He allowed Stephen to open the passenger door of the Opel Astra where the seat of his damp tweed culottes slid unpleasantly across the plastic seats, and responded with silence to Stephen's brave babbling as he twisted knobs and pressed buttons and tried to make light/better of the ghastly situation. 'Oooh, lovely – a bit of heat, now that's nice. We'll be warmed up again in no time. Look! A CD player! Oooh, that *is* posh. Whoops! Foot off clutch – start again. There now, that's better. Off we go! Wonder what this button does . . . oop . . . the horn – excuse I—'

'SHUT THE FUCK UP!'

So Stephen did. Wilson did not ask where they were going, sparing his booker the torture of explaining the merits of bed and breakfast as a holiday accommodation option.

The sun, such as it was, was going down as they drove westwards towards Killa. Mercifully it was well signposted, as Stephen had rightly assessed this was not the best time to test Wilson's map-reading skills.

The road was high and flat and past its horizon the mass of the sea threw a soft bluish light in their path across which floated splashes of orange and red. It was the type of magnificent landscape that gives men hope. But from behind the windscreen of an Opel Astra the best either man could manage was a fleeting moment of quiet respect. After half an hour's silent driving, with the light fading, they passed an old-fashioned sign that read 'The parish of Killa'. Stephen chanced a word.

'Nearly there now.'

Wilson raised his eyes to heaven, as if there still was a heaven to raise his eyes to, because if there was how come this stupid person was further torturing him with fatuous comments.

Over to his left, something caught his eye. High on a hill, atop a landscaped lawn, lit up against the darkening sky, was a small castle. It had turrets, it had stone eagles on podiums flanking its drive – and inside, surely, everything an internationally renowned pop star could possibly want. It wasn't perfect, but it would do.

'Stop the car,' Wilson said. Stephen stopped and eyed him nervously.

'I want to stay *there*,' the diminutive singer said, pointing towards the castle on the hill.

17

Superstar DJ, here we go!
He's OUT-rageous.
He's COUR-ageous.
He's the Mix-master of deck-dexterity, the hip-slick
champion of cool himself – can you please put your hands in
the air, and wave them about like-you-just-don't-care,
because that's our way of saying – He-llo to Mr Yellow!

That, Alfie decided, would be his DJing name. It wasn't great but it had a ring to it. He wrote it all down in the notebook and popped it into his new bag.

Talk about a freaky twenty-four hours. Helen was quiet during the four-hour journey, so Alfie spent his time rifling through Mal's records in the back of the car, deciding on his track list for the show and plotting his disguise. He had thought about where he was going with this whole disappearing thing, and had decided that, if he was going to make it work – get this time-out that he felt he needed – he was going to have to let go of Helen's apron strings and start taking responsibility for himself. First up was his appearance. It had to change and dramatically if he was going to get away with fronting up this fashion show as a DJ. There was the beginnings of a beard with a few days' growth so, as he was normally clean shaven, Alfie was going to let that be. Next was the hair. Driving through Ballaghadreen, he asked the driver to stop outside a large chemist's where he ran in and bought himself a box of ladies' hair dye in 'Beach Blonde', a packet of razors, some fake tan, a bag of cotton wool balls, a pair of scissors and a bottle of CK One just for the heck of it. With the CK One he got a promotional baseball cap and a generously large branded 'cosmetics sac' which, as an avid consumer who had not had the experience of an exciting new purchase in over two days, Alfie thought was a delightful gesture. Forgetting himself, he relayed as much to the teenage assistant with one of his winning celebrity smiles who returned it with the look of pity she reserved for old people capable of wetting themselves with excitement over a free hat.

The B&B was another pleasant surprise. There was an en-suite shower and even a small basket of toiletries laid out on the shelf above the wash-hand basin, which reminded him of his mum's house. There was a TV mounted on a wall bracket opposite the bed. Another excellent invention and one which MoniKa had refused to incorporate into their new house. She had commissioned special cabinets to house all their entertainment units: 'Old French style – like they had in the Lancaster in Paris. Remember?' He had suggested the brackets then and she had laughed at him and said, 'So *tacky*, Alfie – God you're *sweet*!' Patronizing him like he didn't know how to decorate a house. TV brackets were not tacky. They were nice and normal. They were what ordinary people had in their homes, and he was an ordinary person now and wall-mounted television brackets were good enough for him. There were tea- and coffee-making facilities too. Alfie remembered the very early days of U&Us. They had been doing a schools tour and it had been too late to drive back home from North London one night so Dave, in an uncharacteristic act of generosity, had booked them an overnight stay at the Moat House in Elstree. 'Have they got tea- and coffee-making facilities in the bedroom?' Sharon had asked when Alfie rang to say he wouldn't be home. 'Yes, Mum,' he said. She explained later that she was worried Dave might have booked them into some flea pit. For some reason, Sharon had always considered tea- and coffee-making facilities as a measure of respectability in paying accommodation. She would have liked this place with its basket of cosmetics in the bathroom and its chintzy curtains. That is, she would have before she got a taste of the Dorchester and the five-star lifestyle he had introduced her to. Fame had ruined everything for him and his family. It was the simple things in life – tea- and coffee-making facilities, the telly right up at an angle where you didn't have to even sit up in bed to watch it – these were the things that were important.

'Beach Blonde' turned out to be a disaster. Alfie followed the mixing instructions on the packet, but decided to put it on naked in the shower in case any of it should fall on to the carpet. Within the confines of the tiny cubicle, the fumes were quite overwhelming and as a waft of it suddenly hit his nostrils, Alfie turned his head quickly and a clump of dye fell on to his bollocks. He wiped it away with a towel, but he couldn't have done too good a job of it, because five minutes later it started to burn like fuck. He ran back into the shower and switched it to cold. The shower was overhead and not detachable so splashes of freezing cold water started to run the bleach off his head and into his eyes and all over the place. So he reached blind for the cosmetics basket and washed his hair in 'bath foam' before he could safely open his eyes and see that, the bleaching process cut before its prime, his hair was a nasty shade of orange – including a patch below his belt. It was all a bit of a trauma but then, Alfie told himself, at least it was different. Although not different enough. If he was going out in public tonight, it was going to take a lot more than a dye job to disguise him. He was going to have to be creative and he was going to have to be brave. Taking a deep breath, Alfie moved the tea and coffee accoutrements on to the bed, and replaced them on the dressing table with the instruments of disguise he had bought earlier.

It was early evening the night before the show and Alfie had to leave for a meeting with the production crew. Helen and her co-committee members – a person called Karen, or maybe Colin, and a model with one of those funny Irish names you can't spell that Alfie had a funny feeling he might have slept with once at a party.

His transformation complete, Alfie's hair had dried up to a crisp, dark yellow – hence his new DJ name. As for his persona, he would be cocky, he decided. Full of himself. One of those swaggering young I-know-where-it's-at DJ types, so very much at odds with his low-key down-to-earth, humble self that nobody would ever guess who he really was.

Brim full of confidence and looking forward to his challenge, Alfie pulled the CK hat down over his new hairdo, slung the 'cosmetics sac' over his shoulder and headed out the door.

18

This wasn't the first time that Corrine had worked hard in her life. The music industry had involved 24/7 devotion, and then as a journalist and writer she often burnt the midnight oil to meet a deadline.

However, the day of putting together the fashion show wasn't work in the sense that Corrine had ever known it. This was graft. This was Helen Doherty giving instructions: 'Corrine – the hairdresser needs fifty Kirby grips and a tin of Elnette hairspray five minutes ago. Do you think you could organize something?' and Corrine having to follow them because she knew she had no choice. Running around getting Kirby grips for hairdressers was not exactly what Corrine had planned. What she had planned was greeting VIPs as they arrived at the venue and having them ferried to their hotels. She had a full-length chiffon Galliano number that had stood the test of time, and had taken the precaution of driving to Galway to purchase a pair of low-slung mules from Brown Thomas, as she rightly suspected that high courts wouldn't be able to take all the running about. What Corrine had not really prepared for as well as she might was the logistical aspects of how and who was going to do the actual ferrying. While she had persuaded chosen key 'players' to buy tickets, she had neglected some of the more basic elements, such as applying for use of land to the county council in whose park they had erected the marquee and underestimating the number of 'bodies' required to help ferry the seemingly endless boxes of stuff from one place to another. Many of these jobs had been allocated to Aoife but perhaps, Corrine thought, looking at the empty marquee and the smattering of curious locals standing around while Helen looked disbelieving on at the not-happening-ness of it all, they could have thought a bit more about the organizational side of things in advance.

'Who's chair of your local G.A.A.?' Helen asked. Corrine shrugged, only vaguely aware of the existence of Gaelic sports, never mind that they had a local club.

'Derry Byrne,' Aoife said and she had her mobile out already.

'Ring and tell him we need men, kids and women too, down here asap. There's a free ticket for Godot's September show in it for anyone that's here within the hour, and if they don't like the band then they can refund them for the money.'

The knowledge that she might not have done all that she could have done to prepare for today did not make it any easier for Corrine to take instructions from her ex-lover's wife. Especially when she realized that fetching Kirby grips and hairspray was just about as good as it got. Programmes had to be put on each seat, ditto goody bags which first had to be filled from skyscrapers of boxes that Corrine thought would never be emptied by the end of the week, never mind in a few hours. Sapphire and Enda showed up, thank God, as little-miss-popular Aoife had somehow managed to land herself the plum job of overseeing backstage and had recruited an army of helpers from the early hordes of willing G.A.A. players hopeful of finally getting into a genuine fashion model's knickers. Hence, all the big burly men were fetching cups of tea from the catering tent for pretty American make-up artists and taking over Kirby-grip sourcing, while Corrine was left with their wives and children to help her carry mountains of heavy boxes out of the endless queue of trucks and vans that were pulling up at the park gates.

All the while Helen was running about, shouting in and out of an earpiece:

'WHERE ARE THE FUCKING FAIRY LIGHTS, DOM?

'Thierry. THIERRY! Don't fuck with me today, I'm begging you . . . I need those canapés ready for the catering staff an hour ago! I don't care about your fucking scallops today, Thierry . . . it's for *charity*, nobody's going to sue.

'These chairs need to be moved back from the catwalk – look – I can't see a fucking thing from here. What do you mean I'm sinking? Fuck, you're right! Dom – DOM! Where's fucking Dom? (Shit, my shoes.) Dom, we have chairs sinking into the grass in the front row. We need planks. Now! Everything under control there, Corrine? Good girl.'

It was unbearable. She was supposed to be in charge of all of this. Helen had come in and taken over. Vaguely,

Corrine knew that that was the way it had to be. That in reality, she was way out of her depth and that Helen was, in fact, saving her from what could potentially be an appalling fiasco the likes of which she dare not even contemplate. However, that did nothing to alleviate the mounting sense of fury that Helen was taking centre stage on a day that Corrine had earmarked as her social 'comeback'. Fury gave way to terrified panic as the day wore on and Corrine realized that she was not going to get the chance to go home and get changed. She missed her nail and hair appointment at four which was a pain, but she had washed her hair the night before and could throw it up into a makeshift chignon tonight without too much bother. As for her nails, well they were fucked anyway after the day's carting about, wrapping and unwrapping things. She'd pop into Flynn's and get Molly to stick on a packet of those fake . . . damn! . . . she was backstage with Aoife helping out – that little bitch had it all sewn up today. Never mind, if she had a couple of hours on her own in the house—

'Corrine, guests have started to arrive at the airport. I need you to go out there right away and start ferrying them to their hotels. The bus driver's waiting.'

What! Was it that time already? No. No way, Corrine thought, looking down at her scruffy jeans and old sweater, no fucking way was she going to greet people looking like this.

'But I'm not dressed.' As she said it, Corrine realized that it sounded like a teenage whinge. Helen at least had the courtesy not to respond to it as such but, in fairness, there was no way she could have responded that would not have upset Corrine. What happened next really did make Corrine wish she had kept her mouth shut.

'You look great to me, Corrine.' (Yeah, right, says she in her plain black ensemble, with no doubt a diamond choker hidden in the handbag to glitz it up for evening.) 'But if you don't feel comfortable meeting the guests I can send Aoife.' (And you can go home and get ready?) 'Besides I really need somebody I can trust to keep an eye on the DJ. You'll see when you meet him. I'll explain later.'

What was this shit? Not able to get dressed because she had to 'keep an eye' on the DJ? Except that when she first clapped eyes on him Corrine was so shocked that she was temporarily distracted from her own troubles. It wasn't just that he *looked* vile, or that he was monumentally arrogant, the really creepy thing was that he was somehow familiar. Like someone you might once have met in a terrible nightmare. That shaved hairline – no eyebrows; eugh! – the badly dyed crispy hair; a puffed-out jaw, and he spat when he spoke – 'My nhyame ith Misther Yellow' – like his mouth was full of cotton wool. He elicited a weird *déjà vu*. And it wasn't just her. She could see it in the faces of the technical crew: immediate horror followed by a self-doubting quizzical look.

One of the sound crew approached her while his short-straw friend ran the terrible-looking creature through the system.

'Aren't you the singer Sapphire?'

'Used to be.'

'Ah yeah – that's right. You quit, went into TV?'

'Journalism.'

'Ah, yeah. I was studio runner on one of your last albums . . .'

Jesus. He only looked in his twenties.

'. . . you wouldn't remember me.'

Corrine wondered if she should pretend just to be polite, although studio runners were the kids that fetched you your coffee and sandwiches. They weren't people who registered.

'Well, now you come to mention it . . .'

'Trust me. *You* wouldn't remember.'

And he said it in such a sideways way that Corrine wasn't sure that he didn't mean to suggest she hadn't said something to offend him way back when in the distant Eighties.

Fuck him, anyway. Who was he? Only some nobody button-pusher—

'Ahhh, Corrine – you've met Sam. Sam owns the Grass Studios in Dublin.' (And half the pubs and clubs there, Corrine discovered subsequently.) 'He's down helping out for the night.'

'Got my tent pitched in the next field.'

Corrine didn't doubt it.

'Sam, could you keep an eye on the DJ for me? I need to spirit Corrine away.'

'Mr Yellow, yeah? What's the fucking story, Helen?'

'Just keep an eye and make sure he doesn't fuck up.'

'What? He's a fuck-up *as well*?'

'Just cover him for me, will you? I'll tell all later.'

'Sure thing, boss lady.'

The thing that bothered Corrine more than Helen's lording it around, more than her elegant black Anne Klein two-piece, more than the fact that she obviously knew every soul worth knowing in the universe, and that even the humble folk of Killa who had known her less than twenty-four hours were responding to her 'charms', was the fact that Helen had somehow got hold of the idea that herself and Corrine were 'friends'. That was fine as far as it went. Corrine had found that name-dropping Helen was useful enough in terms of making new contacts, but when it started into this girlie, conspiratorial 'wait until I tell you' chummy nonsense, Corrine felt uncomfortable. And that was before she even considered that she had slept with the woman's husband. Corrine had no idea how she had become complicit in this fake friendship, but she had found herself inviting Helen to stay with her for a few days after the show. Why? Why had she done that? Helen had been on the phone and going on about how stressful her life was at the moment, and about how she was longing to get away and was thinking of staying on for a few days after the show when Corrine had suddenly blurted out, 'You're welcome to come and stay with me.' But then, that was Corrine. Why had she slept with Enda? Always putting other people first.

Helen had her arms around Corrine's shoulder and was guiding her away like a kind schoolteacher. She smelt floral and old fashioned, Corrine was gratified to notice.

'I have got someone who is dying to meet you.'

Chairperson of the Estonian Orphans' Society or some ghastly person from an airline who'd sponsored flights, no doubt. Helen had been parading these bores in front of Corrine all day, introducing her as 'the woman behind it all'. (So fucking far behind you can't see her.)

'Corrine, Jack, Jack, Corrine.' Jack had a broad smile and extraordinary teeth. He was wearing a baseball cap. American. How boring. 'Jack is the new commissioning editor of *Rolling Stone* magazine – he has been so supportive of us.' Jack looked adoringly at Helen, as if it were a privilege to be breathing the same air. Puke. 'So I said to him, "Jack, let me give you something back, because have I got a girl for you to meet?" '

Helen sure had the patter off pat.

'So I believe you're the best interviewer in Europe,' Jack said, giving her the best opening line she was likely to hear that year.

But Corrine wasn't listening. Behind Jack she had seen a limo pull up at the entrance of the town park and a figure emerge from its back door, pushing sunglasses to the top of his tousled head so he could look around. The frantic expression under his frown was a look she had seen before, as Corrine convinced herself that Mal Doherty had come looking for her.

19

Molly had to literally pinch herself to keep reminding herself this was all happening. The best day of her life? It didn't even feel like her life. It wasn't her life. Was this her? Molly Walshe? Little Molly Walshe from Killa, Co. Mayo, at the centre of this glamorous celebrity circus? Well, it surely wasn't possible. It was just too good to be true. All of it.

Where to begin? At the beginning. Right. First there was the marquee.

'A *tent*?' she had said when Aoife had first told her they weren't holding the event in Donlan's Hotel again.

'A *marquee*, Molly.'

'Yeah – I *know* what a marquee is, Aoife.' Actually, Molly had only seen a marquee once. Doing make-up for a friend of a friend's wedding in Cavan. The wealthy farmers had attached one to the back of their large house. It was, to all intents and purposes, '. . . a tent. We are charging people one thousand euros a head to sit in a tent?'

'Two thousand.'

'What?'

'Well, some people are paying two thousand euros.'

Molly had given up at that stage. The whole thing was beginning to sound like an elaborate lie. Like knowing Bono's wife and saying that this woman Helen was married to Mal Doherty. Maybe Aoife did know a few famous people and maybe she didn't. But one thing was for certain, if she did and some of them turned up to this fashion show, they'd surely prefer the comfort of Donlan's function room with its 'Italian-style' indoor fountain and its lush monogrammed carpets than a cold tent pitched in the middle of the town park.

How wrong she had been, and for the first time in this twenty-four-hour glamour fest, Molly was open-mouthed in awe at how blasé Aoife was about it all.

'Right,' the model had said, snapping shut the swanky mobile. 'The marquee has arrived at the park, Moll. Helen's not down until tomorrow so it's you and me gotta get this tent up.'

As they reached the entrance of the town park, Molly saw the biggest truck she had ever seen in her whole life. It had an English reg. and was as long as a row of houses. Two men climbed down from the driver's rig and one of them came over and kissed Aoife while the other lit a fag and leaned against the back, eyeing the curious locals who were beginning to gather.

'Where do you want us to put this thing, baby?'

'Anywhere you can, Sonny. There's a flat patch there in the middle. We don't want to pull up any trees.'

The man laughed, although Molly didn't doubt he

would have pulled up a tree with his bare hands if Aoife had asked him.

'How do you *know* those guys?' she asked as they started to unload.

'Sonny does the marquees at London fashion week. Lights, seats, rigs – the lot.' Molly nodded like she had a clue what she was talking about. 'We had a night out spring/summer last year – ended up at the Hippodrome. Talk about Eighties retro. What a laugh!' Moll looked at her like, 'What the fuck are you talking about?' and Aoife looked back like she was slightly irritated at Molly's innocence.

'Anyway, that's just what you *do*, Moll. You meet these guys and you call in favours.'

'He's doing this for *nothing*?'

'He wasn't going to. But then I told him I had this friend who was a real innocent doll and went wild for English men. Said she'd show him a good time if he pitched his tent in her park.'

'You didn't!'

'Jesus, Moll. Sunny is loaded. This is like a holiday for him. Driving over to Ireland, taking a couple of days out. His way of putting something back. No skin off his nose. He can afford it. He'll have loads of mates coming over for this gig, Helen's lighting guys, sound guys. Might even make a few new contacts if he does a good job.'

It all sounded a bit mad to Molly, but nothing could have been as mad as that day. Sonny and his partner David had hired a Dublin marquee company to come down and help them rig the 'big top'.

That first day, Corrine or Helen hadn't been around at all, so Molly and Aoife were in charge, and it felt great to be.

That evening Molly and Aoife had stood alone in the empty tent. The seats were coming from a Galway theatre in the morning, so they stood on the cool grass and looked up and around them at the enormous white silk ceiling and walls. They were in another world, where everything was white and soft and clean. Things would happen here inside this pod in just twenty-four hours' time. Glamour and glitz the likes of which Molly didn't even dare dream about. Aoife hoisted her up onto the wide catwalk and she stood there and shouted 'LOOK AT ME!' and spun around and around like a silly girl. She didn't care. She could be excited in front of Aoife. Aoife found a stool and leapt up to join her and they did a few turns of the catwalk singing Tina Turner's 'Simply the Best', which had been their anthem at school, collapsing in laughter.

If it had ended there, that would nearly have been enough for Molly. Enough excitement and fun for one year. But it didn't.

The following day, it was preparations and hard work. But it was brilliant. Molly was in charge of the make-up tent, insofar as preparing things so that all the hair and make-up artists knew where they were going to be working. Were the lights bright enough? Were there enough 'work spaces' for the artists' materials? Cotton wool, tissues, wet wipes (allergy-free), make-up remover all on hand in case of emergencies. Bottled water, real glasses for the hair and make-up artists, plastic for the models (in case of tantrums). Each model had their own 'rack' for clothes and Molly had to make sure the right clothes went on the right rack and were labelled – and that the model's names were spelt right. 'Trust me,' Aoife said, 'you don't want to offend Araminta.'

And that was just the beginning.

Helen arrived and guess what? She really was Mal Doherty's wife. First up, Molly recognized her from the social pages. Secondly – the first most unbelievable event of the show – Mal Doherty himself actually arrived. In a car. At the town park. In Killa. Then – *then* – he goes straight over and he talks to Corrine, who Molly knows really well. So now Molly knows Corrine and Aoife and now Helen, and Aoife is talking like 'Mal this' and 'Mal that' to do with him doing some kind of a speech or something and Molly's saying, 'Yeah, Mal this that and the other' like she knows him. Then – *then* – he comes over – Mal Doherty comes over – and he's like 'blah, blah, blah, great job' and all to Aoife and she's like 'blah, blah, thanks' and everything and all that and then – *then* – she goes, 'This is my best friend Molly.' And Molly thought the feet would give from under her, but they don't and she holds her hand out and she goes, 'Hi.' *Hi*. Just like that. Like it's no big deal. Like it's not just the most mind-blowing, freakish, mad mad mad mad mad thing that's ever happened to her ever.

She thought to herself, standing there in the grip of Mal Doherty's hand, This is mad. Surely it can't get any madder, any more like she had just stepped out of her own life and into some parallel universe of celebrity glamour. Punishment or reward for reading all of those magazines. *Hello!* comes to Killa.

Then it did. Get madder. And the rest.

'Molly, this is Sheryl from *Hello!* magazine. Can you look after her and make sure she has everything she needs?'

Sheryl was only the same age as Molly. Pretty and casually dressed with a large camera, nearly as big as herself, hanging around her neck.

There were so many questions Molly wanted to ask her. Are Victoria and David as in love as they look? Will Alfie's marriage to MoniKa last? Was that *really* Dale Winton's house, or is it true that Cilla lent it to him for the *Hello!* shoot?

'I'm a freelance,' Sheryl kept saying. 'I only do the social pages.'

'But you must *meet* loads of famous people,' Molly enthused.

'I photograph them,' Sheryl said, 'it's my job. It's different from actually knowing them.' Then she said something really, really weird: 'You probably know a lot more celebrities than I do.'

Who did she think Molly was?

'How long have you been working for Helen?'

'Oh. Not long!'

That was all it took. A small white lie and Molly was somebody else for the next thirty hours. It wasn't that she wanted to be anybody else, that she didn't like who she was. That she didn't think she was 'good enough'. It was just that other people seemed to expect it of her. Or rather, there was an opening to be somebody else, and she just saw it and walked in. Not somebody else even. Just a more confident, interesting version of herself. And boy did she need it when Mr August started proceedings.

'Clicky fingers! Clicky fingers!' he shouted whilst doing the same. 'Assistant? Assistant? Where is she?'

Molly presented herself.

'Hi. I'm Molly.'

'Creds?'

'Pardon?'

'Credentials? Qualis? Who trained you? Where? Why? How? Hurry, hurry girl! We've got to get started and I need to know what you can doooooo.'

'Why – *you* trained me, Julian. Do you not remember?'

She was taking a mighty chance and she knew it, but after an afternoon hobnobbing with the bright and famous, Molly was feeling cocky. Besides, innocent and all as she was, she had begun to realize that working in a chemist's shop in Killa did not exactly qualify her to this level of make-up artistry. She was intimidated, but she was determined to prove herself all the same. As luck would have it, Julian's long-term memory was temporarily on the blink due to his last cocaine binge. All he really knew were this season's colours, how to apply them, and that he needed somebody well connected in this rural hole to get him some drugs before nightfall. Molly looked smart enough, and he knew her, allegedly, so that was good.

'Millie!'

She didn't correct him.

The rest of her working night was so intense Molly almost forgot how to breathe. Julian 'did' the first face on a bland-featured young girl from Co. Cork who had only been modelling two weeks and looked as over-awed as Molly felt. By the time the self-acclaimed 'maestro' had finished with her, her eyes had been striped across from temple to temple with a khaki 'Zorro' mask and her lips were a washed-out beige, heavily glossed. She looked truly vile. Or, as Julian put it, 'Totally Now!'

Molly, who had been studying the magazines and practising various 'looks' into the night on Aoife in preparation for tonight, had to throw all that practice away and replicate the 'Zorro' look on a production line of models while Julian stood at the back opening of the backstage tent smoking fags and trying to identify and make eye contact with various passing young men. Every time Molly finished a model, she called Mr August over and he would scrutinize them, occasionally flicking a brush across a nose or cheek and waving them on to 'hair' with a dismissive wave. Molly was disappointed not to get more feedback on her work, but then she could not have known the level of her boss's anxiety, nay *disbelief*, that nobody had organized 'a little something' to keep them going backstage. When he had asked his assistant for same, 'Millie' had swiftly arranged delivery of a pot of horribly strong tea and a plate of sandwiches made with that awful white chewy bread and sliced ham. Julian, like every self-respecting drug addict, was vegetarian and only drank herbal.

When the make-up was finished, with a full ten minutes to showtime, Molly had no time to sit back. She was being pulled this way and that by everyone. 'Has anyone seen a pair of size-eight shoes?' 'I put a roll of tit tape down here two seconds ago and it's gone.' 'I'm hungry. I want an apple.' 'Can you get these women to use the ashtrays provided? This place is enough of a fire hazard as it is.' 'OmiGod – this milk is *full fat*!' 'Don't touch your eyes! Don't touch your eyes!' 'I don't care if your Mammy is out in the audience. You are *not* wearing a bra!' 'Flesh thongs? Flesh thongs? Who has them? Where are they? Now!' 'Thought MoniKa was doing this gig?' 'Nobody's seen her.' '*I* heard she was in Tangier.'

There were models whining, hairdressers hollering, firemen fear-mongering, and at least one make-up artist reduced to a shivering lump of nerves in a corner.

'Fucking eejit . . .' Aoife said when Molly pointed to Julian and said, 'I don't know what's the matter with him but he looks very upset.'

'I do – here give him this,' and she handed Molly a small bottle out of her handbag which Molly knew was poitín. Aoife's Great Uncle Padraig from 'out the mountain road' was too old to bust these days, and kept a few treasured regulars supplied with this potent high-proof potato-based beverage, including his wayward niece who used the odd drop as a 'more natural alternative' to the appetite-suppressing drugs favoured in the fashion industry.

'I don't believe you, Aoife. What do you think . . .?'

'He'll love you for ever.'

'I don't know – he doesn't look well . . .'

'Promise!'

Molly wandered over and tentatively touched Julian's shoulder.

'Mr August?'

'WHAT?'

'I thought you might like some—'

'What's this? More fucking tea?'

'No,' Molly said, 'it's an illegal substance,' Julian's face brightened considerably, 'called poitin. It's extremely dangerous and I'd better warn you that . . .' But the bottle was out of her hand already and half its contents down the American's gullet.

By ten thirty, when the show itself was over and the real part of the night – the party – was about to begin, Molly was already suffering from mental and emotional overload. On a busy day, Molly would have to wipe down a display, do a couple of five-minute facials and, if she had to replenish the tea and coffee baskets, squeeze in a lunch with Fonzie and a drink with Aoife, that was about as much as she could cope with. Since that morning, Molly felt like she had lived a whole life. A life.

'Alive! That's all it is, Molly. You're feeling fucking *alive*, girl.' Aoife's eyes were sparkling under her khaki mask and Molly felt a bit scared of her, as if she was someone Molly didn't know. 'Weeeeaeeeeew . . . come on, chicky, it's time to partaaay!' and with that, champagne snipe aloft, she launched through the fabric wall that separated backstage from front stage expecting her friend to follow. But Molly was tired. She had drawn a picture in her mind of what the rest of the night would entail: Aoife and her thin friends being 'freaky' and her feeling left out. Molly wasn't wild like that. It had been an amazing day – the best of her life – that was enough for now. She decided to sneak off home. Nobody would notice, and that way she could leave on a high.

She left through the back of the marquee and took the river road home. On the way she ran over and over the day, from the amazing well of shock when she first saw that truck and realized that this fashion show was *actually* happening to the thrill of sending the first girl out through the lit screens on to the catwalk. As the sounds of the party behind her faded and gave way to the chirruping plop of the water, it already seemed to have been a dream.

Her parents weren't in the house. They were back at the party along with every other inhabitant of the town. The B&B was fully booked, but surely nobody would be back there yet? So Molly was surprised and briefly alarmed to find the kitchen light was on at the back of the house, and there were noises coming from within.

Imagine her shock as, walking in to investigate who had left the party of the century behind, Molly was confronted with the figure of her favourite pop star (in the world *ever*!) having a good old rummage through her parents' fridge.

Offices of Justin McIvor, Press Agent and Impresario, Watford Way, Hendon, London NW4

FORWARD URGENT ATTENTION:
Justin@McIvorManagement.co.uk

To: mnKa@hotmail.com
From: Hettie@2day.co.uk
Re: Where RU?

Mon, am *not* happy chick here, babes. Waited for hour at GO!SUSHI – in the end Jez and the gang turned up and, got 2 tell U-guys, U missed a *great* night! Give me a ring soonest and we'll arrange a replay.

Hugs Hettie.

PS That nice man at Volkswagen was on to me just now about your car.

Soonest xxx

To: Justin@McIvorManagement.co.uk
From: Hettie@2day.co.uk
Re: Pink Beetle

Got your message, Just. and I'm *really* sorry but I just can't deal with *anybody* over this Beetle thing except for Mon. Or

Alfie. Get her to give me a bell on the mob. Or better still mail me back.

Hugs Hettie

To: Justin@McIvorManagement.co.uk
From: Hettie@2day.co.uk
Re: Pink Beetle

Sorry, poppet. Know UR *really* important and everything but no can do re Beetle unless I speak to Mon herself. Or Alfie. Get her to give me a ring. No reflection on u, babe.

Soonest, Hettie

To: Justin@McIvorManagement.co.uk
From: Hettie@2day.co.uk
Re: Pink Beetle

Justin!!!!???!!!! What part of 'no' do you not understand? Man at Volkswagen is *really* keen to deliver it to her himself so I really need to know where she is. Or Alfie.

Best Hettie

To: Justin@McIvorManagement.co.uk
From: Hettie@2day.co.uk
Re: Tangier . . .

. . . on the *Vogue* shoot, of course! *Why* didn't I think of it and *you* are a big silly Justin for not telling me right from the get go, because now my friend MoniKa had lost the car of her dreams and it is *all* your fault! Plus *2Day* magazine now have to fly out there to apologize which on top of all the money they have paid already is going to make Lucy *really* cross.

Anyway, still sending hugs although you are a *very* silly man!

PS Am even crosser with Gary at LipsInc. Because *really* it was his job to tell me first! Men are *so* silly!

20

Enda was taken aback when Corrine asked him to go easy on the sex thing. Things had been a little hectic in that department, but he had assumed that Corrine had been enjoying it as much as he had. Which, now that he thought back on it, was terrible because he hadn't really been enjoying 'it' at all.

Sex, if you'll pardon the pun, had proved to be something of an anticlimax for Enda. But then, his expectations had been high. And why wouldn't they be? It's not every man loses his virginity at forty-five.

By which age Enda had turned 'self-love' into something of an art form, elevating it out of a mundane habit and making it a sustainable enough activity to keep serious temptation at bay.

He could not quite work out how it happened but somewhere along the line Enda's musical tastes became divided into songs that could soundtrack his own personal porn movie and songs which would, under no circumstances, elicit even the remotest question of sexual arousal.

In recent years the former list had grown from a few

obscure disco hits and George Michael to include almost every song on the radio, and a few worrying 'off-siders' such as the *Coronation Street* theme song, which sent him to a state of tight-trousered-ness that defied explanation. So it seemed that, far from his appetites fading with age, Father Enda was living in a constant state of low-level sexual arousal. 'Self-loving' had turned into a punishment, as the priest fought his constant compulsion to self-relieve. He had to close down the youth club disco. No more naps in the confessional box as privacy became the enemy of his better judgement and he had to open the whole thing out and introduce face-to-face confessions to his resistant parishioners. Enda was in the grip of a terrible addiction, and music was his 'trigger'. Anywhere there was music, every café, every pub, every shop and every passing car – everywhere he went – Enda was in a constant state of discomfort. The only relief Enda had was in the listening to certain music that elicited no reaction in that department whatsoever. In fact, it could be said to have the opposite effect. And so Enda stocked up on Enya, Christy Moore, Joan Baez, Neil Young and redeveloped his musical tastes in the direction of folksy moral dronings that would remind him of poverty and politics and God and things that were guaranteed to quash any hope of sexual arousal. *Sounds of the Spirit*, Enda's local radio slot, which was now his only source of income, was born as an exercise in self-control. Basically, if it didn't give Enda an erection, it was on the show.

The obvious line of reasoning, and one to which Enda himself subscribed, was that it had been living in the unnatural state of celibacy that had caused this perverse state of wanting to hammer his lad to within an inch of its life at every given opportunity. Now that Enda had left the priesthood and was free to sleep with women, this problem (if not the problem of how he was going to earn a living and what he was going to do with himself for the rest of his life) would surely right itself.

But it was not to be so.

He had always believed that the first time would be unimaginably magnificent. Corrine was naked, her skin felt good, she made all the requisite breathy oooh noises, a lot like Andrea TC or the lady in the Orgasm Song. He didn't (as he feared he might) end up at the tradesman's entrance, but while he was engaged in the actual marriage act his mind began to wander. Enda had experimented widely in order to replicate what he thought a female vagina might feel like. And to his very actuate alarm, he found himself comparing 'the real thing' with a lukewarm beef tomato, a jar of tightly packed peach slices and, it has to be said, a vacuum cleaner. It was not that Corrine did not measure up. It was just that the act in itself was not so far removed from what he had experienced before that it transported him away from himself.

Sex with a woman, the very thing he had dreamed about, craved at times and stoically avoided always, was not, as he had heard trailer-trash wives complain to Jerry Springer, 'All That'.

After six months of sleeping with his beautiful, accomplished sexy neighbour, Enda realized that, when it came right back down to it, he preferred doing it himself.

Officially, that made him a sexual pervert. Perhaps his vow of chastity hadn't been such a sacrifice after all.

Then again, it was all so awful that it didn't bear thinking about. So Enda didn't. Instead, he tried to concentrate on the good things. Move forward. Embrace this new life he found himself living. He had recently been appointed Station Manager at K WEST FM, the local radio station, so as well as continuing to host *Sounds of the Spirit*, he got to look after the other contributors on this small, but profitable media outpost. He left the presbytery, as he found that even though he had resigned, people were continuing to call to the house and treat him as if he were still their Church representative, and was renting a two-bedroom terrace in the village centre for the princely sum of ten euros a month from an ex-parishioner whose mother he had comforted up to her death. The house was still full of the old woman's belongings as the family had not yet had the heart to clear the house and Enda did not feel he had the right to move anything. In any case, he had few belongings of his own – just clothes and some sex toys – and ownership wasn't something he cared about. It was just before these two God-given gifts – the job and the house – presented themselves to him that Enda had met Corrine. She had seduced him (well, she had been quite drunk so Enda wasn't sure if that counted, and he certainly hadn't objected) after a fundraiser at the station. He had been flattered by her attention, gone back to her house and one thing had led to another. Whatever about his high expectations, beef tomatoes etc., the whole experience of having a 'girlfriend' (Corrine hated being called that, but she also hated being called his 'lady', and she said 'partner' made them sound 'too serious') had certainly given him a confidence which he knew had contributed to his getting the station manager's job and moving out from under the wing of the Church. So now he was a working guy, out there in the big bad world, with a 'lady' to look after. It was a big change. And while he might have been struggling to adapt to things sexually, Enda found that he was enjoying the whole aspect of giving in a special way to one special person. That, after all, was the important thing. To be able to show Corrine how much he appreciated her by being especially thoughtful and attentive to her needs. That Corrine had expressed a need for him to not have sex with her for a while, well then that was a small thing to ask of a man who had had his first 'real' sexual encounter only six months beforehand.

In any case, there were more important things going on in her life at the moment. The charity show. In moments of doubt about his new life, Enda was given to wondering if Corrine was the right woman for him. The rare time that he had dared to call into question her refusal to publicly announce him as her 'other half' or gently half-defend Sapphire against her sharp tongue, Corrine was quick to remind him that he was an expert in neither relationships nor parenting and occasionally threatened that perhaps it might be best to call the whole thing off. Enda sometimes questioned whether it was a genuine desire to stay with Corrine that made him snap back into line, or just that the fear of failing at this relationship might mean he really did still belong to the Church. He missed being a part of it sometimes. The ritual of daily mass. The security of his spiritual routine. The sureness it gave him. There was nothing sure about Corrine. In either her commitment to him or, if he was honest, in his feelings for her. He showed her love in every way he could, and Enda believed that love was a choice – not a given. It was something that you did – not necessarily something that you felt. Sometimes, he just wished it was easier. Although, for the weeks that Corrine was working on the charity show, the fears seemed to fade. She was so committed, so *driven*. Really, he could never have imagined how very much she cared about orphans. And then, here was the really terrible thing in all of this, while Corrine was doubtless suffused with a spiritual light (he could virtually see it pouring out of her), Enda felt himself becoming jealous. Yes. Jealous. Of Estonian orphans! How awful was that! Corrine was on the phone day and night in the lead-up to the show. Enda, of course, did everything he could to help. He looked after Sapphire, tried to keep her entertained – although at times he found the pubescent girl's attention exhausting and cloying, which in turn made him feel guilty. He offered to do lots more, from DJing to selling tickets on his show. But it seemed that anything he offered was irrelevant. Then the big night came, and Enda felt, at last, he would get his reward. He didn't want much. Just to be seen alongside her, giving Corrine the support that she needed. Showing everyone, all her friends from Dublin and New York and London, that he knew what a special lady she was, and that nobody need worry because he was going to appreciate and love her from high heaven and to kingdom come. Enda could almost feel himself becoming more worldly by the minute as he picked out his favourite blue jeans and a bottle-green blazer with navy piping he'd bought from Killa's Handsome Homme shop in the early Eighties. 'That jacket's a classic,' the owner Josie had told him, 'it'll never go out of style.' Enda took him at his word and slid it on over a cream cotton polo neck. The 'genuine' cowboy boots he had bought with his first lay pay cheque, waiting three months for them to be custom made by the American catalogue firm, came last. They still pinched a bit but they were getting there, and they had softened at least enough for Enda to be described as 'sauntering' as he reached the park entrance at four p.m., half an hour later than Corrine had said he was to be there, and a couple of hours before the show was due to start.

'Where the fuck have you been?' She had Sapphire with her, and put the two of them to work straight away unloading boxes and packing bags.

The rest of the day didn't really pick up after that. Sapphire and himself hardly saw Corrine. She certainly didn't introduce him to anyone, aside from that one lady, Helen, but then she had come over and introduced herself. It seemed like she was running the event, or at least taking the credit for running it, which perhaps had put Corrine's nose out of joint. In any case, just before the show started Enda searched around and found her talking to some hip-looking man.

'Are you still here?' she asked. 'It's past Sapphire's bedtime, I thought you'd have taken her home.'

Sapphire didn't have a 'bedtime', none that Enda had ever noticed anyway.

Enda stuck around for a few seconds hoping for an introduction to the man, but none was forthcoming.

'Enda,' he said, sticking his hand out. The other man didn't even get a chance to reply before Corrine snapped, 'Yes, well, *off* you go!'

And he did. Humiliated and rejected. As he walked off Enda overheard her say to the man, '. . . babysitter.'

It hurt.

The following day, Corrine called and said she had had an offer of some journalism work and might have to go to Dublin to conduct a few interviews. She was all sweetness and light, and could he mind Sapphire if she went away?

'Why not? I am only the *babysitter*, after all.'

'Oh, *don't* be like that, Enda.'

Enda had a horrible feeling that she might go and leave Sapphire behind anyway, so he agreed.

But there was something fishy about Corrine suddenly wanting to go to Dublin like this, and he didn't like it. He did not like it at all.

PART THREE

**_Vogue_ Suite, The Hilton Hotel,
Tangier, Morocco**

To: mnKa@hotmail.com
From: Hettie2day.co.uk
Re: U and Me and Alfie

Dear Mon,

God it was _soooo_ amazing to c u and spend time in Tangier.
U r a V. SPECIAL woman and I was BLOWN AWAY with
how brilliant and BRAVE u r being about this whole Alfie
business. He is _such_ a bastard but at the same time we all
know that he is amazing really and that God – he loves you
soooooo much? Don't worry, girl. I won't tell _anybody_. I _so_
understand and I _so_ forgive you for ignoring me for the last
few days. It is _so_ scary to have the horrid press following you
around. So I just need for you to know that while I may be
the Celebrity Co-ordinator at _2Day_, I am first and foremost
your friend. And Alfie's. You can _so_ trust me. _Of course_ I will
help u find him. We are _all_ concerned for Alfie, and we _all_
love him very much and want everything to be OK between
the two of you. It was interesting what you said about that
fashion show in Ireland. I don't know Helen Doherty _that_
well, but there's that Irish girl – Eva? The one Gary took
on last year? Bet she was involved so I'll chase it up.
Anyway. You leave it all to UR bestest chum and _don't_ be a

worry bunny. We'll find him and U'll both live hippily ever afters.

Hugs and kisses and be in touch soonest –

Friends forever, Hettie xxxx

To: mnKa@hotmail.com
From: Gary@LipsInc.co.uk
Re: favour for Uncle G?

Biggie to ask you, babe. Favio swung by with the *Vogue* pics after lunch and I spotted a little gem. Local lad, six one I'd say – Favio says he worked in the hotel you were staying at and he got him to stand in on one of your shots. You've got to know who I'm talking about because he's a pure stunner and I've got an inkling when the issue comes out they are going to be queuing up to book him. If you get him back to London for me I'll love you for ever.

Gary xxx

21

It is so funny, Helen thought, looking out on the field behind Corrine's house, how things really do work out for the best. If she hadn't stuck to her guns and come down to do the show, then Mal wouldn't have followed her down like he did.

Then, Mal wouldn't have hooked up with Corrine and cemented that whole *Rolling Stone* freelance job with Jack, and Corrine probably wouldn't have had to rush up to Dublin to sort things out leaving Helen with the *perfect* excuse to stay behind and mind her house for a couple of weeks. It wasn't that Corrine's house was magnificent, or that Killa was the most buzzy place on the planet but, for some strange reason, it felt good to be away from her own life. So good, in fact, that Helen did not feel in the slightest bit guilty.

Mal had wanted to stay on with her: 'We'll book a hotel. It'll be romantic. The twins are with Mum. They'll be fine. We won't go back until we're OK again.' Helen assured him that they were: 'Fine. Really, babe.' And she kissed him in that way that she had kissed him hundreds of times over the last few years. A tender lie they were both trying too hard to believe. Enough love to keep panic at bay, but not enough to make either want to take it any further.

Mal went home angry straight after the show, but he rang her the following day and every day since saying, 'I miss you; I don't like you being away; come home or I don't know what I'll do.'

Corrine had been brilliant.

'Hey! Don't let him guilt-trip you. Quite apart from the fact that you'd be helping me out, you *deserve* a break. Let him look after himself for a change, it'll do him good. Sometimes relationships need room to breathe.'

That was what was so great about Corrine. She understood.

'Pressures of rock 'n' roll, Helen? I don't know how you do it. I mean it's one thing putting up with all that shit when it's your name up there and you're getting the glory, but being in the background like you are? It's like – *why?*'

Helen's gut flinched at the truth contained somewhere in her new friend's words. So she smiled apologetically and shrugged in that 'I love my husband' way, the way that tells you if you stay loyal and faithful the love will follow. And love often does follow; but once it's come and gone, it rarely comes back.

'Don't you worry about that husband of yours. I'll drop in and keep an eye on him!'

'Drop in? I thought you'd be *staying* in our house?'

Helen felt disappointment as Corrine insisted that she

wouldn't. Although she knew it was petty, she didn't want Corrine to be staying with anyone else. Helen had formed an attachment to Corrine which she suspected herself might be both premature and childish. Born out of something lacking in her life. An immaturity perhaps, a loneliness. Whatever the reason, she had a need to be liked by this woman.

'It's too far out of town.'

'Our driver can bring you in.'

'Honestly, Helen, I'd rather not.'

'But I'm staying *here*.'

There was a pause.

'You are helping me out, Helen. I don't want to impose . . .'

'You won't be imposing . . .'

'Yes, but Mal will be working and . . .'

Fucking Mal! The moody tight shit. Didn't want anyone invading his precious, private space. Well, Corrine was her friend and . . .

'Fuck Mal!'

Corrine let out a laugh, and Helen was pleased to have made her smile. She seemed stressed out lately. But then, Helen didn't know her very well so maybe Corrine was like that all the time.

'I mean it, fuck him. It's my house as much as his – *more*, actually. Besides, it's big enough for plenty of guests to stay and—'

'I'd rather not – ' Corrine said with a new assertion, then seeming to make some distinction added, 'stay in the house.'

The conversation ended abruptly there, and two days later Corrine left for Dublin.

Little Sapphire was the sweetest thing, although Helen found it hard to believe, not to mention a bit depressing, that she was only a couple of years younger than the twins. Their childhood had seemed dreadfully short, and she still regretted the time she spent away from them as toddlers, when she had to go chasing around after their father. Perhaps she would have been better off letting him run off with that woman and reared the twins on her own. She practically had anyway. His influence had been largely a bad one: how can you tell a thirteen-year-old that smoking pot is only for adults when his father and his cronies are influencing the fashions and minds of half the kids in his class? Down here, in Killa, things seemed so different. Like another country almost. Certainly another life. Helen had always found relaxation and relief in doing 'ordinary things'. For her it was one of the advantages of not being famous herself. Living with Mal meant that everywhere they went together, they were at risk of being followed or photographed. On her own, or with the twins, she was only of minimal interest to the press. Unless she was daft enough to, say, openly have an affair or get drunk on a plane, neither of which she had ever done, she was more or less invisible. She had sent Frank home the day after they arrived in Killa and hired herself a car. She stuck a 'Mr A. Smith' down as a named driver, and told Alfie to call her if he needed it – although he was still staying in the B&B in the village and Corrine's house was a good twenty minutes' drive inland so her need was greater.

The house was set back from the road by a short tree-lined drive. At the front was a wooden veranda, an unusual feature, more American than Irish, and one which made it noticeable to passing cars. The back of the house over-looked a lake and was overlooked itself by one of those flat boggy mountains that is really a glorified hill. It was in a beautiful location, and on her way there from Killa, Helen had to pass by the convent that herself and Mal had bought, which she noticed, rather sadly, was still empty and rotting away. Would things have been different, she wondered, if she had breathed life into that old building and moved down here? But then different how? There was nothing wrong. Nothing for her to complain about. Their life in Wicklow was good. Rural setting. Beautiful house. Mal came home when he could, and in any case it was often enough for Helen. After three months of his lounging about the place, she was generally happy to see the back of him. So the twins were wild but then, would they be any less wild anywhere else? There was nothing for her to want to get away from, to want to escape, and yet that is exactly how Helen felt. She was relieved to be living somebody else's life rather than her own. Looking after somebody else's child, living in somebody else's house, filling somebody else's fridge. She told herself that she was 'on holiday' but in reality, it was a pretty poor holiday for a woman who had a fully staffed mansion in Marbella awaiting a phone call.

Corrine had told her that a friend of hers would

probably pop in and was on hand to look after Sapphire 'anytime. Enda, he's a priest – well, used to be a priest.'

Helen had met him at the fashion show with Sapphire, and he had seemed nice enough. So with the house tidied, the evening's meal prepared and Sapphire still out at school, Helen looked Enda's number up on the pad next to the phone and gave him a bell.

He sounded strange and worryingly breathless on the phone, but she invited him round for his tea. Just a casual arrangement, somebody else to talk to. He was polite, but seemed puzzled that she was calling.

'When is Corrine off to Dublin?'

'She went two days ago.'

'She's gone?'

'Didn't she tell you?'

'No, she didn't.' He said it like it might be Helen's fault.

'But what about Sapphire?'

'She's fine. I'm here looking after her.'

'You've moved in?'

'Well – until Corrine gets back.'

'But what about . . .' Helen was waiting to see what he might object to next '. . . me?'

What an odd thing to say. It was a bit awkward so Helen just did the best she could.

'Like I said, Enda, would you like to come around for your tea?'

The odd bod made an excuse and Helen was surprised to find herself slightly hurt at the rejection of this complete stranger. Perhaps it was just that Helen Doherty was not accustomed to having her social invitations declined.

Despite, in fact probably because of, Enda's refusal, Helen decided to indulge herself anyway in an afternoon of something she loved but seldom had the time to do: baking. Earlier in the day she had wandered around the local shop in Killa and been charmed to find a section given over to cake-making. Hundreds and thousands in little pink boxes, baking soda, dried fruit as well as icing bags and biscuit cutters. On a whim she had bought a bag load of ingredients and accessories and had half-hoped she might do something as charmingly innocent and old fashioned as invite the priest to tea.

And so, sod the priest, she thought, I shall bake without him!

It had turned into a glorious afternoon and Helen decided to set a table on the veranda out front. She dragged out a small wooden table and some chairs from the house then rummaged around in cupboards for a table cloth. At the centre of the table she put a stone pot from the kitchen and filled it with roughly bunched bluebells picked from a wooded area at the side of the garden. She put out teacups and saucers, and left a rack of scones fresh from the oven to cool in the crisp late-afternoon air.

She was inside glazing an apple tart when she heard a car pull up on the gravel drive. It must be the neighbour dropping Sapphire off from school. When Sapphire didn't come bounding in to her at once, Helen went out to investigate.

Sitting on the veranda, on the two wicker chairs, were two men – tourists if their rental Opel Astra and their chic 'weekend in the country' cashmeres were anything to go by. One squat and older, one younger and good looking. Gay.

'Afternoon tea for two, please,' the older one said, lasciviously eyeing her cooling scones.

'I'm sorry,' she said, not knowing whether to be irritated or amused, 'but this isn't a tea shop, it's a private—'

'Helen?' the younger one said.

'Who?' the older man asked, reluctant to swivel his eyes from the scones.

'Helen! Helen Doherty! The woman we've been looking for, you stupid shit, and you can take your eyes off those scones for a start – you've *had* your cholesterol intake for today.'

'Wilson?' Helen knew the singer better than his partner.

'Well – a fat version of him,' Stephen helpfully added, 'take your hand *off* that if you know what's good for you.'

'It's only bread,' the older man cried.

'It's a cake, Wilson. A cake. And what do cakes do . . .?' Stephen turned to Helen, his face sliced with genuine despair. 'I take him to the middle of nowhere for a break, and what do I find? We're in the Cake Capital of Europe – put the scone down, Wilson – WILSON!'

But it was too late. It would have been better with a slab of butter and a dollop of jam, but it had gone down his gullet none the less.

'Hmmmmmmmf – deliquoussh!'

Helen didn't know what they were doing there or why, but she knew she'd find out. Either way, she was feeling so mellow, she didn't think she'd be able to drum up giving a shit one way or another.

'I suppose I'd better put the kettle on.'

And she did.

22

Mr Yellow had been neither as successful nor as anonymous as planned.

The sound man Sam, who owned the Grass studio in Dublin, was also – by the fucking way – a shit-hot mixer who had worked up one of the tracks on Alfie's last album. There was this terrible half-hour where Alfie was trying to keep his face down and explain through spit-balls of cotton wool what he wanted to do musically that night, and Sam was continually saying 'Yes, Mr Yellow', 'No, Mr Yellow' like he was blatantly taking the piss. Alfie did not like having the piss taken out of himself, especially when he was trying to be serious about his music – which, despite the fact that this was something a bit different for him, he was on this occasion. Eventually he decided that the only way Sam was going to take him seriously was if he confessed who he was. It was only fair, after all, to let the guy know he was dealing with a seasoned professional.

'No fucking way . . . you are shitting me, man . . .' Sam stuck his face right up to his, then bounced back in his chair in shock.

'Shit, Alfie. what the fuck have you done? Shit, man, you're a fucking mess – your hair, man! Your eyebrows! What's this . . .?' He slapped Alfie's cheek and a mound of sodden cotton wool squelched out. 'Oh, fucking Jesus, man. I mean – what the fuck have you . . .?'

'I'm trying to *hide*,' Alfie spat at him in explanation, annoyed he was making such a fuss and afraid that people were looking over.

Sam let out a half laugh.

'At a charity fashion gig with every supermodel and celebrity clinger in Europe? Nice one, Alf.'

'That's why I'm in disguise.'

Sam leant back and gave him a look.

'Are you for real?'

Alfie was starting to feel a bit of a fool. He began to flick through Mal's records determinedly, like he was here to do a job and if Sam was going to take the piss well then—

'Shit,' Sam said, but quietly to himself this time.

He went over to the freakish-looking kid and put his hand on his shoulder.

'Listen, Alf, all I'm saying is, if you really want to disappear just do it.'

Alfie looked up at him, and even he was aware how pathetic he must have seemed.

'Take off to the Caribbean or something. I been in this business – I seen people disappear all the time.'

'How?' Alfie asked.

'Just forget the whole scene for a while.'

'That's what I'm trying to do, but—'

'Nah, mate. I mean – step the fuck aside.' He looked at Alfie like he was slightly exasperated, but not in an unkind way.

'Look. Go home, yeah? Leave me your bag and I'll do the job tonight.'

Then Alfie realized that he had been looking forward to being 'Mr Yellow'. Fame in disguise. Glory by another name. Silly really. Downright stupid actually, he regretfully noted from Sam's sympathetic but disbelieving expression.

So he went back to the B&B. As he left it all behind, Alfie felt, not regret, but sort of mournful for what he would be missing that night. Then he started to feel sorry for himself. Why could he not 'have it all' without 'having it all'? Why couldn't he have just a bit? Be a superstar DJ for one night, have a few beverages like any lad and maybe bed down with a model – then go back to being ordinary Joe in the morning? You see, Sam could do that. He was a technical head. Funky glamorous job, but not so glamorous that it would never invade his privacy. What had he meant by 'forget the whole scene', 'step aside'? Had he any idea what bollocks that was? Sure. Alfie could do that but would the bastards let him forget? The press? The tabloids? Would they step aside? Not likely. This place would be teeming with them by now if he hadn't been smart enough to hide away from them.

It was early evening when he got back, and the B&B was eerily empty. Alfie went up to his room and made himself a cup of tea. He ate the packet of shortbread biscuits and watched some TV. Then he had a shower, washed the teacup in the wash-hand basin and made himself a cup of coffee. He watched some more TV, then decided to go downstairs and explore. At the front of the house there was the Residents' Lounge. Not much in there except for a large TV with videos piled on top. Nothing that interested him. The Breakfast Room, where he had indeed enjoyed a very nice fry that morning, was to the left. Beyond it, through a pair of French doors, was what he had heard described as the 'Reading Conservatory'. Mrs Walshe, his very nice landlady, had invited him, with a dramatic sweep of the hand, to 'feel free and enjoy the delights of our conservatory – a favoured place of refuge for many of our discerning guests'. On a cane-and-glass coffee table, flanked by two generously cushioned floral armchairs, was a pile of celebrity magazines, the glass shelf underneath it groaning with the familiar red and white of *Hello!*, *OK!* and *2Day*.

Unbelievable, Alfie tutted to himself, that people could be so shallow. Nothing better to do than sit around reading this crap. Did they not realize the invasion of privacy, the . . . oooh, now *there's* that wedding they weren't invited to. We'll have a quick peek at that – MoniKa had said it was going to be a tacky affair and by Christ she was right. State of that bridesmaid? He could almost hear Sharon and Mon warning his sister: 'It's going in *2Day*, so if you don't do Weightwatchers, love, we'll have to hire someone to replace you.' How right they had been! And here was that rock-head that'd blanked him big time at the MTV awards last year. Fuck me! House full of puffy flowery furniture your maiden aunt wouldn't live with. Oh now please. Who turned the lights up on that poor cow? One of his contemporaries – kept him at Number Two for three singles running – seven months pregnant and trying to 'do' a 'Madonna'. Result? Call the skin-care police or better still sack the press agent!

Three hours of not being able to *believe* what some people will do for publicity, and many hundreds of *Now! OK! More! Heat!* magazines later, Alfie realized that he had not had any dinner. His 'hosts' were still out at the show. Their daughter or something was helping organize it and they had apologized to guests for there not being an evening meal available. He thought he could go out and try to find a chip shop, but then again there was another pile of magazines in the TV lounge, and he had an idea he might like to try and find his own wedding in there. Have a look and see how good or bad it was in the light of all his new-found education. Alfie wandered into the kitchen and was perusing the contents of the fridge, guessing that there must be the ingredients for a bacon sandwich on the premises, when the kitchen door opened and a young woman walked in.

'Alfie!' she exclaimed.

'No, I'm not!'

If that had been the case, and the young man with the badly dyed home haircut and the shaven eyebrows had *not* been Alfie Smith, he might have reacted differently. He might have been confused – 'Alfie?' – or even, if he had known she was comparing him to the pin-up pop star, might have been quite pleased – 'Well, no, but actually some people do say there's a resemblance.' The one thing that a man who was not in reality Alfie Smith trying to pass himself off as A. N. Other would definitely *not* have done is immediately leap into a defensive position. Of course, she recognized his voice then.

'OHMIGOD! It really *is* you!'

'No, it isn't,' he said, raising his voice a few octaves.

By this time, the girl – the intruder – had more or less fallen into a chair next to the door and was muttering, more to herself than him, 'OhmiGod – Alfie Smith is in my kitchen, ohmiGod, ohmiGod, it's you, it's him, ohmiGod . . .'

It was a look he recognized. Fan hysteria. Fucking marvellous. He had never had much sympathy for the dribbling mounds of emotionally pulverized teenagers that stood in their hundreds around the stage door. Even less so now that he was trying to consider himself a 'serious' artist as opposed to a teen pin-up.

'OhmiGod . . . hee-haw . . . hee-haw. OhmiGod . . .'

Hyperventilation. If he didn't act quick, she might collapse and die on him. What to do? What to do? *Just Seventeen* competition-winner date. Name: Shaznay Tate, thirteen-and-a-half-years-old, from Wigan. Went into breathing convulsions when he turned up at the Hard Rock on Piccadilly. What did the press agent do? Think! Think! Ah – she made her breathe into a bag, gave her a glass of water, got me the fuck out of the room. He looked round. No bags. Thinking via panic, Alfie grabbed a glass from the draining board, filled it with water, flung it in Molly's face and ran out the kitchen door.

'Yaaaah!' he heard her scream as he high-tailed it into the TV lounge and she came chasing after him.

'What did you do that for?'

'To calm you down.'

'Well, it *didn't* work!'

Actually, it had, but Alfie didn't like to point that out, not while she was very annoyed indeed at having her hair and make-up ruined. Molly was no longer in a state of heightened shock. However, it would be an exaggeration to say that the fact that her favourite pop star (in the whole wide world!) was sitting in the TV lounge of her parents' B&B was no longer of interest.

Sweeping aside her soaking fringe, Molly sat and regarded Alfie as if not quite sure where to go with this next. She had so many questions.

'What are you doing here?'

'I am the DJ for the show. My name is Mr Yellow.'

'What have you done to your hair?'

'It's always been like this.'

'Your eyebrows are gone.'

'I have never had eyebrows. I was born without them.'

Molly was getting annoyed now. Alfie could see it. She had come home, found her favourite pop star (in the world ever!) in her kitchen, and now he was denying he was who he was. Finding him there in the first place was bizarre enough. Having him deny it, and his queer get-up, with the horribly dyed hair and the shaven eyebrows and the orangey tan, was making her feel dizzy. She had dreamed, so many times, of the moment when she might meet Alfie. She'd fantasized, of course she had, of walking into the

B&B one day and he would be there, just trying to escape from all the celebrity nonsense. They would strike up an immediate friendship and perhaps that might lead to something else. The fact that it would never, *could* never happen made it sweet to dream. Now it was *actually* happening. But in a horrible off-the-wall sideways way, at the tail end of a day which had contained enough excitement, thank you very much.

Molly decided to give up.

'You *are* Alfie Smith. I know because I know *everything* about you. I am going to bed now, and in the morning, if you are still here, and if you are still Alfie Smith . . .' Well, then what? Nothing. She couldn't think of anything, she was too tired. '. . . well then, that'll be that, then. Good night.' And Molly headed off up stairs.

Ten minutes later, after trying six of the guest rooms, Alfie knocked on Molly's door.

'Yes?' she shouted. She was halfway through her nightly skin-cleansing routine, but he took it to be coolness.

'I *am* Alfie Smith,' he croaked as loudly as he could without alerting the neighbours to his celebrity status.

Molly said nothing through the door.

'You won't tell anyone, will you?'

He had no reason to expect her to, but she called through, 'I won't tell.'

God. It all seemed like a lifetime ago, even though it was just a couple of days really – less than a week since he left Holland Park. If Molly hadn't turned out to be all right, introducing her to Fonzie and all, he'd have never got to where he was now. Which was living the low-key life of an unsuccessful London DJ called Albert Smith (Al for short. Ingenious. When lying, stick as close to the truth as you can), aka Mr Yellow, crashing in the crib of his new best friend Fonzie Mallarkey, and basically enjoying the carefree existence of a regular drifting bloke in his late twenties. On the advice of his new friend – 'If you don't mind me saying so, Al, I think you should lose the hair dye. Doesn't go down too well on fellas around here' – Alfie had had the blond sheared down to a number-one crop revealing a pleasantly oval-shaped scalp of whose smooth velvety finish he was inordinately proud. The eyebrows were growing back at a great rate and he had managed to shave in a piece of slimline elongated tash/ sideburn face topiary that was, frankly, rather elegant. He looked vaguely like himself, only older and more mysteri- ous. Which was wasted really on the people around here because they didn't seem to respond to the 'mystery' vibe at all. They took Albert Smith at face value. A young man with no particular place to go, just hanging out for a while over at Mallarkey's. Out and about. Having the crack. Zooming around on the back of Fonzie's bike, scooping the few pints. Even the local girls seemed uninterested. To them, he was just some biker mate of Fonzie's that he probably picked up at a rally; would probably be around for a while then bugger off back to England with himself. Nothing to get excited about. Gossip and speculation were perpetrated by locals for and about locals. If you wanted to sink your teeth into a good story, you'd better have some history first. Top of the list, these days, was 'Father' Enda – the really terrible DJ on the local radio station. As his alter ego, Alfie was slightly put out that such a musically ignorant person could get, what seemed to Albert Smith at least, an excellent job opportunity. Enda was apparently knobbing some local writer called Corrine, who used to be a pop singer called Sapphire? Alfie vaguely remembered seeing one of her singles in his mother's old record collection. Whatever. At least the story was keeping the heat off him. Molly had been as silent as the grave, although she was always trying to squirrel him away into quiet corners where she could call him 'Alfie' and share the contents of their secret together. He thought she was probably slightly in love with him, but then – that was a fan thing – and she would just have to live with it. In the meantime, her silence was allowing Albert to thrive in his new life and who knows, perhaps even launch himself on the airwaves of Killa as a superstar DJ.

**Offices of KLM Management,
Grosvenor Square, London W1**

To: Karl@KLMManagement.co.uk
From: Hettie@2day.co.uk
Re: Alfie

I *totally* get UR only trying to protect Alfie, Karl. And we all know that you R one of the v. few agents who actually cares about his clients. That's why *me*, and *everyone* in the media, has such respect for you, Karl. I mean – Wilson's coming out? Need I say more? U were fab then, and UR fab now. A legend. The very last thing I want 2 do is show you any disrespect, but the thing is MoniKa is a *really* good friend and I am totally doing this with *not* my *2Day* hat on. U know how Mon and Alfie R? They *really* love each other and she is *really* hurt and *really* worried about him. She just wants to know he's all right but she just can't make this contact herself because, well, it would just be *really* hard for her because if you didn't tell her well then that might mean a 'no' from the next closest person to Alfie and that would be *really* hard. So she is making me to ask instead. Phew! I know they'll get back together sometime anyway. As their close friend, I just would like to be part of making that happen. Thought u might be 2. Anyway, u can call me anytime.

Deepest respect and regards
Henrietta Flinthrop

To: Karl@KLMManagement.co.uk
From: Justin@McIvorManagement.co.uk
Re: Alfie

Look, Karl, I don't want to be awkward but there is a lot riding on us finding Alfie right now. Both our clients are big names, and now that MoniKa and Alfie are married, I think it's time you got off your high horse and started to work with me on this thing. The reality is that I am MoniKa's press agent, and right now the big story around her is: Where is Alfie? Alfie is your client – so the two of us should at least be *seen* to be pulling together. I'm not daft. I know you know where he is and how to reach him. If you don't, well then you must be some shit manager. In the meantime I've got Ron Parker up my arse here and I need to give him something, otherwise – well, you know Ron. He's talking about bringing Wilson's name into it and you know how he hates queers.

See what you can do,

Call me back soon, Justin

To: Karl@KLMManagement.co.uk
From: StephenSilke@hotmail.com
Re: Alfie

I know you are well able to handle all this shit, Karl, but at the same time I think I'll keep Wilson away from the tabloids this week. We're a long way from Honest Ron over here and I'd just like to keep it that way for a while. Justin is a known scumbag and I am astonished at MoniKa taking him on, although, as you and I have discussed before, there's more to her than meets the eye. Don't know about that Hettie one. Doesn't she work for *Hello* or *2Day* or one of those mags? So you just crack ahead at your discretion, darling. Alfie is still here mixing and mingling with the ordinary folk, as are we. We're just letting him get on with it for a couple of weeks or so. He'll wear himself out soon enough and doubtless we'll all arrive on your doorstep to a glittering fanfare before the month is out.

PS Can you *believe* the Corrine thing?! Tho' her daughter is a peach. Yep that's all fine for tour spring/summer next year – will check dates on return. You are patience personified – no other agent would put up with any of us! Thank you.

23

They say that ownership is nine-tenths of the law. And that was certainly a belief that would have appeared to hold true for one Constance Heany, erstwhile housekeeper to the most senior cleric in the parish of Killa, Bishop Simeon Dunne.

Every summer it was Bishop Dunne's habit to take himself off to America for a six-week secondment where he could enjoy the edifications of Californian Catholicism. Under the spiritual guidance of his learned cousin, Monsignor Edward Dunne (or 'Ed the Head', as this people's priest preferred to be called), Simeon was able to cast aside the formal dictate of high-ranking clerics in small-town Ireland and party. Tanned, togged and trainered sitting in a beachside café nursing last night's sushi hangover and wondering how on earth Ed managed to maintain such a lavish lifestyle – 'It's a *cash* business, Dunne. You always take recreational spend out of the *plate*, man' – His Lordship could not possibly have known what abuses were being perpetrated on his property back home.

Constance was not the best housekeeper a bishop could hope for but she was adequate. Simeon was an exacting master when it came to cleanliness and privacy, and while Constance Heany had acquired the position from his predecessor on the grounds of her baking skills, the incumbent had a delicate digestion and little interest in the hearty home cooking she offered him. Instead it was often required of him to point out small jobs which she had overlooked. On no fewer than three separate occasions he had had to remind her to vacuum underneath the sofa in his study and, while her scones were good, she had proven slow when it came to cleaning away tea things from the study after they had had guests. In the spirit of Christian humility and servitude, Bishop Dunne was prepared to straighten the occasional antimacassar and he understood that symmetrically aligned towels were not a priority for everybody. But when a bishop's socks are put back into his drawer in loosely scrunched balls – unironed, unfolded – sometimes with not even enough care to ensure they were matching . . .! Well, suffice it to say that living under that pressure, it was no wonder he needed a holiday.

After he had left, Constance decided to give the office a good going over. Hoover under the sofa, seeing as how she had absolutely nothing better to do. Plus, this summer break was the only opportunity Connie got to have a bit of a rummage through the parish papers as His Lordship kept the key hidden on his person at all times. Just as well she had had one cut while his predecessor was in charge otherwise she would never have known what was going on. Being fully up to date on Church affairs was as much the duty of the Bishop's housekeeper as being able to bake a cake fit for a cardinal. She had been the first to know of Father Enda's departure – but that was pure fluke. Imagine if she had heard it from Rita Cooney first? It was a possibility that Constance lived in constant fear of. No. She might not have the old goat's confidence, but she wasn't going to let that hold her back.

Imagine her horror then when this most committed and respected of housekeepers found neatly written on the top of his On Return Home To Do jotter the words 'Heany' and 'retire' directly one after the other.

And try to imagine then the mood in which this person might have been a few moments later when, in an almost dreamlike state, they were to open the front door of the palace to reveal two strange men standing on the marble steps and professing a need of warmth and shelter. For Constance Heany, the convention of her Catholic upbringing, the fortitude with which she had sacrificed marriage and children in order to work her way from humble parish presbytery to the Bishop's palace, simply melted away. With it went all official protocol in relation to members of the public fraternizing with high-ranking religious, i.e., requesting audiences in writing, kissing of rings, etc. These were replaced with a new set of rules, the rules of an affronted housekeeper, which were more along the lines of letting complete strangers come and live in the Bishop's home while he was on holiday. In other words, the worm had turned and it was Constance Heany (Ms), who, through means of allowing other people to use his towels, slippers and anything else they fancied, was now inviting Bishop Dunne to kiss *her* ring.

And thus it was that Wilson and Stephen came to be staying in the Bishop's Palace in Killa.

It was not, by anyone's standards, the mansion in Herts. It was, however, a far cry from a council flat in Colindale and thus, in a nice rounded way, a perfect compromise between Stephen's 'folksy' holiday plans and Wilson's celebrity pampering requirements. Plus, Wilson had discovered that there were compensations to keeping his trap shut about Stephen 'forgetting' to pack his slippers and the lack of bespoke flower arrangements over the breakfast table. They came in the form of being permitted to partake of their new hostess's talent for cooking in general and baking in particular: tarts, pies and cakes of every permutation and in quantities too copious to contemplate, as Constance savaged her way through the housekeeping account. On the first morning, Stephen came down for breakfast to find Wilson polishing off a plate of potato bread dripping with 'low-fat spread, I hope?' The cook shot Stephen a look which left the junior partner in no doubt as to what she thought of 'low-fat' alternatives, and the die was cast. Constance Heany, starved of praise from her cold Bishop, blossomed under Wilson's adulation. She had no idea he was the internationally acclaimed rock singer Wilson and when he did tell her, well she just didn't believe him with that chirpy 'don't mind him' tolerance that seasoned old ladies save for the half-touched. She did not know, or care, that he and Stephen were gay lovers. All she knew was that there was this charming man who lavished her with praise and couldn't get enough of her buns.

For his part, Stephen was both relieved and happy that the holiday was working out as it was. Wilson seemed to be relaxing in a way which he did not seemed able to do back home. When everything was at his fingertips, Wilson could not help but indulge – and Stephen, while he undoubtedly enjoyed elements of their extravagant life-style, sometimes found his partner's constant pursuit of perfection spilling over into neurosis. Wilson was a work-aholic whose gruelling self-imposed work schedule had to be carefully controlled. His manager Karl and Stephen had taken to appointing certain months as 'off' – no writing, recording or performing by order of the doctor. As a musician, Wilson tore himself apart creatively to get things perfect. When he wasn't working, Wilson hounded every-one else to create perfection for him. There were too many options open to them and Stephen, even after all these years, was still astounded at what people were prepared to do for money. Could the hotel please paint the walls in their suite a particular shade of grass green as Wilson had been told by a healer that green was a good colour for him this year? No problem, sir. When Wilson complained vaguely of a sore ear/toe/elbow, there were always specialists willing to fly themselves in for the right fee. In fact, Stephen had been quite surprised at how easily Wilson had seemed to accept this new, albeit temporary, circumstance. He continued to confront Wilson about his addictive consumption of Constance Heany's cakes, but the two of them knew that his badgering was only half-serious. An old-fashioned back-to-front expression of love, like your mother insisting you wear your coat buttoned between October and March. And while Wilson was a far cry from laundering his own smalls, he seemed to derive some amusement from the novelty of watching his new hero, Constance, around the house.

'*Look* at this shirt . . .' he had announced to Stephen before they retired on their second night. 'I mean just look. It's *perfect*! The woman is a genius!'

The following day Stephen returned from his morning jog to find Wilson at the ironing board. His tongue protruding in a point from the side of his mouth, he was deep in concentration. 'Daw. I can't do it, I can't do it. I'll melt the button, I'll melt the button.'

'Keep going – that's it. Hook the fabric under the little line there at the point . . . now look . . . you've done it perfect,' Constance encouraged from behind him.

'No. You're just saying that.'

'I mean it. I cannot believe you have never ironed a shirt before.'

'Never.' Wilson puffed up with pride.

This was a side of Wilson Stephen really loved: a naïve boyish delight. Too often the pop singer used it to manipulate, putting on a spoiled, pubescent pout when he couldn't get his own way, making it unattractive to his partner. But there was some childlike element returning that Stephen found adorable again. He couldn't remember the last time he had seen Wilson like this. Probably not since the early days of lavish gift-giving when his face had been eagerly expectant of his young lover's approval. Stephen rarely gave him that approval now.

Although a truce had been called, the two men had not discussed the child issue again. It had been easy enough, their energies having been focused sideways on to a new charge: Alfie.

'He is such a fucking child!' Wilson had announced after they finally caught up with him. He refused to be summoned to the palace, so they met him in Corrine's house the day after they arrived. They had tripped up at her place by accident. Helen had been foolish enough to bake scones whilst the wind was pointing in the opposite direction to an open-windowed car containing Wilson. She had found Alfie, telephoned him to come over, and Wilson had spoken to him, alone out on the veranda. He only stayed for ten minutes, and wouldn't even come in and say hello, which Stephen found unnerving.

'He won't go home, and he doesn't want anyone to know that he's here.'

'But what about Mon?'

'He says he doesn't care. He is enjoying his "new life" of anonymity.'

'But it's been less than a week!'

'That's youth for you. A week seems like a lifetime.'

'He's twenty-nine, Wilson. He's hardly a teenager.'

'Well – that's what he says and I just didn't think it was a good idea to argue with him.'

'I think he's having a nervous breakdown.'

'He'll be fine. I told him that we'd be sticking around for a while and he seemed sort of relieved.'

'Really? And are you OK with that?'

'With what?'

'With sticking around for a while?'

Wilson ignored the question in a deliberate, pointed way by standing up and walking towards the kitchen where he had intuited Helen was about to relieve the oven of another batch of goodies. It was his way of reminding Stephen that although this break had been his idea – and although things might be going according to his plans – the senior partner was still very much in charge.

That had been a few days ago now, and they hadn't seen Alfie since, though they had called around to Helen every afternoon. And then there had been the *other* drama to contend with: when Wilson found out who the house Helen was staying in belonged to, he nearly swallowed his own teeth.

"That fucking c . . .'

Helen wasn't what you'd call a foul-mouthed fag hag by any stretch. There was too much of the lady about her. Fine-weather camping is all well and good, but Stephen knew Helen wouldn't go in for the rough stuff. In other words, don't use the 'c' word, especially not in relation to Corrine, who was clearly a friend of hers. Wilson tended to spit everything right out and not much care what anybody thought. But then, the rules state that one should not get offended by anyone richer and more famous than you, and Wilson was richer and more famous than most.

Stephen correctly understood that Helen did not sing to this hymn sheet, and as Wilson was disabled from such intuitions by his cripplingly large ego, it was left to Stephen to ensure that he didn't say anything regrettable. By Stephen at least.

'Corrine! What a coincidence! Wilson used to go out with her in the dark ages! Didn't you, darling?'

Mercifully, and in the truly classy style of a Class 'A' socialite, Helen grabbed the hint immediately and with great 'more tea, vicar?' panache changed the subject until twenty minutes later the drama flared up again with the entrance of—

'Sapphire. These are two friends of mine . . .' Helen looked pleadingly at Stephen.

He put his hand out confidently and announced, 'I'm Stephen. Pleased to meet you.' He'd had enough bailing for one afternoon. Let Wilson figure this one out for himself.

The rather awkward-looking girl limply allowed him to shake her hand but her eyes were fixed on Wilson. For almost thirty full seconds the stout lumpy schoolgirl and the stout lumpy pop star eyed each other until she finally said, 'You're Wilson. You used to go out with my mammy but you're not my dad.'

Stephen saw Wilson's expression disintegrate into a filthy poisonous sneer from which he knew something appalling was about to escape. He bounced out of his seat and grabbed the child. 'Sapphire, I don't know about you but I've been here for three whole days and I haven't seen a cow yet. Why don't you take me outside and show me where all the cows live?'

There were no cows, but it gave Wilson a chance to take it all in re Corrine, and Stephen was able to field most of Sapphire's more terrible questions.

'Why did Wilson stop loving my mammy?' 'Are you his boyfriend?' 'If mammies and daddies make babies, what do boyfriends and boyfriends make?'

After a short while, Stephen decided to cut the crap.

'You ask a lot of questions, Sapphire, and I think you know the answers to a lot of them already.'

The young girl turned her face away, and Stephen felt instantly bad for having shamed her.

'I think there might be some cows over here . . .' she said very quietly and began walking towards a field at the back of their house. Stephen followed and as they walked, he began asking the questions and Sapphire opened up to him quickly, telling him about Father Enda and his radio show and about how she hoped he might become her dad, because then she wouldn't have to go to boarding school. She said that her mum wasn't like other mums because she liked to be called Corrine and that she was very beautiful. She told him how Corrine used to be a famous pop singer, but now she was a brilliant writer and that people took her seriously not just for her looks but for her intellect as well. From what Stephen knew of Corrine – from Wilson's descriptions and the legend of what a ruthless bitch she was back then – he didn't fancy poor Enda's chances. From what he was hearing from her daughter, he didn't fancy Sapphire's chances at escaping being sent to boarding school or, indeed, surviving it when she got there.

'Why did your mum call you Sapphire?' Stephen asked.

The girl was matter of fact in her answer. Not a flicker of hurt on her face as she said, 'She wanted me to be beautiful like her.' Then she shrugged the answer to her own question away.

'And you don't think you are?'

Sapphire looked away and skipped slightly saying, 'Sorry – no cows here. Hey, if we go down to Tara Mulrooney's they have some sheep! Will they do?'

Stephen understood.

'Sheep? You're joking.'

He waited for Sapphire to turn around then he grabbed her plump little hands and shouted, 'OhmiGod, I *love* sheep! That would be *fantastic*!'

Sapphire grinned and her flat face lit up like a miracle. Stephen had made a new friend and yet he could not remember ever having felt so sad in his life.

24

When Corrine saw Mal step out of the car she felt like she did after her first cigarette: sick and dizzy and instantly addicted. He had come for her. She could feel her blood thicken, the colour rise to her face and her eyelids flicker and drop with desire as he approached. It was as if the others weren't there. Mal made a show of kissing Helen and giving out a 'buddy' to the American rock journo, but the look he gave her was sly and awkward and full of statement.

'Corrine – nice to see you again.' And he held out his hand.

Corrine could sense Helen's irritation.

'For God's sake, Mal – you haven't seen Corrine for years!'

So, on his wife's instruction, Mal gave her a kiss. His discomfort and the strain of holding herself back sent a shard of desire shooting through her. She knew she would have to wait, but by Christ she wasn't going to wait long. He wouldn't hold her eye while Jack and Helen were there, so she knew he wanted it as badly as she did. Jack went to find them some drinks, Helen got called away and for a few brief moments they were left alone together.

'How have you been?'

His voice was strained and his eyes were darting around, checking for imminent interruptions. The first came in the form of Enda. He was dressed more appallingly than usual in a green jacket and was limping slightly in those dreadful cowboy boots he thought were so cool. Sapphire was loitering somewhere behind him and their sudden appearance felt to Corrine like her passionate fantasy had been dunked in lukewarm shit. She could barely contain her loathing, although she knew it was more directed at herself for having slept with Enda than the poor hapless creature himself. Sapphire, she tried not to think about. She just used her as an excuse to get Enda the fuck out of there. By the time she turned to explain to Mal that he was her babysitter, Jack was back with the drinks and their moment was lost.

From then on and throughout the show Helen had Mal following her around like a lapdog. She put him up on stage where he was the epitome of low-key cool and where he delivered a casual broad thank you which indicated he hadn't a clue what the whole evening was about. For want of something to say, he acknowledged Helen for all the work she did for charity and for one terrible moment Corrine thought he was going to turn it into a public declaration of love. She was sitting next to Helen, who seemed to freeze the moment Mal mentioned her name. There were problems in that marriage. Corrine could smell them. But the thought that she might be doing Helen a favour was one she quickly put to the back of her mind. The feelings Mal and she had for each other had to prove themselves greater than the sum of his marriage. Otherwise it was just some sad sexual affair. Corrine knew it was more than that. She needed to know it was more than that.

Meanwhile Helen seemed determined to fix her up with journo Jack, who was irritating her like fuck with his 'Mick this . . .' and 'Sting that . . .' name-dropping. However, once the urgency had gone off her and Corrine had accepted that herself and Mal would have to wait, she had enough room to realize that a commission from *Rolling Stone* could be a very good thing indeed.

Once the show was over, and Mal was released from his position at Helen's right hand, Corrine thought he would find a way of being with her. But he didn't. She waited around, holding Jack enthralled with just half of her brain and body language, whilst the other half tried to compute what the fuck was going on. The party had started, and with the thumping music and the ensuing chaos of candles being drunkenly toppled by stoned designers and models squawking and hopping all over the place, Mal had every opportunity to spirit her off to some private corner. After about an hour, Jack and herself moved outside and the fool tried to kiss her. He was drunk and so Corrine pretended she was drunk too and kissed him back. What was the worst that could happen? Mal might come out and find them? Would that be such a bad thing?

And so that's what happened. It was a good and a bad thing.

'Mal has to go,' Helen said, her words clipped, her voice tight.

Or, 'I have to go,' Mal said hurriedly, his voice breaking over the words.

Corrine must have been slightly drunk after all, because afterwards she could not quite remember the chain of events between Helen and Mal suddenly interrupting her kiss with Jack, and the three of them waving Mal off as he disappeared back to Dublin in the limousine he had arrived in less than three hours earlier.

There were other questions lurking around over the next few days as Corrine planned her move up to Dublin. Questions nibbling away at the edge of her conscience, like: Why hadn't Mal called since he got back? Why had he made no effort to see her on her own that night, made an excuse to stay over? Had Mal been sent back to Dublin by Helen, or had he wanted to go back himself? Corrine picked off each one of them, finding reasons to believe in her favour, until they finally disappeared.

Jack was smitten. Based in London, he was e-mailing her every day until she finally conceded to a meeting in Dublin to discuss a commission to interview the top five names in Irish rock. She would need to base herself in the capital for a few days, but Corrine said she had nowhere to stay so Jack suggested the Clarence Hotel, where his publishers had an account. Corrine said that she would be delighted, although she suspected, correctly, that Jack himself would be expecting to provide some room service.

Helen had offered to stay in the house for a week or so and look after Sapphire.

'The boys can manage without me for another while,' and Corrine felt a pang of hatred as she realized that Mal was probably included in that maternal grouping.

In the few days that Corrine was preparing for her trip up to Dublin, she tried to put Mal out of her mind. She had to. What with his wife buzzing around her, helping her pick out seductive outfits which Helen assumed were for Journo Jack.

'Here – take this,' she said, holding out an exquisite silk robe with a lace panel, 'I'll hardly need it down here. God knows why I packed it. He will love it and it'll make you feel as sexy as hell.'

Corrine doubted Helen had ever felt sexy in her life. She had a face that said 'pragmatist'. Certainly she must have been pretty in her youth; but it took a certain bone structure to carry one through with elegance into one's forties. And Helen didn't have it. Tough, Corrine said in her mind. What she was doing wasn't nice, but then, whoever said life was nice? One life, one chance. You had to grab these opportunities when they came along. And worse things could happen. She wasn't murdering her children or maiming her body. She was going after her husband. Helen had allowed herself to become jowly and complacent. She was married to a rock-star genius who was driven by passions that poor Helen could not possibly understand. If Corrine didn't step in, somebody else surely would. In the long term, perhaps Helen would be pleased to have Mal taken off her hands by a 'friend'. Then again, perhaps not. Either way, it was going to happen. It was fate, and Corrine convinced herself she was as powerless over what was going to happen as Helen was.

'Thanks,' she said, taking the robe, 'it's beautiful.'

'So are you,' said Helen and her eyes were full of a female-bonding/friendship vibe that made Corrine, frankly, want to puke. 'I'm sure you'll knock him dead!'

Having to sleep with Jack was a pain in the arse, but he didn't make himself unmanageable and, in the end, he worked out useful. Plus, he *was* a trade-up from Enda, although the virgin ponytail priest was a happening that Corrine was working very hard to demote from regret to complete denial. The sex was tolerable, and once she got into it, it was quite satisfactory. Refreshingly normal after Enda's emotional plungings, and while she could tell he liked her a lot, Jack wasn't about to fling himself at her feet and sew himself on to her for all eternity.

The hotel suite was fantastic, and Corrine felt relieved to be back enjoying the standard of lifestyle she had more or less grown up with, but at the same time regretful that her life had moved so far from all this that she should feel excitement at being there. Jack ordered room service so they 'wouldn't be disturbed' and Corrine had to stop herself from over-ordering. Without the baseball cap and in these elegant surroundings, Jack did not look too bad.

'I have to go back to London tomorrow,' he said with a hint of regret and Corrine said, 'I wish I was coming with you.' They both knew that wasn't true, but when a man likes a woman more than a woman likes a man, it's polite to pretend. There were egos and a hotel bill at stake, which was why Corrine had to set her voice at just the right casual tone when she said, 'Jack – you know Mal Doherty pretty well, don't you?'

'Well, I've met him a few times. You must know him pretty good yourself though, seeing as how you're all chummy with his wife?'

'Yeah, I just find him a bit, you know . . .'

Jack put down his coffee and looked at her.

'No. What?'

'Wee-ll, you know . . .'

She was on the verge of blowing this. Jack's face lost its innocent post-coital softness and became instantly hard and suspicious. Fucking journalists. Nasty cynical beasts. You couldn't get shit past them. Corrine had to double-bluff. There was no way around it.

'God, this is awkward,' she said, looking away, then flicking her eyes back at him to see if he was biting. Jack's eyes narrowed. She had better be good.

'I think Mal fancies me.'

He laughed.

'Ha! Yeah right! Mal fancies everyone.' Corrine looked hurt. Genuinely. 'Hey, sorry, babe, I don't mean it like that, I mean – you are special and all . . .'

She could really fly now.

'Yeah well, Jack. You don't know what it's like. I mean it. He really keeps coming on to me, and I am *really* good friends with Helen, you know? Why do you think I'm not staying in the house? It's shit awkward, Jack, really. I mean, now I have to interview him for you guys and, I mean, I can't do the article without him but really I . . . I just don't know what to do. I need this commission, I can't give up on my career but, you know—'

'Calm down, babe, . . . it's OK . . . it's OK . . .'

Jack came and put his arms around her. Christ, she gave good histrionic. She should do it more often.

'You are not going to give up on this commission, babe. We – I – will find a way.' And he moved around and faced her.

Corrine allowed herself a small smirk disguised as relief.

'Look. Mal's an old dog – but I know him well enough. He doesn't fuck around with the journalists . . .'

'Well, I don't know about—'

'Listen, babe.' Jack was in his stride now. Mr Sort It Out Big Stuff. Men were *such* children. 'I will call Mal and arrange for the two of us to meet him tonight for a drink.'

'No, I . . .'

Corrine put her face onto its vulnerable setting. She felt like she must look quite comical, but Jack was buying into it.

'No, wait, hon. If he is around, which I think he is, he'll come down. Then you and me will be together and as far as Mal is concerned, you are my new lady, yeah?'

'Yeah, OK,' she squeaked gently.

'He won't mess with an editor at the *Stone*'s girl. No way.'

Corrine nuzzled her face into his bath robe.

'Thank you, Jack.'

Jack stiffened slightly as she knew he would.

'Hey now, Corrine,' he said really quietly, 'you know this doesn't mean that you and me . . .'

Stupid prick. Like, as if. She tried to sound disappointed, and it was difficult not to snap.

'Yeah, I know.'

That was one rock journalist that wouldn't be invited to Mal's second wedding.

'Honestly,' Jack said as Corrine got up to go the bathroom, 'why would a man married to a fantastic woman like Helen want to fuck around anyway? Defies belief, babe – don't you think?'

Corrine was in the en suite and he didn't quite catch her response.

⬭

It had all gone so smoothly, it had to have been fate. Mal had met them in the bar of the Clarence and Jack had played a blinder: touching her face, and calling her 'my lady'. Mal was not the type to play gooseberry and Corrine could sense his discomfort. After Jack had gone to the bathroom, reluctantly tearing himself away by running his hand gently along her shoulder blades, Corrine and Mal sat looking at each other in smouldering silence until finally he cracked and said, 'I want you.' She shrugged and said, 'You should have thought of that before.'

'Before what?' he said.

'Before you turned your back on me after the fashion show.'

'My wife was there.'

Corrine looked away, then made a great show of

welcoming Jack back into their company and whispering, 'Take me upstairs and fuck me,' just audible enough for Mal to hear.

Mal found himself having to leave the hotel while another man went off to enjoy something that he wanted. Such injustice was beyond his comprehension, as Corrine knew it would be. After she had seen Jack into his airport taxi the following morning, she checked her messages and there were over ten frantic voicemail and texts on her mobile. He must have rung Helen the night before to get her number. Cool. She left it until after lunch and she could hear him almost swallow the phone.

'I want you here now. I'll send the car.'

They went straight to bed and stayed there for the best part of the afternoon. It was amazing and Corrine realized again that no man could ever make her feel the way Mal Doherty did. He pushed aside the mundane nothingness of the past ten years and brought her back to a time when she felt passionate and adored. Only true love could feel this good. As they emerged in the late afternoon from their lovemaking, Mal put on Godot's as yet unreleased album. As his singing flushed through the air it felt to Corrine like they were in a dream (rather than simply experiencing the most state-of-the-art integrated music system that money could buy). Emotion echoed through her: here you are again, loving him, needing him. Except that, this time, the pain of his inevitable departure was thrumming already at the back of her head. This was temporary.

She was in Helen's house, Helen's bed. When Helen came home, it would all be over. Helen. Fucking Helen.

She had been angry with Mal for being weak, for not having the guts to walk out on his marriage and pursue his passion for her. To follow his own heart, fulfil his own destiny and make hers complete. But now, as he walked naked around the room, pottering in and out of the bathroom for clothes, touching her affectionately on the head as he passed, it all just felt so right. Even being in this house felt right. Helen wasn't here and Mal seemed so comfortable and happy, as if he really wanted her there. Surely if he were committed elsewhere he would be acting shifty, anxious for her to leave. He was weak but Corrine now knew that she could not live without him. She could not let him go this time. She would do whatever it took. She had the power to keep him, she knew that. It was just a question of biding her time, sitting tight and waiting for that moment to come.

NOSEY PARKER

'I'M JUST HONEST – THAT'S ALL'

IT'S OFFICIAL. ALFIE IS GAY!

I have got nothing against homosexuals. Readers of this column know that I regularly support high-profile bum bandits like Elton and his like for the work they do for Aids and such. But what I really hate is people who try and hide what they are. If you're 'gay', come out and say it. At least we all know where we stand then. They call me Honest Ron – I'm a right randy bastard who likes beautiful women. I'm not ashamed of it, but clearly Alfie is ashamed that he can't give that cracking bird MoniKa a regular going over because he has done a runner! And who has he gone to with his 'Oh help – I can't get it up with the most beautiful woman in the world' whingeing? None other than the Queen of the homos, Wilson, and his 'partner' Stephen Silke. Exact details of Alfie's whereabouts have yet to be confirmed by our sources, but there is no doubt that the three men are 'holed up' together in some secret location.

They say: Give us our privacy. *We say:* What are you ashamed of? You're happy to take the money fame brings, now you've got to pay Ron's price for fame, which is THE TRUTH!

THE TRUTH TRAIN: Honest Ron is driving, and it only stops when it gets to THE TRUTH!

Do you want to see Alfie in the Truth Train tomorrow?
Phone 080027821 for Yes, 080027822 for No and 080027823 for Not Sure.

<small>(Calls charged at a rate of £5 per minute.)</small>

25

Molly had changed. Her mother couldn't quite put her finger on how, but something about her daughter had altered lately and she could not decide if it was a good or a bad thing. She had become distracted and withdrawn, and that was not good. But at the same time there was a quietness, a new sedateness about Molly that suggested to Mary Walshe that her daughter might be finally maturing. Because, while Molly appeared to the outside world as a responsible enough young woman, she could be pettish and pouting with her parents – reluctant to let go of her girl-hood. She did her chores, but rarely without being asked, and it was as much her parents' fault, Mary knew, that Molly knew so little about the cost of living that she believed a couple of hours a week in light housework against full adult board and lodging was a fair deal. All things considered, Molly was a good daughter and her parents loved having her around the place, but Mary did worry that Molly was wasting her life mooching about Killa. She could get married young, start a family and Mary would have been happy with that, but there seemed to be precious little happening in that department. And, while Mary did not regret her own circumstances, she wanted her daughter to have the adventures that she had never enjoyed. There was still Miss Mannings' money sitting there, but Molly seemed to have no inclination for travel. She was a homebird. Happy with her job in the chemist's, her tea at home with Mam and Dad every evening and those wretched magazines which had finally spilled out from her bedroom and were littering every surface in the house.

'I'll throw every last one of them out one of these days, I swear!' Mary would frequently complain to her husband as she tried to arrange them into tidy piles.

'Leave it alone, Mary. Sure, what harm are they doing? It's not as if she's off doing drugs or worse.'

'Worse' in her father's eyes meant fooling about with Fonzie Mallarkey, although Mary would have been relieved at such a display of healthy young womanhood. She knew that the magazine thing wasn't right. Molly still offered to give her room up for extra guests, and the few nights around the fashion show they could certainly have done with the space. The reality was that Molly's room looked like the stockroom of a newsagent's shop. There was no way the Walshes could ever put a guest in there, or clear it out sufficiently to hold one. There were magazines everywhere, piles and piles of them, most co-ordinated by date and title, some awaiting 'filing'. There were the teenage titles; these piles were the highest because she had been collecting them the longest. *Smash Hits* and *J17* were floor-to-ceiling in the far corner with the wardrobe jamming them into place. Then there were the newer titles: *2Day*, *Heat*, *Now!*, *Closer* – their piles were smaller. The large-formats – *OK!* and *Hello!* magazines – had their own shelves; *Woman*, *Woman's Own* and the 'older titles' also had their place, but Mary didn't like to think about that. The one time Mary had complained about the chaos and asked Molly to clear up her room, the twenty-something had laughed brightly and begun to explain her complex filing system. Mary had been alarmed by what she saw as a growing obsession, but Jack had fobbed her off, saying, 'It's only a hobby, love. Sure, look how I am about my cooking?' Granted, her husband had enough culinary implements to open a shop, and since he'd gone 'on line' hardly a week went by without him taking delivery of a new-fangled garlic press or its like. But Mary had kept a close eye on her daughter's magazine consumption none the less, and had been relieved to see her 'hobby' being overtaken with Aoife and the fashion show. When it had turned out to be the huge glittering event that it was, covered by the national newspapers and even *Hello!* magazine, nobody could have been more proud or delighted than the Walshes at their daughter's involvement. And if Mary had to trace back the subtle change in Molly's behaviour, it would be back to that event.

'I'm off out now, Mam. Don't bother with tea, I don't know when I'll be back.'

There it is there, Mary thought. Nothing specific – just something missing. A kiss for your mammy? A childish sunniness? She's growing up and she'll be gone soon then you'll be sorry to lose her, Mary said to herself. But on the next layer down, the layer of truth where sometimes mammies dare not tread, Mary Walshe suspected that Molly's change in personality might indicate that she was just plain unhappy.

∎

It was an anticlimax. Molly had never experienced an anti-climax before because she had never been high enough to come down. Sure, she had had her uptimes: winning the prize, going on the make-up course with Julian August in Galway, even, in the early days, realizing that Fonzie, the best-looking lad in town, was after her – they were all highs in her life. Except they were more like steps, really. Good things that afterwards would make her feel better about herself. Like: now I know I'm a good sales-person, a qualified make-up artist, the best-looking girl in Killa. What's next? That was really the problem. After the show there was nowhere she could go. Oh, Aoife had the usual big ideas: 'Come to Dublin; I'll get you loads of work. You have Julian August on your CV now . . .'

'I'd worked with him before then.' Molly knew the make-up course in Galway wasn't the same thing, but Aoife was *really* getting on her nerves. Where Aoife had always irritated her in the way that Molly wished she would take more care with her appearance and stop getting on her case all the time, she had found that since the show there was a distance between them. Molly knew it was herself driving Aoife away, but she just could not seem to help herself. She felt suddenly angry with her oldest friend. Knowing that her anger was irrational just made it worse. What it came right down to was this: Aoife was famous.

Not really famous, like Alfie or Mick Jagger or Mal Doherty, but sort-of famous. That is to say, she knew loads of famous people, had appeared in loads of magazines and had kept all of this quiet from Molly. Except that she hadn't. Kept it quiet. As such. Aoife had hinted at knowing supermodels and famous people in Dublin and Molly had not believed her. And the reason that she hadn't believed her was that Aoife made out that these things weren't really important and so she played them down. And Molly thought that if Aoife were really as famous as she had hinted at, then she would be making a really big song and dance about it because, of course, being famous and knowing famous people was a really big deal. Everybody knew that. People bought *2Day*, *Hello!* and *OK!* magazines in their millions. Not just Molly, as Molly was at pains to point out to her a few days after the show, because being famous was a 'REALLY BIG DEAL!'

Aoife did not get it. 'Molly – you were at the show. It was a laugh, wasn't it? Everyone was the same. Nobody was looking at you going, "She's not as famous as me." Did you not get it? It's not like you freaked out when you met Mal Doherty or—'

'Is that what you think I'm like? Like I'd *freak out* in the same room as Mal Doherty. Like I'm some stupid teenager who'd be like, "Oo-oo-oo, can I have your autograph, please?"'

'That's not what I meant.'

Molly knew that, but she didn't know what she meant herself any more. She was confused. Something had changed. And while her life looked almost exactly as it had done before the show, Molly felt as if everything was somehow different.

'I want a mascara. By that French "Saint" fella. I don't care how much it costs.'

'We haven't got any – we're all sold out.' And she turned her back on Eleanor Jackson. When she turned around again, the old woman had gone and while Molly had dearly wanted her to go away, she had not believed for one minute that she would take the snub to heart. But that was the way things were turning out these days. The same, but different. There was this new feeling of vague dissatisfaction with her life, and then that familiar feeling of apathy – an unwillingness to do anything about it. If Molly were to self-analyse, which was not her bag at all, she might have connected this feeling with her anger towards Aoife.

The show had really turned her life upside down. Molly had enjoyed a simple ordinary life, spiced up with a weekly dose of fantasy. But now the fantasy and the fact had become confused. Alfie Smith – ALFIE SMITH! – had stayed in her parents' B&B and was, in disguise, living in Killa – IN KILLA! – with Fonzie Mallarkey, who had been supplying her since she was sixteen with her weekly Alfie Smith – ALFIE SMITH! – magazine fix. Except that after a few days, the capital letters and the exclamation marks had gone. She wasn't allowed to use them. The only person she could trust to tell was Aoife, and she just said, 'So what?' which was really, *really* annoying.

But Alfie himself was the worst element. Not being able

just to get him on his own, away from Fonzie, which of course was her fault for introducing them in the first place. The first day, the day after that terrible night where she had made a complete fool of herself, she had found herself being caught up in the aftermath of the show. Julian August could not be found, and she was given the job of extracting him from Moran's pub where he was asleep and glued by his own drool to the bar. Fonzie had called round just as she was leaving and Alfie had introduced himself as 'Albert' – she had left them to it. When she got home, 'Albert' was gone. Bag, hat – the lot.

'Struck me as a bit of a drifter,' her dad had said. 'That nice woman Helen came round and paid his bill for him, and I think the Mallarkey lad has taken him. Seems he wants to stick around for a bit.'

Jack shot his daughter a sideways look that made it clear he sincerely hoped the English lad's decision to stay wasn't anything to do with her. Molly was wondering, hoping the same thing. She could not have been more wrong. Over the coming days she barely saw Alfie *or* Fonzie. Fonzie was into awful heavy-metal-type music, and had a collection of horrible old electric guitars in his shed. It seemed that Alfie was helping him 'do them up' and was going to teach him how to play them. That was Alfie. Putting himself out for other people: 'Can't stop now, Moll – Al's just on his way back from Castlebar with some strings and paint and stuff, so I said I'd meet him back at the—'

'Are you sure he really wants to do this, Fonzie? I mean Al's a big London DJ, isn't he? Has he really got time to be . . . we-ell . . .?'

She trailed off because what she really meant was, Alfie is far too important to be hanging out in your garage, and what she really, *really* meant was, If he is going to be hanging around with anyone around here, it should be me.

What Fonzie had heard was, You're such a dull arsehole that not only do I not even fancy you – despite years of unrewarded dumb admiration – but I don't think you are even up to making a new mate. Fonzie didn't say anything, but he looked at her like she had seen him look at Eleanor Jackson, like he thought she was stone fucking mad. That was all Molly needed. She did not love Fonzie Mallarkey, but she needed for him to love her. A pretty girl needed an unrequited admirer following her round. Life in a small town in the West of Ireland was not complete without one.

Aoife was pissed off with her, Fonzie was going off her and now she had managed to upset Eleanor Jackson.

No. Molly Walshe was definitely not herself these days. Her comfortable, same-old life in Killa seemed to be coming apart at the seams, and it didn't feel like there was a damn thing she could do about it.

26

Helen was confused. Or rather she wasn't, and that was the problem. She wasn't confused any more. She knew the answer to the question she had not been asking, and she didn't like it.

This was not supposed to have happened. She was supposed to have left Emily in charge of her mounting pile of responsibilities and received a phone call within the week telling her that she had to come home. She'd get a few days out, a short holiday, then have to go back and get on with everything. Instead of which Emily had informed her during her daily phone call that everything had been filed, there was nothing going on and frankly, she was bored. When a rock star's wife leaves a message on their answering machine saying that she is on holiday until further notice, people leave her alone. Voluntary work, it seem, is just that. If you don't feel like doing it, nobody is going to twist your arm. Pragmatic and charming, Helen was the charity's first-choice celebrity fundraiser, but she was not indispensable. There were any number of glamorous wealthy wives dying to be seen to 'give something back'. Their contribution was mainly holding catered 'committee meetings' in the business suites of fabulous hotels where they would compile lists of other rich people also anxious to be seen to 'give something back'. Everyone was basically working off the same list and the competitive edge was defined by who knew the airline magnate/conglomerate namesake best.

'We've been invited out to Tony's garden party next month. I'll talk to him. He'll take a table for ten, at least.'

Fifty-plus red chignon gives thirty-something honey highlights a stark look, says, 'He won't come, but he'll make a contribution and we can sell the table on – same as last year.' One or two offer the blonde newcomer a thin smile of sympathy for not knowing that fifty-plus red chignon was Tony's sister-in-law.

Most of the charities themselves knew that Helen Doherty was one of a very few outsiders who were prepared to turn charity fundraising into actual work, beyond making a few pressure phone calls and posing for the society photographers on the night. If Helen was organizing a fundraiser for you, she would be there all day on the day, up to her elbows in canapés and sponsored champagne, clipboard groaning with receipts, barking instructions and begging favours right up to the last minute. She'd get changed in the hotel ladies' fifteen minutes before countdown and be there to grip-and-grin every guest as they came in, looking as relaxed as if she had just spent four hours at the hairdresser's. She was a real treasure and the charities loved her, but she was a volunteer and worked at her own pace on her own projects. She was answerable to no one and nothing except her own conscience, and right now that was busy with other things.

Helen had been twitching around looking for distractions. It wasn't as easy as it was at home where, aside from there always being a new cause to jump on, there were any number of rooms to redecorate or reorganize. In somebody else's space, there was only so much you could do without being intrusive. And so, in the past forty-eight hours Helen had stripped and sorted Sapphire's bedroom, cooked five batches of fairy cakes, hemmed and re-hung a set of curtains, polished the red tiles in the hall until they shone and then unpolished them with scouring pads after Stephen nearly broke his neck on them when he came to pick up Sapphire. She had called on the two men a couple of times, but only to pick up Sapphire. There was a field behind the Bishop's palace where Stephen had found a disabled donkey. Sapphire had correctly diagnosed the neglected animal as needing its hooves cut and a friendship was developing between the two of them. Helen could see that Sapphire was a lonely child, one who would seek out the safe company of adults rather than try to compete in the belly-tops teen-mag culture of girls her own age. It was strange how the three of them – Alfie made four – had ended up in this social outpost. Killa, it was clear, was no secret celebrity retreat. There were places like that in Ireland – beautiful locations littered at their lakesides with vast modern mansions where the great and the good would helicopter in for weekend house parties, the more adventurous deigning to frequent some local pub that had long since used its celebrity clientele to turn itself gourmet.

If she and Mal had stayed in the convent here, Killa would doubtless have fallen into that category by now. Locals treating them with casual friendliness whilst charging them double price for a pint of milk and pointing their house out to those fans who were obsessive enough to make the journey down. It was a country weekend getaway with full security attached. The only thing casual about it was, in reality, the wardrobe. If you counted cashmere as casual.

Killa was different. Perhaps because it bore out a theory which Helen had long since learned and often put into practice. Which is that, if you don't act famous, people rarely treat you as such. Take Alfie, for instance. The world's press were doubtless searching for him by now, and yet here he was, with no more protection than a different haircut and a slight alteration in name. He certainly was not in hiding, as he had been in their house in Dublin. Helen had seen him flying around on the back of his new friend's motorbike. He had even served her in the newsagent's shop that morning, for God's sake! Alfie was not behaving like a famous person and, crucially, he did not expect people to recognize him. And so they didn't. Wilson was another case in point. Helen did not know him very well, but the few charity benefits she had attended in his name had borne out the flamboyant camp high-maintenance image. There had been live swans walking around at the last one. Now, here he was, locked in the local Bishop's palace, feasting on buttery scones and, if Stephen was to be believed, ironing his own shirts and developing a fondness for Irish daytime television. To someone in the know, Alfie's helping a mate out in his shop and Wilson's desire to iron his own shirts seemed bizarre. Only fame, Helen thought, could take ordinary, everyday activities and warp them into novelties. Only fame could make someone want to escape a house and a husband who was the envy of millions of women the world over and take up temporary residence in the home of a woman she barely knew to look after her pubescent daughter and voluntarily hem her curtains.

Or perhaps not. Perhaps it wasn't the pressures of fame, the stress of keeping it all going. Perhaps it was something else. In fact, 'perhaps' was the luxurious position Helen had been in as short a time ago as yesterday. The nebulous state of perhaps-ness was something which, in her new state of certainty, Helen longed to go back to. The discomfort of not knowing, the constant seeking out and achievement of distraction, seemed like a privilege she had once enjoyed.

There had been no blinding flash. No incident had set it off, there had been no catalyst, no sudden moment of truth. It was as if this knowledge had been crawling around inside her head for – how long? Weeks? Months? Years? – She had just been too busy to pay it any attention.

The twins had called that morning. 'When are you coming home? We miss you.'

'I miss you too.'

It was a lie, and guilt rushed through her in the act of speaking platitudes to her own children. Missing her kids was part of the physiology of motherhood for her. She had let go of the twins as they grew older because that's what good mothers do. As much as she had encouraged their independence, Helen still felt as close to the twins as if they were a part of her body. Helen looked confident, her life as it appeared to the world giving her every reason to be. Only she knew that the confidence she displayed was no more than a weapon. Helen carried her sure, unaffected charm as an open holster over the hips of her Gucci jeans to protect herself and the family from the invasive glare of the public and press. For all their wealth and influence, Helen had always felt powerless over her family's privacy; she was constantly wary of people who might betray them. Mal was thick-skinned. He shrugged off bad reviews and press-informers as part of the job and so it fell on Helen to vet their circle and keep their family from descending into a perpetual party. Sometimes it worked better than others, but through everything Helen had one thing she felt entirely sure of: her position as a mother. Biology aside, the confidence she had as the boys' mother was indisputable. Her love was unflinching and complete. They drove her mad, frightened her, worried her, sometimes they even made her wish they had never been born. But everything she did, she did for them. Now here she was lying to them. If she missed them, wanted to be with them, then that feeling was weaker than her need to stay here in Corrine's house.

'How are you getting on with Corrine?'

She had called the night before and Corrine had answered the phone.

'I was just going to call you. I bumped into Mal with Jack the other day and . . .'

Helen was pleased that she was there. For no reason in particular, just that it seemed to even the score somehow.

'All right. I suppose.'

The boys sounded unsure about their new house guest. But then, they were fifteen and, Helen thought, probably following their father's surly lead.

'You be nice to Corrine now. Make an effort to be friends with her. For me, yeah?'

Fionn sniffed a vague reply; she snapped and the conversation ended badly. She knew that meant they were not really coping without her, but still that did not make her want to go home.

And in staying away Helen knew she would be pushing herself that final inch towards the truth.

Over the past few days it had been creeping up on her like a bad case of flu. She had known it was there, but (unbelievably now she was face to face with it) she had thought there were other more important things to attend to. Like hemming a set of someone else's curtains. Or baking fairy cakes for nobody in particular. Helen had always known she would have to confront it eventually, just not now. 'Now' being a loose term for 'ever'. Over the past few days the compulsion to escape had become stronger and stronger until, eventually, rational thought overtook her desire to bleach the insides of Corrine's kitchen cupboards, and she faced the demon.

Long since used to the dark comfort of denial, it cowered in a corner under the spotlight of her conscious mind. *You don't love Mal.*

And then once she had seen it, she could see nothing else but this truth in its every gory detail.

You have been married for twenty years and instead of growing to love him more, you have come to love him a little less every year. Now, you do not love him at all. You do not love the way he looks, the way he talks, the way he dresses, the self-conscious pouting way he carries himself. You do not love the way he feels; you recoil when he touches you.

The more Helen looked at the truth, the worse it got until she felt paralysed, trapped by its dreadfulness.

You are disappointed when you see a part of him in your sons, nauseated at the idea of making love to him. You would have liked more children – but not with him.

And on and on, staring at this gaping wound as its sides flailed back and all the poison came pouring out.

He organized the wedding without consulting you; he went on tour when you were pregnant; he was unfaithful, insincere; he fell in love with another woman and made you feel responsible.

In fact, Helen decided, it was not as simple as her just not loving Mal. She realized that, actually, she despised him. She traced it back to the affair he had had when the twins were small. The wedding, his being on tour when she was pregnant – she had coped with all that. But the affair had finished her off. And it was how long ago? Thirteen years?

Helen stalked around the kitchen looking for something to smash. She put her fist down briefly on the top of a boogie box and kicked off some awful party CD she had got free with yesterday's Sunday paper. The sudden warbling of some forgotten disco hit reminded her that she was in somebody else's house and smashing things wasn't an option. She decided to knead bread. But first she needed to make dough. *The fucking treacherous big-headed bastard –* no yeast, she'd have to make brown soda – *she should have left him then. She should have taken off with the twins and left him to rot with the filthy slag he nearly chose over her.* No brown flour, she'd have to use white. *Like – who the fuck did he think he was?* Self-raising, she might as well make scones. *People go around telling him he's God and he believes them. Stupid weak-willed shit.* No margarine, she'd have to use . . . *'My wife and kids keep my feet on the ground.' Yeah right – so how bullshit is that.* . . . Butter. *WHAT THE FUCK AM I DOING MAKING SCONES?*

Helen threw the bag of flour at the window above the sink and screamed, a huge powerful howl, fuelled with the pent-up rage of a dozen years. Then she slid to the floor and banged her fists on the flagstones until she thought her wrists would break. After a few minutes, Helen found herself suddenly calmed by the pragmatic realization that now this revelation was complete, she would have to do something about it. If facing the fact that she no longer loved her husband was frightening, the idea of leaving him was worse. Now there really was something that didn't bear thinking about.

Which was why, despite the mascara streaks and herself and the entire kitchen being covered in flour, Helen was almost glad when she heard a polite tap on the back door followed by the figure of Corrine's neighbour, the priest.

27

'Why didn't Wilson come?'

Because he's a moody, selfish, lazy, self-pitying shit-head.

'Wilson decided to stay and help Constance make some cakes.'

'Wilson likes cakes, doesn't he?'

'Yes, he most certainly does, Sapphire. He most certainly does.'

'I think he's fat.'

'I think you're cheeky – and too grown up to be saying rotten things like that about people and getting away with it.'

Sapphire and Wilson didn't get on. As the adult, Wilson took the lion's share of the blame for behaving like a petulant ten-year-old. The middle-aged wealthy-beyond-measure rock star was jealous of a plump twelve-year-old girl, and felt he was perfectly entitled to make poisonous comments to Stephen about his new rival's appearance and personality.

'She's a fat loser kid who will never amount to anything. Just like her miserable cunt of a mother.'

Stephen generally ignored Wilson's more vicious remarks with the dignified air of one who is so far above such bilious bitchery that they can barely hear it.

'Did you say Alfie was calling around this afternoon?'

But Wilson rarely let go until he had got a reaction.

'You'll get no thanks from that bitch for babysitting her retard.'

'I shan't be late – we'll be back for supper.'

'I mean, she's *Corrine's* daughter. She's got bile for blood. You can tell by just looking at her. That big face and the eyes too close together . . .'

'Do you want me to pick you up anything in Galway? I called Brown Thomas ahead and they've put a few things aside but if there's . . .'

Talk of services provided seemed to send Wilson over the edge.

'*Don't* you try and pretend you are going to Galway for *me*. I know what this is all about. You trotting off with your fake kid playing let's-pretend parent. Well let me tell you something, *Daddy*—'

'I'm not listening to this . . .' Stephen gathered his bag and car keys and headed for the door.

'Oh, that's it – walk out. Run away. Can't face the truth. Well, you just go ahead and live out your little fantasy, Stephen. Just don't expect me to play along with it. Don't expect me to pretend that the fat kid—'

'SHE HAS A NAME!'

Result. Wilson was delighted with himself.

'Yeah, right.'

'Sapphire. Namesake of the woman that you were hiding with in your closet until your late thirties? So don't you *dare* lecture me about fantasies, you brutal little hound, or call her fat. If the poor child comfort-eats she has an excuse with both her age and her appalling upbringing, which is more than can be said for *you*. I will be back before nightfall, and I may – will, probably – have Sapphire with me. In the meantime, I expect you to have done some growing up!'

It was a brave attempt at the last word, but it didn't work.

'And a gay man playing fake Daddy to a stranger's daughter – that's mature, is it? Have you any fucking idea what trouble you are getting yourself into here? Getting us *both* into? When Corrine comes back and finds out who her precious little girl has been hanging out with . . .'

Now Stephen had really had enough.

'Fucking STOP right there, Wilson. First, I can guarantee you that Corrine does not give a shit about who is hanging out with her daughter who she has not even bothered to speak to on the telephone since she went up to Dublin. I think that is fucking shocking and so, because the kid is missing her mother and because I am a fundamentally nice person, and because I have nothing better to do than sit around here watching you STUFF YOUR FACE, I have become Sapphire's friend. Not her "pretend parent" or her "fake Daddy" because, unlike my spoilt, deluded, eating-disordered partner, I am *not* a dysfunctional fantasist. You may think it is strange for a gay man in his thirties to become friends with a twelve-year-old girl, but then again, I have yet to meet a person you bothered to become friends with whom you did not want to fuck. I have ordered you in Egyptian cotton linen and some Jo Malone from a department store in Galway. I'll do what I can to get you slippers and if you think of anything else I'm on the mobile! Goodbye!'

But the triumphalism of having wrenched the last word from Wilson's grip was short-lived. On the way over to Corrine's house, Stephen could not help but wonder if there was some grain of truth in Wilson's cynical accusations. Was this child just another project? A way for Stephen to achieve the rounded familial intimacy that a male partner alone could not supply? How much was the time he was spending with this confused, immature adolescent about his own need to be needed, his latent, or perhaps even imagined desire to be a parent? Surely he was not so shallow, so mean spirited as to be pursuing this relationship with the primary purpose of annoying Wilson?

As he pulled up outside her house, Sapphire threw herself into the front seat next to him and Stephen's doubts melted away. She was wearing a horribly bobbled pink jumper with a lace collar and a long denim skirt which looked like it had belonged to her mother back in the dark ages when it was fashionable. Her short bobbed hair was pulled back from her face with a nasty plastic hair-band clearly picked up from a one-euro bargain basket at the local chemist's. She was grinning from ear to ear, fizzing with excitement and adventure. This sad, inelegant, tragically charmless overgrown child trusted him. And he saw in her open adoration of him not only her vulnerability, but his own capacity for good. Yes, Stephen was beguiled by the innocence of children. He had yet to meet one that he did not like, nor one that did not take to him. But Sapphire was different in that she was unhappy; he could read her insecurity as clearly as if it was tattooed on her face. Stephen was no expert in twelve-year-old girls, but he knew that they didn't normally favour their mother's cast-off clothes and they generally tried to present themselves as older than they were. Sapphire's clumsy attempts to appear younger than her few years were a desperate cry for affection. Corrine was competitive instead of nurturing. Nothing made Stephen madder than a bad mother. These bitches that just blew out babies then didn't bother with them – when, by virtue of his physicality, Stephen's own parental instincts were completely denied. It wasn't fair.

***

'I'm fat too, so it doesn't matter if I say Wilson is fat.'

'Who told you you were fat?'

Obvious. Sapphire didn't reply.

'What shall we get in Galway?'

'Can we go to McDonald's?'

Eugh.

'Of course we can – but what else would you like?'

'I don't mind. Can I put on a CD?'

He would have expected a request for pink tiara-type accessories, but Sapphire seemed uninterested in the whole shopping thing. Stephen suspected she was just happy to be spending the day with him. Or rather, to be at the centre of somebody else's day.

※

'I'm going to play one of Fat Wilson's.' And Stephen could not help a smile.

The two of them sang along loudly to one of Wilson's love anthems and the tiny atmosphere that had inhabited a corner of both their minds cleared and the freshness of their adventure hit them anew.

'What's your biggest wish in the whole wide world?' Sapphire announced. Stephen could not answer that one honestly so he said, 'Driving to Galway with a special friend and shopping for shoes.' True enough on both counts.

'And you?'

'The same.'

That wasn't true and Stephen wondered why she had asked the question if she didn't want to answer it herself.

'Really?'

'Yeah.' She turned towards the window. She was one odd kid. After a few seconds she turned the music down and said, 'It's not really. But if I tell you you'll laugh at me.'

'No, I won't.'

'Yes, you will.'

'I won't, I promise.'

Shit, she wanted to be a fashion model or a ballet dancer; impossible dreams fed to her by that deranged mother.

'I want to play soccer for the Killa under-sixteen girls' team.'

'Is that all?' Stephen let out a little laugh.

'What do you mean?' Sapphire looked like she was going to cry. 'I said you'd laugh at me. You think I'm stupid. You think I'm too fat to play football. That's what Mrs Kieran said. She said I was too clumsy.'

'She did not.'

'She did!'

'Well – the next time I see Mrs Kieran I shall tell her she is *completely* wrong.'

'Well, she's the football coach and what she says goes. And she says I can't go on her team.'

'We'll just have to see about that. Because I think you would make a marvellous soccer player, and I should know because getting people on to football teams happens to be my job.'

'I thought you worked for Wilson.'

'Oh, that's just a hobby. My *real* job is training people to be fit enough for football teams.'

'You're lying.'

'Em, excuse me, young lady. Am not. I am a professionally qualified highly experienced fitness trainer. I have helped hone some of the finest bodies in the world.'

'Well whose bodies have you honed then that I would have heard of?'

'Wilson.'

'That doesn't count!' She gave him a look like he might tell her off, but she knew he would laugh and he did.

'Madonna.'

'Does she play football?'

'Alfie, then . . .'

'And what team does he play for?'

Sapphire was genuinely unimpressed, and Stephen was impressed that she was unimpressed. Perhaps Corrine's parenting had had some grounding side effects. Or perhaps Sapphire couldn't stomach celebrity because she had been fed on a diet of her mother's glorious past. More than likely it was a trick she used to infuriate her mother. Stephen could only imagine how irritating a faded star would find a child's nonchalance at their glory days.

'I don't care what you say, Sapphire, you won't put me off. I could *so* get you on that team.'

'Bet you couldn't.'

'Bet I could.'

There was a few seconds' silence while Sapphire mulled it over.

'Could you *really*, though?'

'It'll be hard work.'

'I don't mind.'

'You'll have to train every day.'

'Will you be with me?'

'Every step of the way.' But even as he said it, Stephen could feel his nerve endings tingle, turning him into a liar. They were only here on a couple of weeks' vacation. Now here he was making a commitment to get even more involved in this kid's life than he was already. He was encouraging her, inviting her to bond with him further.

A needy, helpless child – what the fuck could she benefit from a friendship with a queer rock star's sidekick? Sure he could train her on to the local football team. Probably nobody else could. The kid looked like she hadn't taken a bit of exercise in her life and, in all fairness, she carried herself like she was clumsy as hell. But in promising to do this thing he was also promising that he would be sticking around for what, two weeks, three? Wilson would flip – and rightly so, actually. He had taken a step too far this time. But what could he do? He could feel Sapphire gazing at him as he drove. A kind of burning admiration, fanatical, hopeful – he was right up on that pedestal and, although he felt terrible, Stephen just knew it was the place for him to be in that moment.

'When are the trials, then?'

'In the middle of October.'

Fuck! Six weeks! What the hell had he landed himself in? Only last night Wilson had shown signs of wanting to go home.

'Karl was on. He said MoniKa is back and she brought some Moroccan boy home to Holland Park with her? I don't like the sound of it. I think perhaps we should check him out.' Plus, he had flipped his lid when he had seen the Honest Ron 'Alfie is Gay' piece – which was the type of thing he would normally laugh off. Stephen could sense that Wilson was starting to lose touch with his 'normal' life. As if being away from it was softening his defences and making it that bit harder to handle.

At the end of the day, if Wilson wanted to go home, then—

'Could I be ready by October, Stephen? Could I, do you think? Could I?'

'Well, I most certainly cannot see why not. But first, young lady, we had better get ourselves to Galway and buy you some kit.'

NOSEY PARKER

'I'M JUST HONEST – THAT'S ALL'

Our man Honest Ron Parker reports on the stars and their scandals

NEW MAN FOR MONIKA

MoniKa – supermodel and wife of pop singer Alfie Smith – was snapped with this tall dark handsome stranger outside her Holland Park house at seven a.m. yesterday morning. Nosey Parker can exclusively reveal that the young man who has become a regular fixture in the stunning six-foot brunette's life is Ahmed, who has just been signed to the same model agency as MoniKa.

Our source revealed to us, however, that despite claims that they are 'just friends', MoniKa first met Ahmed in Morocco when she was 'taking a break' after her split from Alfie. Maybe Ahmed provided a shoulder (or something else!) to cry on? MoniKa, who lives alone since the disappearance of her husband last month, recently told this paper that she was 'missing Alfie', but that she had not given up hope for their marriage and was 'expecting him home any day'. Tip for you, Mon. I'd hang on to the pretty boy cos I don't think Alfie's worth it!

Tell us what you think! Phone 080027821 if you think MoniKa should take Alfie back and 080027822 if she should tell him to **** off!

(Calls charged at a rate of £5 per minute.)

Yesterday's survey revealed 42% of you think David Beckham's new hair is cool and 58% of you think it looks stupid.

So tomorrow: David goes in the Wank Tank!

294

28

Hang on in there, baby . . . hang on in there, darling . . .
oooh right there, right there, baby don't you move it
anywhere.

Enda was just being polite really, popping round to let
Helen know that he was going to Dublin to call on Corrine
and wouldn't be around for a few days to help with
Sapphire. Not, indeed, that she had been calling on him to
help much. His real motivation was to find out where his
'lady' was staying, as he had not spoken to her since before
she went away. He had bought himself a groovy new
outfit that morning that Jamesy had assured him would
'Carry you as far as Paris, man, never mind Dublin.' Now
all he had to do was call in, have a quick cup of tea and
get the information he needed from Helen, before whizz-
ing up to the station and catching the six o'clock train.

It was most certainly *not* his intention to be still sitting
here at ten past seven — all hope of catching trains and
reuniting with Corrine gone — listening to yet another
unhappy housewife whingeing about her lousy marriage.

Enda had gone to the back of the house after a short tap on the front door yielded no luck. He had his hand poised to knock when he was temporarily thrown off kilter by the Orgasm Song suddenly belting out of the open kitchen window. It was so very unexpected that Enda was virtually flung backwards and left wondering if he had been caught in some kind of space/time continuum in one of his madder sexual fantasies. He looked through the window to give a cursory check that the house had not become temporarily occupied by lovemaking American soul singers, and was faced with the sight of Helen balancing her considerable cleavage over a large mixing bowl. As she ground her hands into the flour her arms stiffened and her breasts squished together into a magnificent X.

Enda took a moment to rearrange himself mentally from lecherous love-god to lovely priest-type person, and gave the briefest of taps. As he entered, Enda was just in time to see Helen hurl a bag of flour across the room and make carnage out of Corrine's kitchen. Violence is frightening whether perpetrated by man or woman and judging by the state of Helen's face she was having some kind of a breakdown. Enda was an expert at reading desperation in women's faces. This was just so not what he needed right now.

'Are you all right, Helen? Shall I come back another . . .?'

'Fuck no,' she said, then quickly, 'Fuck! Is it all right to say fuck in front of a priest or . . .? Oh fuck, I've said it again!'

This was not the poised, elegant creature that had so expertly stolen Corrine's limelight on the day of the show.

'Anyway you're not a priest any more – oh, fuck it! Would you like a cup of tea?'

'That would be nice.'

'And a fucking fairy cake?'

Enda smiled weakly, unsure if she was joking or in the grip of a swearing seizure.

'Sorry,' and the smile that answered his made it obvious it was probably a bit of both.

Through force of habit, Enda clicked into kindly priest mode. He would miss the train, probably, possibly lose his girlfriend to the big city – if he hadn't already – and what for? Another act of Christianity for which he would be neither paid nor appreciated.

'I'll tell you what, Helen, why don't I make us both a nice cup of tea and you can tell me all about it?'

So she did.

There wasn't much he hadn't heard before. Standard marital stuff. Man consistently selfish over protracted period of time; taking his lovely wife for granted. Enda had been listening to this crap for years. As an arbiter of the Catholic Church it had been his moral duty to make the women stay with their husbands. 'Keep showing your husband love, communicate, tell him your needs and he will come around. He loves you.'

Right. How many years had he been saying that and how many times had it worked? Enda had come to the conclusion that men did not know how to show love. The only time they ever seemed to learn it was in retrospect. Their wives would leave them, they would be devastated and next time round – and there was always a next time for the man – their second wife/live-in girlfriend would get a much better time of it. Women in their forties with children found themselves less inclined, or in demand, to get involved again. They hung around the church and developed crushes on 'good' sexless Enda. The man who would come to their houses and make *them* cups of tea. The man who encouraged them in their aromatherapy/Reiki/counselling courses and made them tapes of his Christy Moore CDs and listened to them moaning about their bastard ex-husbands.

You're a saint, Enda.

He had endured that description for too many years. But who was he to tell them he was no saint. That he was a man who had been known to empty himself into a variety of household appliances and would do the same to any of them at the slightest invitation. But here it was. Enda wasn't entirely sure any more that he would. Empty himself. Into any of them. What galled him was that he never felt them looking at him in that way. Enda knew he was easy enough on the eye, certainly compared to the lazy beer-bellied retards most of these lonely women had been, or still were, married to. But it seemed to him that women did not know what they wanted. They left their husbands because they were selfish (often it would have taken as little as a man bringing them up a cup of tea on the occasional morning to save a marriage). Now, here was a guy who would have worn holes in the stair carpet bringing them cups of tea and you would have thought they'd be rushing him to the ground and tearing at his trousers with their teeth. But the most Enda ever enjoyed from any of them was the occasional coy confession that they had 'needs'. Sometimes Enda suspected there was an invitation hidden in there somewhere. Once he had taken one of his parishioners up on her offer of an 'aromatherapy' massage. 'I need to practise, Father,' and he had rather hoped that they might be practising something more than some mimsy, vaguely irritating shoulder-poking. Afterwards she had adjusted the top button of her white overall and blushingly asked if he had 'enjoyed' it. He had felt like telling her he would have enjoyed it a lot more if she had worn a see-through nightie and sat on his face.

Years of listening to needy women giving off about their husbands, and never having enjoyed any physical recompense for same, had made Enda rather cynical about these 'open your heart' sessions. So he sat and he made all of the right noises while Helen bleated on about her loveless marriage, and at the same time he mentally sang along to the CD which he had switched on to a low volume whilst he was up making the tea.

'. . . and then I discovered he had been having an affair. Well, not just one of his usual trysts with groupies, you understand – no, this was the Real Thing? Like a full-blown . . .' blah blah. Sooner or later the Orgasm Song was bound to come along again. Would he get away with getting up and having a quick flick through the tracks? Was there any excuse?

'I mean . . . I was upset. *Sure* I was upset, but then there were the *twins* to consider . . .'

Helen – I fancy another scone. No this wasn't the right time. There'd be a lull soon, surely. Maybe she'd say, 'Would you like another scone?' Then that would be the time to get up and—

Now that we've caressed . . . hmmmm . . . kissed so warm and tender . . . I can't wait till we reach . . . that sweet moment of surrender . . .

Oh dear. Enda had been waiting for the Orgasm Song through sheer boredom but he hadn't really thought about what he would do when it came on. Or rather, what circumstance it might bring on in him that was quite beyond his control. Given his very recent experience in the back garden Enda had felt himself probably temporarily impervious. He was wrong. Not to put too fine a point on it, he was so hard it hurt.

Helen stopped talking for a second then said, 'You're a good listener.'

'Yeah, I know. I'm a saint.'

What an awful thing to say! This poor woman, pouring out her heart and soul, and this sudden burst of sarcasm. No need for that kind of nastiness. No need for—

'Not from where I'm sitting you're not,' and her eyes peeled themselves away from his face and moved deliberately down his torso until they took up residence, for what felt like an unseemly length of time, on Enda's crotch.

He coughed, by way of a plea, and Helen, smiling slightly, moved her eyes back up to his face. And when she did he rather wished she hadn't. Two conflicting desires were already battling it out for supremacy. One was to plunge his hands into his trousers and the other was to stand up assertively and say, 'What about another nice cup of tea there, Helen?'

This look. This staring at him across the room, this letting him know she knew what was going on, mocking him – it was making him feel kind of weird. Angry actually; and then this anger seemed like it was making him harder and one voice was saying, 'Get up, Enda. You get up and put the kettle on and put an end to this terrible nonsense.'

And the other voice was saying, 'Nonsense? What nonsense would that be now, Enda? Would that be the fact that some babe in a low-cut vest top with no bra is staring lasciviously at your monstrously huge cock?'

Then Helen said, 'We used to call this the Orgasm Song,' and she gave him such a look. A look like he had never seen before. Her eyes sparkled, as though she was laughing at him, but not in a bad way. Well, in a very bad way actually, but in a good bad way. There was no coyness, no shyness, nothing that could be classed or classified as anything remotely resembling love. This was desire. For him perhaps? For something certainly. Enda knew he ought to say something. But his mind had gone into temporary suspension. Even the music escaped him. All that was left of him now was his cock. And this woman's bad, bad look.

'Is there something you need to do, Enda?'

He knew exactly what she meant and it was not to get up and make them both a nice cup of tea. So, with a flutter of shock and shame, Enda released himself from his prison of shop-fresh slim-fit denims and took hold of himself as he had done less than one hour beforehand under very different, and yet, in some bizarre ways, almost exactly the same, circumstances. Except that Helen was not kneading bread in a low-cut vest top, but rather pulling self-same over her head confirming her admirer's no-bra theory. And what magnificent breasts they were! Perfect – and Enda should know because he had studied breasts widely in a variety of publications over the years. These were not the manufactured pneumatic balloons so favoured by sanitized top-shelf *Playboys* and *Penthouses*. Neither were they the hardly-worth-the-trouble pert weenies you saw on pretty young pop singers and actresses. Helen's breasts were large, but not overwhelming. Just this side of pendulous, where you wouldn't feel intimidated about getting stuck in. Comfortable, but not enough to make them motherly. They were top-quality Readers' Wives material. Nothing fake or manufactured about them. They were the kind of breasts that you might find on a real woman. Which, of course, was what Helen was. A real woman. She was not Lively Lynda, 39, wife of Kevin Marsh, plumber, enjoying afternoon sexy-undies playtime in their four-bedroomed semi in Weston-super-Mare – or any one of the hundreds of fantasy 'wives' Enda had enjoyed looking at over the years. This was a live one, and she was making the kind of moves that would have put Lively Lynda to shame. Half-lying on the sofa where he had first kissed Corrine, Helen was now topless and while her left hand reached across both breasts to play with her nipples, her right hand was teasing open the fly button of her silky combat trousers.

Her eyes were trained on his; her breathing was getting faster and was punctuated by anxious whimpering cries. She bit her bottom lip as she pulled off her panties and Enda found himself delightfully scandalized as he saw a patch of damp spread across the light cotton fabric.

'I am so wet,' Helen moaned. 'You are making me so wet.'

⬭

Generally speaking, Enda did not like going to places where he had not formally been invited. Perhaps this woman made a habit of public displays of masturbation? Helen was, he knew, married to a rock singer. Quite a famous one. Maybe this was normal social interaction for the music business fraternity. So nice to meet you, please feel free to touch yourself up while I put the kettle on. Maybe Enda was naïve to assume there was something wrong or dirty or at least essentially private about hammering one's lad outside a person's back window whilst they were going about their everyday housewifely duties. And it would have to be said that, certainly in Enda's experience to date, masturbation and fully interactive consensual adult sex were not necessarily linked. None the less, Enda decided to take a chance and interpret Helen's outburst as an invitation. It was not written, but if a woman is fiddling around in her underwear and announces that you are making her wet – well then, instinctively, if not formally, you can take that to mean that you have passed the interview and got the job.

As he walked across the room, though, Enda began to

feel a little foolish. There was too much clothing going on and therefore something vaguely comic, obscene almost about the way he was standing out of his trouser fly. Helen did not seem to notice as she grabbed him down to her. There was a bit of kissing, but frankly, both of them were ready for the main event. More than ready in Helen's case as she loudly proclaimed, 'Fuck me, Father!'

It really was a most dreadful and terrible thing to say. Even Helen, he felt sure, would have been thoroughly ashamed of herself had she been in full possession of her senses.

All the same, and most probably despite and not because of his recent departure from the Roman Catholic priesthood, Enda Devlin followed her instructions with a commitment and voracity that surprised them both.

And in a dark corner in a locked room at the very back of his mind, he secretly wondered what excitement those three terrible words might have aroused in him if he had heard them when they had actually been true.

To: mnKa@hotmail.com
From: Justin@McIvorManagement.co.uk
Re: What's going on?

I cannot fucking believe that you came home without telling me. I thought you were staying out in Tangier for another fortnight? Do you know how I found out? Fucking Ron Parker rang and asked me who the paki was you brought home with you. It was patently fucking obvious I didn't have a fucking clue what he was talking about, and when I rang that shitbag queer Gary he refused to tell me, and you don't pick up your fucking mobile so I had to read about it in the paper. I have never felt so humiliated in my life. I am a fucking professional, MoniKa – and I thought you were serious about your career, but obviously I was wrong. Expect to hear from you by return.

Justin

29

'It's not just that she's a fan of this guy. But she's obsessed? You know what I mean, Al – *obsessed* with the guy. In that kind of a way that you might worry, you know?'

It was such a beautiful day. Alfie could not say that he had ever noticed weather before. He travelled all the time; Alfie knew hot from cold all right, but it was like this was the first time he had stopped long enough to feel it. To breathe in the air; notice the difference between the soft summer rain that lubricates a perfect summer day and the sly persistent drizzle that heralds the beginning of a bad spell. Fonzie and himself were sitting on low flat rocks in a shallow inlet of beach right at the edge of the Atlantic. 'Next stop New York, baby.' He made it sound like he had been there. The boys had been camping on this beach the week before. They'd caught and cooked fish on a makeshift barbecue, drank warm beers and sang along to shite rock music from somebody's broken-down boogie box whose batteries were precariously held in place with masking tape. Today was different. Fonzie had an air of solemnity about him that was bringing Alfie down. And, truthfully, frightening him slightly. The bike was parked up behind them between the grass dunes and there was no sign of human life. No houses, no phone wires, no cars, just the two lads and lashings of nature. This was a place for telling secrets, hoping that the width of the sea might dilute their intensity, or better still carry them off to America and return them in a more glamorized version. The newsagent dug around inside the collar of his denim jacket for his hoodie, then drawing deeply on his cigarette said, 'I love her, Albert. What can I tell you? I. Am. In. Love. With. Her.'

Alfie nodded sympathetically.

'But she is in love with a pop singer. Did you ever hear anything so fucking stupid? This has been going on for years, man. Years. It's making me nuts.'

Alfie tried to make a noise that sounded both sympathetic and non-committal. He did not want to get dragged into this scenario. He did not want to—

'Hey! Hey! *You* know what I'm talking about, man!'

Fonzie leapt up and gave him a big punch on the arm.

'Well, I, um—'

'Yeah! Yeah! Yesterday – shit, I meant to say it to you. The paper! The *paper*, man . . .'

Alfie jumped. He realized that he had been feeling jumpy since he left Holland Park.

'Molly was in the shop and she comes over and starts telling you about this Alfie? There was a column in the paper about his wife running off with some black dude? You gotta remember it, Al, man. She freaked out! She was all like whispering to you about it like you gave a shit.

Weird. I tell you, Al, she is gone really weird and I don't know what to do.'

It had been a break. Really. Hanging out with Fonzie and his mates. The newsagent had taken the last week off work so he could show his new mate around 'the scene'.

'I've been around – I've got mates in London, you know? Went to Boston last year – great city, but you know what? At the end of the day, Al, what have you guys got there that we haven't got, eh? I mean you earn the few quid, have a few scoops with your mates – have a laugh – you can do all that here but without the hassle.'

And that was true. They were a really nice bunch of laid-back lads. Bikers, most of them. They said they liked their music heavy and bought official Limp Bizkit tour T-shirts on the Internet which their mammies ironed inside out so the transfers didn't bleed. But after a few pints their soft-rock colours would come to the surface and they'd sing along to old Eagles tracks and Bryan Adams ballads. Pissed in Bosanova's nightclub in neighbouring Gorrib, they would dance to anything, except for:

'Those shitty boy bands, man . . .'

'Fucking chancers . . .'

'Talentless arseholes . . .'

'I fucking *hate* them, man!'

They knew Al wasn't into rock.

'Al's a dance-head . . .'

'Those DJs . . .'

'They're all into that kind of bang-bang shit.'

'No offence, man.'

They could tell Al was kind of cool in that big city way,

but they didn't like him because he was cool. They liked him because he liked them *and* he was cool. And that made them kind of cool by proxy. The Killa lads talked big, but secretly they feared they were hick.

These were the boys that had never left home, or had come back every weekend from their colleges in Galway and Dublin, afraid to stay away for more than five nights on the trot in case the cities kidnapped their souls. These were the ones that hadn't gone to Boston or Birmingham or London. Who had buried their educations in their uncle's newsagent's shops, the pubs, farms, B&Bs of Killa and its surrounding areas. One or two of them had money. The local GP's son had joined his father's practice, others were also being primed to take over their parents' businesses. But money didn't make too much of a difference down here, not to anyone who wasn't interested in building a huge house with pillars to show off to the neighbours. GP Geoff owned his own house in Gorrib, but he didn't live there. He stayed all week with his parents and continued to enjoy the housekeeping services, using his own place as a glorified crash pad for himself and the lads after a heavy Saturday night in Bosanova's. Their contemporaries abroad sent news of exotic travels and telephone-number salaries on Wall Street. Then there were the adventurous fools hiding out in America with no green cards, getting drunk on labourer's cash-dollars, kipping on tolerant relatives' couches, afraid to leave their hearts in San Francisco for fear the authorities would never let them back in again.

Fonzie, Geoff, Jamesy, Kevin, Paud and Vinny existed

in a small world but it was comfortable and safe and it was easy. Most importantly, it was theirs. Their local, their pool table, their strip of main road between Killa and Gorrib where you could open her up to over one hundred and never get caught. They loved the life they had, but secretly they all wondered if the wide world was more wonderful. Al was welcomed as an arbiter of sorts. It was his job to tell them that their lives were sweet. The tourists they befriended each summer brought news from the front line of life. We're being shot to hell out there, boys; if you're smart you'll stay in Killa.

And Alfie had to admit they had it good. He had enjoyed the very best that the Killa crew had to offer: fishing, camping, playing boy scouts on the beach looking for driftwood to burn. Taking the slagging when they got him rubbing two sticks together while they all stood over him smoking fags. How long would the city-head go before he noticed they had three Zippos between them? Strumming 'Stairway' on the guitar at GP Geoff's gaff; it was four a.m. and they were all wasted after getting back from Bosanova's. Geoff had scored and brought back a girl with long brown hair. She looked very young, and the dashing doctor kissed her gently while she sank into him like all her dreams had come true and Fonzie passed him the biggest spliff Alfie had ever seen.

'Fucking marvellous, lads, where'd you get this stuff?'

They looked at him then laughed in unison.

'This is the twenty-first century, Al . . .'

'You're not in the back of beyond, you know . . .'

'Yeah, man, there's a lot of stuff about round here that you don't know, man . . .'

'Shit like you can't imagine . . .'

'Not in your wildest fucking dreams, man . . .'

They were bluffing and Alfie knew that, but he let them think he was impressed. Shocked. He had seen things that he knew that they would never see. Things that their wildest dreams, their worst nightmares, could not possibly compute. He had walked into a hotel suite in Munich one night and caught two locally hired security men fucking a young fan simultaneously on the promise of an introduction to him. Her tiny body was limp, almost invisible between their uniformed bulk. She was naked, her head lolling and facing him. When she saw her hero the dead eyes filled with hope and in a terrible second he imagined she had thought it was worth it. He could have let her stay the night and maybe the treat of being with him would have made the pain go away, but he called the police instead. She didn't press charges. Perhaps because the rapists had made good their promise and she had had five minutes alone with her hero.

Alfie had walked out onto a stage and faced thirty thousand people. He had stood for a few seconds picking out faces in the crowd and known that they were here to see him. Not the drummer. Not the bass player. Not the keyboard player, the backing singers, the dancers, the manager, the man in the fucking moon, but him. Alfie Smith. You could sell a record and lots of people listened to it and that was fine. But when they showed up in person? That was scary. That was like – hello? Thirty thousand people and they all have one thing in common at this moment in time, and that thing is you. That makes you a pretty amazing person. Thirty thousand people don't just pay money and turn up for anyone. In a funny kind of a way, Alfie had often thought, this is what Jesus must have felt like. Except nobody paid to see Jesus, and they would pay to see him. Alfie didn't think he was Jesus. Although he did think he had more in common with Jesus than most people. He had mentioned this to Karl before, but all his manager had done was warn him, most severely, against ever saying anything like that to the press. 'Particularly Q magazine, Alfie. Even if they say it to you first, do not ever compare yourself to Jesus, Alfie. Ever.'

Alfie knew that his manager and the press thought he was guileless. He talked up his charities too much; he had never gone down that bad-boy hellraiser route. Maybe if he hadn't hooked himself up to the steadying older influences of Wilson and Karl he might have turned freakshow. Then it would have been all right going around saying he was Jesus – people loved a drugged-up loser rock star. Sometimes Alfie felt like the world was laughing at him. Sneering at his success. Waiting for him to fall. He wasn't the crash-and-burn type. Too sensible. No. He would just gradually sell fewer and fewer records until eventually he would be booked for a couple of guest slots on the *Des O'Connor Show* to promote his taking the lead in *Joseph and the Amazing Technicolor Dreamcoat*'s summer season.

Except he wouldn't. Because he was going to give up the ghost long before that happened. Well, he had given it up. Technically. Although Alfie was beginning to realize that walking out of one's own life was not as easy as all that. As the wisest of American pop psychologists would have told him, you take yourself with you wherever you go. Except, Alfie was carrying the additional burden of pretending not to be himself whilst trying to escape being himself. It was all rather complicated and, if truth be known, it was becoming something of a bore.

Fonzie and his friends were nice guys. Nice ordinary guys. And they thought Alfie was a nice ordinary guy too. Being a nice ordinary guy was something that Alfie was proud of, but only, he was beginning to discover, when it was in the context of his celebrity.

Here is Alfie Smith the pop singer having a drink in the pub like the lovely down-to-earth nice person he is. He could be swanning about in Cannes or LA, but instead he is enjoying a half down his local. Wow. What a guy.

The pint, Alfie was finding, was not half as much fun without the flattery of other people's perception of you as marvellous. It was all about choice. He was choosing to hang out and be ordinary instead of being precious and famous. But if the other people did not know he was making that choice then that made him . . . what? Just like them? And you see, try as he might, Alfie was just not like them. He *was* extraordinary. He *was* different. He *did* know what it felt like to be Jesus. No matter what people said. No matter what Karl said. It was just a fact of life. Of *his* life.

'She collects magazines with pictures of him in it. I mean, the woman is in her twenties. I don't know. If

I didn't know her as well as I do, I'd say she was one of them fucking bunny-boilers, you know? But like, she's not. I just wish she'd get this guy out of her head and give me a chance.'

'I don't think she's half as interested in this Alfie bloke as you think she is, Fonzie.'

He had to say something.

'Yeah?' Fonzie sat up, then slumped back down again in despair. 'But then what the fuck do you know? Sure you hardly know her.'

'No, but I do know a lot about women.'

Fonzie closed his eyes and, with a patronizing smirk, he put his hands up for his advisor to hold it right there.

'With all due respect, man, you are talking to the babe magnet of County Mayo here. I have road-tested half the females in this county, and those I haven't got around to are growing old at the back of the queue.'

'It's not all about sex, Fonzie.'

Fonzie looked at his new friend like he was the most innocent person he had ever come across. Alfie felt this wave of adolescent competitive anger sweep over him and was unable to help himself.

'I am Alfie Smith,' he said.

And you know what? It felt good.

To: mnKa@hotmail.com
Cc: Justin@McIvorManagement.co.uk

MoniKa,

I am sorry you had to find out about Alfie the way that
you did but you must understand that Wilson and I really did
think we were acting in both of your best interests. Whether
you agree with us or not, it's done now and we'll have to
work things out and move forward from here. The poor kid is
confused and needed some time to get his head together
and Ireland is great because nobody pays us celebs too
much attention. Killa is kind of pretty and, to be honest,
Wilson and I have enjoyed the break ourselves. Alfie is
coming around to us this afternoon for a chat. I'll let you
know what comes out of it, but promise me, MoniKa, you'll
sit tight. The last thing we want is some nasty press siege,
and you have handled all this so well up to now – let's just
let the land lie as it is and see if we can get Alfie home
without attracting too much more attention.

See you soon and really, everything will work out for the
best,

Very best, Stephen

(Wilson too!)

To: mnKa@hotmail.com

From: Justin@McIvorManagement.co.uk

Re: ooops!

Cc: celebrity@sunnewspaper.co.uk;
showbiz@the daily mirror.co.uk;
bizznizzz@star.co.uk;
gossip@dailyexpress.co.uk;
newsdesk@thetimes.co.uk;
newsdesk@telegraph.co.uk; hettie@2day.co.uk;
veronica@womansway.com

Silly girls should be more careful with their e-mails!

Look what you cc'd to me this morning. Thought you'd like to know I've forwarded it to every showbiz editor in the UK.

See you in court

Justin

30

Molly was not in the mood for work today, but she went through the motions anyway. She used to love her morning beauty regime, but today it just irritated the hell out of her that she couldn't just roll in to Flynn's straight from bed. She had to brush, floss, exfoliate, tone, moisturize, conceal, put on foundation, powder, blusher, eyeliner, mascara, then curl her lashes – hold, two three four – apply lipliner, lip-tint, lipgloss, check her neck for colour match and tide-marks, and check her straightening irons were hot enough, damn! She had forgotten to switch them on. Sod it. Molly hated her hair in its natural curly state and so she blow-dried and straightened it with irons every morning, but today? She just could not be arsed. She grabbed a scrunchie and pulled her damp locks up into a messy bun on top of her head. Who was going to see her, anyway? Eleanor Jackson? Fonzie? Aoife was over in London and she'd probably love to see her looking a mess, the cow. Molly missed her. More this time because she was so annoyed with her. She wished she would come home. When she had called her a couple of days ago half-intending to make up with her, Aoife had said, 'Come over here. There's a party tonight. There'll be loads of people you know from the show. Please come, Molly.'

Aoife hopped on and off planes all the time, but for Molly the idea of flying to London on a day's notice was ludicrous. Molly knew that Aoife knew that and so it annoyed her that she had even said it.

'I'll buy you a ticket.'

'I can buy my own damn ticket!'

'So you'll come, then?'

It was unusual for Aoife to sound so desperate. Normally, when she tried to persuade Molly to do things it was all about jazzing up her unadventurous friend. This time it sounded like she wanted Molly to be there. Like she didn't want to go on her own. Which she didn't. But when Gary invited you to one of his 'parties', you had to attend. It was that or go to the bottom of the bookings list.

The 'office' was a leather-walled fashion-feast of a suite where twice a year their modelling agent gave his girls, and boys, the opportunity to parade around in front of a seamy collection of Gary's 'friends' – who were basically creeps rich enough to buy their pussy from the pages of *Vogue*.

Aoife had been busier than ever since the show and was missing her regular trips home. She felt that bringing the fashion show to Killa had tainted the last bastion of her normality, which was her relationship with Molly.

Her dream had always been to drag her oldest friend into the business; to have an ally by her side to help keep her feet on the ground. Aoife knew that Molly was talented, could have it all in a heartbeat. Except she was beginning to wonder herself if it was worth having.

Aoife had gone to the party alone, taking a nip of her uncle's poitin in the lift on the way up. Poitin made her narky anyway and when the lift doors opened she grabbed a passing cosmopolitan and threw it straight down on top of the poitin. She looked around the room to try and find someone she could pick a fight with when she spotted him. The Moroccan boy. He could not have been more than nineteen and he was stunning. Chocolate-brown with delicate features and cheekbones to die for. He looked almost feminine, if it weren't for the body which was, as she now overheard Gary describe him to one of his flabby showbiz luvvie sidekicks, 'Grade-one meat, darling, and these African Muslims, why they'll bend over the breakfast table, love . . .'

Aoife always felt for the new ones, and this kid, like so many she had seen before, looked like he did not want to be there.

⬯

'That's MoniKa's new squeeze.'

'She dumped Alfie for *him*?'

'No, stupid. Alfie left and she's using Ahmed to get back at him.'

'Brought him back from the *Vogue* shoot in Marrakesh – Gary's put him on The List.'

'The List' was the unofficial roll call of those who 'would'. Nobody admitted to being on it and it did not exist in real terms, beyond Gary's extraordinary powers as a matchmaker of the seediest kind.

'Ugh. But what's his connection with MoniKa?'

'He's *living* with her!'

'In the house in Holland Park?'

'Yes!'

'OhmiGod! Is she *doing* him?'

'I don't know. Look. Nobody ever knows what Mon's up to but you can be sure she has her reasons.'

'That's for certain.'

Aoife plonked herself down next to him.

'Hey, Ahmed. Howzit goin', man?'

Gary was glowering at her from across the room so she gave him the finger. Ahmed had been all dressed up in Gaultier: tight mesh T-shirt and silk combats. He looked uncomfortable, and Aoife could not get a word out of him. She thought she could smell something nasty. Gary would put him up in a flat and plug him for a while, get him bookings for a few horny-homme fashion shoots, but then what? McDonald's? And who was going to pay his fare home – MoniKa? Aoife didn't think so. She was feeling under-fucking-impressed with the whole thing, actually.

'You want to go home, don't you?'

She just asked him straight out like that, and he nodded at her with such open delight that she knew that this quiet Moroccan kid had certainly expressed this wish to, probably, everyone, since he got here. Man. This was bad. This was—

'Can I help you?'

In fairness, MoniKa didn't have to say very much. All she had to do was give Aoife one of her superior do-I-know-you looks and a possessive prodding of her rival's foot to indicate her displeasure at a minion muscling in on her property.

Aoife Breslin did not like MoniKa, most of all she did not like to be prodded. And she was pissed, and upset anyway over her best friend Molly, and annoyed with herself, and feeling especially sorry at being away from home and all of these things combined to make her – she would admit it herself later – perhaps a little more annoyed than she should have been.

'DON'T TOUCH ME, YOU STUCK-UP PIECE OF SHIT!'

That would be very annoyed indeed.

Security perked up. Cat fight in a top London model agency? Well, you have to leave it for a few minutes, don't you – just to see how things pan out? 'Sonly polite.

MoniKa was all wide-eyed shock and her faux innocence sent Aoife thermonuclear.

'Ahmed does NOT WANT TO BE HERE! He wants to be AT HOME! With his FAMILY!'

The whole room was looking at Aoife now like what-the-fuck-is-she-talking-about? Not want to be *here*? Like, who in their right fucking mind would not want to be *here*? In this *fabulous* penthouse? With this *fabulous* crowd?

Aoife knew she had given the game away and was revealing her own vulnerabilities, so she side-stepped and gave everyone in the room exactly what they wanted.

Without introduction or explanation she announced, 'And your precious husband is over in the West of Ireland fucking my friend who works in a chemist's shop.'

The collective gasp reverberated down the King's Road. Half a dozen of the audience had done Aoife's charity show and behind their perfect pouts you could hear remembered facts clanking into place. Milly? Maisie? Molly! The girl who had screwed the sound guy that night had a flash-back that he'd mentioned Alfie had been there but she had been so stoned she hadn't cared. She cared now though. It was so thoroughly awful they all wanted it to be true.

Aoife wasn't going to hang around. Fuck them. She stood up and asked Ahmed, 'You coming?'

It was only when they got outside that Aoife realized what she had done.

<hr>

Molly decided to grab a piece of toast before leaving for work.

The dining room was jampacked. She had never seen it so busy: chairs and folding tables had been dragged in from all over the house and there were even a few people standing. She pushed past them into the kitchen.

'What's going on?' Molly asked her father, who was frantically buttering toast.

'Don't ask me, love, just this mad rush. They're all English as far as I can gather; a few of them arrived last night but then this gang comes in howling for breakfast out of nowhere. What can I do?'

'Charge them a tenner a head for tea and toast?'

'You said it, girl!'

'See you later, Dad.'

'Molly?' her father called at her as she opened the door out to the dining room.

Then the strange stuff started to happen.

The dining room went suddenly silent, and for a split second everyone was staring at Molly. At the full second mark, half of the guests grabbed cameras, seemingly out of thin air, and the other half started shouting;

'How long have you been Alfie Smith's girlfriend?'

'Have you slept with him?'

'Were you a virgin before you met him?'

'Were you seeing him before he married MoniKa?'

'Were you at their wedding?'

'You're a make-up artist. Did you meet Alfie through MoniKa?'

They had got up out of their seats and were crowding around her, flashing cameras in her face, poking her with fists made from microphones, shouting questions.

Molly was scared and she backed into the kitchen.

'What the hell is going . . . Jesus H – GET OUT OF MY KITCHEN!'

Jack Walshe was taken off guard, confused as to why these people were chasing his daughter but mostly he was very, very angry indeed that there were guests invading his kitchen. A *laissez-faire* attitude to guests helping themselves was something that himself and Mary argued about on a regular basis. This assault was too much and he launched himself at them, brandishing the nearest weapon to hand: a wooden spoon coated in scrambled egg which he flicked and flapped in the direction of the oncoming mass. Nothing dampens enthusiasm quite like a lukewarm egg, especially when it is applied just under the collar of a Prada blouse or onto the lens of a very expensive digital camera.

In the brief respite Molly was able to leap up the back stairs and into her room.

Jack Walshe was successful at removing the British press gang out of his kitchen, but less so out of his house.

'If you could just get your daughter to talk to us, Mr Wal—'

'Get out of my house.'

'If she could just make a statement then we would be able to—'

'Get out of my HOUSE!'

'Pose for a few pictures, you've a lovely garden and—'

'GET OUT OF MY HOUSE BEFORE I CALL THE GUARDS!'

One man pushed himself forward and stood square in front of Jack, carving himself into the position of spokesperson and mediator by raising his right hand and saying, 'If you could just let me explain how this works, Mr Walshe.'

'I'll tell you how this works, you fat British scumbag.' (Dennis Fumble, veteran press photographer, was indeed rather fat, indisputably British and, Jack had correctly intuited, something of a scumbag, as the ensuing titters from his compadres paid testament.) 'You are trespassing on my property and if you do not haul your considerable ass out of here pronto I will call the—'

'Listen, mate, you don't know what you've got on your hands here. Your daughter, with all due respect, has been poked by a pop singer and I've got to tell you—'

What Dennis Fumble had to tell Jack Walshe was a wisdom he did not get the opportunity to impart as our intrepid landlord landed a punch to the photographer's nose that rendered him prostrate. The gathered ladies and gentlemen of the British press who had been previously cowed by a splash of warm egg were shocked to their core at this unnecessarily violent outburst. After all, they were just doing their job. Intrepid, truth-seeking soldiers that they were. They weren't budging now. No way – not after one of their number had been assaulted. There were principles at stake.

So Molly was stuck up in her room for however long it took to bore a British journalist off a doorstep, which any one of their countless victims, including Alfie Smith, might have told her, was quite a long time.

For the first while, Molly could not really take it in. Why were the press following her? Had she called them up unbeknownst to herself and told them about Alfie? Had Alfie told them she was his girlfriend? As a kind of a decoy? To get them off his back? What on earth was going on? Maybe they had gone, but when she opened her door, she could hear them cawing downstairs and her father roaring. This was a nightmare. She had never heard her father sound so angry. Somehow, this was her fault. Punishment – but for what? Then she looked around the room and she saw them. Hundreds, no thousands of magazines. They covered every surface of the room. How could she not have noticed them before? Cilla at home, Paula Yates before her tragic death, Diana, Princess of Wales' memorial book, J-Lo and Ben, Jennifer and Brad, Michael and Catherine Zeta, Alfie and MoniKa – what was it all about? All these celebrities were just people. Like Alfie, who was not the thoughtful selfless saint she had once thought, but was actually an immature daft eejit in the style of Fonzie Mallarkey. Here she was, imprisoned in her room, surrounded by the lives of people she could only ever fantasize about meeting, and when she did meet one – the greatest one of them all – he was ordinary. Not nearly as interesting and fun as her friend Aoife and about as intelligent as Fonzie Mallarkey but not nearly as good-looking. Alfie Smith, when it came right down to it, was, by Molly Walshe's standards, an average lad. And she had spent how many thousands of pounds following his career? She had wasted how many years of her life drooling and dreaming over him? She had been stupid, stupid, stupid – but more than that. She had been lied to. By the press. She had been sold this idea that Alfie Smith was special and different. She had bought magazine after magazine after magazine, stored them, filed them, treasured them and for what? A great big fat lie. And now these people were harassing her.

Her mobile rang.

'I've done something awful, Molly.' It was Aoife. The rift forgotten, Molly burst into tears of relief at the sound of her old friend's voice.

'I don't care – just come and get me. The house is full of newspaper journalists and photographers. Dad is shouting and I'm locked in my room and I don't know what to do-ho-ho-ho-hooo!'

'My plane is just after landing – I'll need to make a few phone calls. Give me an hour.'

One hour. It seemed like a lifetime. She opened her door slightly as her father was just coming up the stairs.

'Stay in there, Molly. I've called the guards, they'll be here shortly.'

Molly and indeed Jack knew that Sergeant Leonard was the laziest guard in Ireland and could rarely raise much more than a smirk and a shrug in the face of most crimes. It was going to take more than a mild-mannered 'careful now' to move this lot. Molly hoped that Aoife had a plan.

In the meantime, Molly had to wait. She went to the window to get some air, but as she opened it a woman's voice called up, 'Molly! Molly! How much do you want to talk? Name your price!'

She closed the window quickly and sat on the bed. She had never been aware of feeling claustrophobic before, but Molly felt really trapped. Here, in this room which was hot and stuffy and cluttered with stories of other people's lives. People she had never met and one whom she had: holidaying in the South of France, getting married in castles in Scotland, having their cellulite/spots/surgery scars highlighted with red arrows so that the world could be told they were only human.

A few weeks ago, Molly could have sat in her room for

days going over these magazines. Now one hour seemed like a lifetime in their company.

Molly had filled her bedroom with stories about other people's lives. Where, Molly wondered as if wakening from a dream, was her own life? It was here, in this cluttered poky bedroom in her parents' B&B and a small chemist shop where she sold cold cream to old ladies and prayed that somebody with a clue might come in and purchase this season's lip gloss.

That was no life. No life in comparison to the ones she had been reading about. Molly had thought she was happy with her lot before the fashion show shook her at the roots. But her roots were wobbly before then, she now realized, otherwise why had she been so obsessed with the lives of all these glamorous people? Perhaps that was what she had wanted all along. And there it was. The truth. She wanted to live in a house in Minorca with a swimming pool shaped like a dolphin. She wanted to be photographed with a rock-star husband in a Gucci dress at a premiere. It was what every little girl wanted. Except that Molly knew that it didn't happen to ordinary little girls like her. It happened to special people like Alfie Smith. Except, except – Alfie wasn't special.

And so Molly Walshe made her decision.

She rang Aoife and told her what she had decided to do and got her friend to make the appropriate arrangements.

One hour later, Jack Walshe heard a tap on the door he was guarding.

'Go back up, love – guards will be here in a minute.'

She tapped again and called, 'I'm coming out, Dad. Open the door.'

It had been three hours and Jack was done fighting, even with his daughter. The vision that stood framed by the narrow stairwell hardly looked like his own flesh and blood. Her hair hung poker straight and shining down her shoulders and she was wearing her low-cut, short-cut black Bosanova's disco dress (every father's nightmare) with stiletto boots. Her skin was perfectly tanned and shimmering, and beneath the (original!) Gucci sunglasses that Fonzie had bought duty-free in the States last year, her glossy lips were set in a determined pout. Jack could only gawp in horror as a dozen cameras snapped up his daughter's skirt.

Resolutely, Molly began to walk down the stairs, silent in the face of the questions being fired at her and impervious to the pleas of the photographers to 'Smile!' 'Stay where you are, love!' 'Look, Molly!' 'Here, Molly!' 'Molly! Molly! Molly!'

She walked in a straight line, and the seemingly impenetrable gang parted in the way that they always do in the face of somebody with the confidence to brave them. To Jack Walshe, who had been battling the bastards all morning, it looked like his daughter was walking on water.

With canny timing, just as she reached the end of the driveway Derek Mallarkey (Fonzie's uncle) arrived with the limousine. He kept the engine running, as instructed, and Molly saw her friend Aoife fling open the door.

Inside were some of the people she needed to make all

of this happen: MoniKa, Aoife, the African boy and the journalist.

As they drove away, Molly looked out of the tinted windows and saw the photographers still hopelessly flashing and she felt the same delightful confidence she had enjoyed at the fashion show.

'Happy now?' said Aoife.

'Born to it – *darling*!' she replied. And they both laughed.

31

Helen woke with a start. She checked her watch and saw it was gone nine.

Shit.

Stephen must be dropping Sapphire back. It was pretty early, although who else could it be? She thought she had heard the doorbell ring, but she wasn't sure. In fact, throughout the past few hours, Helen had come to not feel sure about anything. It was a kind of relief, actually. A level of confusion where the only option was to let go. And let go she most certainly had.

Helen had never had casual sex before. Mal had been the third and the last man she had ever slept with. She did not know what had come over her seducing Enda like that. He wasn't exactly what one might describe as irresistible, but then Helen's husband was, allegedly, the sexiest man in the world and she didn't fancy him any more. If there was lust involved it was less towards this gangly earnest ex-priest and more to do with this sudden urge Helen had to prove to herself that she was still alive, still interested and able for love. Well, not love exactly – more sex. Just like that, in the middle of the afternoon, with a virtual – no, actually a *complete* – stranger. It was like, the ultimate proof that she didn't love Mal. Although the ultimate proof was how she felt, right now, the following morning. And that was tired, a little confused, but utterly without regret. As for Enda? Well, he was just there. Helen had had a couple of moments; felt an inadvertent longing at one point when he had touched her face before kissing her. Experienced a strange feeling when she realized that this probably meant something to him. Nothing as terrible as guilt, a short-lived sickly sweet sensation, like she had gorged herself on chocolate. There had been moments too when she had wished the night would never come to an end. Not because of the sex itself, although it was good – but because of the way a night of passion puts reality on hold. The morning meant things were back to the way they were before. There were consequences, responsibilities to face. The thought of it made Helen feel old.

Half asleep, she gathered the cheap candlewick dressing gown she had bought in the local discount store around her sticky, naked body and padded across the hall. There were papers on the floor, although it was early for the postman to have been. Through the bevelled glass door Helen could make out that the figure outside was a woman. Vaguely concerned that it might be a teacher from Sapphire's school, she opened it without hesitation.

'Did you know that your husband is having an affair?'

'Helen! Helen! Over here, Helen!'

'How long has your husband known Corrine Coen?'

Corrine had recognized her moment when it came, snatched it, and gobbled it up like a hungry animal.

'Helen Doherty?'

She was alone in the house when the office phone rang.

'No. Helen is away at the moment. Can I help?'

'Are you her secretary?'

'No.'

'Her sister?'

'No.'

'A friend?'

'Look. Who is this?'

There was a slight pause on the other end, as if the person was unsure whether it was safe to reveal themselves.

'Catherine Crown from the *Mail*.'

'And you are looking for Helen?'

Corrine pitched her tone as reticent, as if she was hiding something. This was going to be so easy and so never be traced back to her. The bastard press could always be blamed.

'I'll be straight with you, em . . .?'

'Sapphire. Oh, I . . . Corrine. My name is Corrine, er, Caroline.'

'Right, em Caroline. We are looking for Alfie Smith, the

pop singer, and we understand that he recently stayed with Helen and Mal there in Dublin.'

'Oh, I wouldn't know anything about that, I'm just, em . . .'

'Would that be Sapphire the singer?'

'No, well, I . . .'

'Wilson's ex?'

God, that hurt.

'And you are a friend of Helen's? Well, could you just let her know that the press are well and truly on to the whole Alfie Smith thing. We'll find him sooner or later and to be honest she's better off—'

'I can't. That is, I'm more a friend of Mal's.'

'Right, well then, maybe you can get him to tell his wife that we are willing to—'

'Can I be frank with you, Catherine? I know that the *Mail* is a serious paper otherwise I wouldn't dream of telling you this.'

There was silence and the click of a mini-recorder.

'Go on.'

'It's really awkward, but I would just as soon be kept out of this whole thing.'

'What are you saying?'

'Nothing. Goodbye.'

And Corrine hung up.

Mal Doherty had long since been on the tabloids' list of ones worth watching and within an hour Ms Castle had all the information she needed.

'Helen?'

She did not have time to turn around and warn him. She did not even have time to regret having fashioned him a dog collar out of a Kellogg's Cornflakes box the night before and making him wear it as part of a fun/kinky sex game, let alone regret the fact that Enda had forgotten he was wearing it. In any case, the short silk kimono he wore on top did nothing to soften or disguise it. If Helen photographed off guard looking dog-rough could be construed as classic press invasion of privacy, Enda was a walking headline. A dog-collared priest in a nightie was too good to pass up, by anyone's standards.

Between Enda taking a step forward to see what the noise was about and Helen slamming the door on Catherine Castle not ten seconds passed. Hardly a photo shoot, but sufficient for the likes of Dennis Fumble to get a front-page shot. They were still standing looking at each other when he was downloading it on to his mobile for e-mail.

'Fuck. Fuck, fuck fuck . . .'

Enda did not like to hear a woman swear out of context. He didn't know exactly what was going on but he knew it wasn't good and he knew he wasn't currently in a position to moralize.

The letterbox flap opened and a pair of women's lips spoke in a loud whisper.

'Helen? I'm just going to stick my card through. This must be really hard for you, but—'

Helen snapped the metal flap down hard on the girl's fingers and heard a loud yelp, followed by copious swearing and sympathetic noises from more experienced doorsteppers who had neglected to warn this first-timer about the dangers of exposing one's extremities to letterbox flaps.

Helen ran frantically around the house closing curtains and pulling down blinds.

Enda bent down and picked one of the journalist's notes up off the floor.

'Maybe you should talk to—'

'Get away from the letterbox, you fucking fool!'

Dennis Fumble's smallest lens was already poking through. Thankfully a close-up shot of an unidentified man's testicle wasn't of much use, and the damage Enda caused with his shock-flap-snap caused Fumble more pain than the girl's finger.

'That's a two-hundred-pound lens! I'll fucking sue!'

'Whoops! Sorry . . .' Enda shouted through the door, with not a hint of irony in his voice.

Helen, by now half-dressed, grabbed him and dragged him into the bedroom, slamming the door behind them.

Enda had the notes in his hands and held them out to her.

'What?'

'These are for you.'

She waved him off, and in all his life he did not think anyone had ever looked at him with such disgust.

'For Christ's sake, Enda, get dressed, just get out of my sight.'

Enda found his clothes in the living room where he had shed them the afternoon before, then he made them both a nice cup of tea. When he braved the bedroom again Helen was wearing an expensive-looking trouser suit. Her hair was tidied into a sleek ponytail and she was wearing make-up. She was perched on the edge of the freshly made bed and looked terribly unhappy.

'I suppose I had better face them.'

Enda didn't know much, but he could see that Helen was fraught with worry.

'Leave it for a minute. Have some tea.'

She didn't argue, and took the cup quietly from him.

'I'm sorry,' she said.

Maybe Helen was a little bit sorry, but there was too much else going on. Sorry or not, she needed him. Even if he was just the nearest person to hand that wasn't a journalist.

'Forget it,' he said. 'Do you want to tell me what's going on?'

She sighed deeply.

'Not really.'

'OK,' he said, but he didn't get up. He wanted to kiss her and be naked in the bed with her again. Less than an hour ago they had been asleep together, their bodies wrapped in an intimate puzzle of limbs. He had woken throbbing, proud of his virility, ready to surprise her – Mr Voracious Appetite looking for another slice of fun to finish her off. But sex was just the foreplay to what he loved best. The feel of this woman's large, lazy breasts as she lay on his chest sighing; the way her strong breathing turned to gentle wisps of sleep; how his forearm against her skin looked heavy and strong. This was real. This was the Blessed Virgin and Andrea TC all rolled into one. This was love. For the first time in his life Enda had had the feeling that she was his woman and he was her man and everything was right with the world.

But everything looked very wrong now. And Helen didn't look like his woman any more. She looked like somebody else's worried wife. In the half-hour since Enda had left her, Helen's face had worn the look of an old hurt come to life. Born-again pain. Something awful had happened to her, and Enda knew that he had to try to make it go away.

'I love you, Helen,' he said.

'Oh no, Enda, please, I . . .'

He stood and put his hands on her shoulders and looked into her eyes.

'Really, Helen. I. Love. You. Everything is going to be all right now.'

Helen shot to her feet, shoving his hands aside with the full weight of her upper body.

'For crying out loud, you stupid *stupid* man! Have you ANY IDEA what is going on here?'

Enda could not be certain as he had never done it before, but he was pretty sure that this was not the correct response to a declaration of love.

'My husband is having an *affair* and those . . . those,' she pointed at the window and although her voice was high pitched with anger, Enda could see her small hand shaking pathetically, 'vultures are not going to go away until they have tasted my fucking blood.'

Helen sat down on the bed again. 'Sorry.'

Enda did not react. He hated that he was just falling back into this role of kind priest. He wanted to fling her down onto the bed and make love to her; damn her husband and his seedy affairs, they didn't matter now, they didn't—

'It's with Corrine, Enda. He is having an affair with Corrine and you know what? It was Corrine before – the mystery affair all those years ago? Corrine. I can feel it. In here.' And she thumped her beautiful breasts. 'The timing is right. That interview she did with him, it all started around that time. Then later, a few years ago, I never told you about that because, well, I didn't like to think it was true myself. There were these two weeks when he was away, down here – we had a house. Dreams about moving down here. I know she was in Ireland at the time because I saw her. When he came back from that trip, he wasn't right. As soon as they said it to me out there I knew. You know how you just know?'

Enda didn't actually. He didn't know just where to begin with it all until Helen helped focus his mind with a rejection.

'So the last thing I need now is some bloody man telling me he's in love with me. I'm sorry, Enda, but . . .'

And then Enda saw what he was dealing with here. An epiphany of sorts. Maybe the Man Upstairs throwing out a few hints.

Helen was trying to be tough but she wasn't. Corrine, now she *was* a tough cookie. But Helen was only pretending. She could not cope with this on her own. She needed a friend, a kind capable person to listen and to help her through to whatever place it was she needed to be. A spiritual advisor, a trusted soul. Enda knew he could do that. He would rather be a sex-machine distraction, but you know? Sometimes you can't always have what you want when you want it. First rule of celibacy.

He sat down next to her on the bed and reached for the tight double fist she had dug into her lap, laying his own large hands over them. They felt cool and dry and comforting, like a compress.

'Helen,' he said, his voice full of the kindness of a seasoned counsellor, 'why don't you try and tell me what it is you want to do in this life?'

She studied his face for signs of sarcasm or condition or investment. There were none. Only the steady sureness of someone who knows how to give.

And so she did.

32

The atmosphere at breakfast was not good. Even Constance felt it, and she was a woman whose thoughts should have been diverted by the attentions of that very nice Englishman she had met the day before. She had been enjoying her weekly day-off routine of a lunchtime bowl of soup in Duffy's followed by a browse around Killa's dozen or so shops. Well, forget the shops! At fifty-plus with a belly upon which one suspected he had parked many a pint, Dennis was hardly what one might describe as distracting. But then Constance Heany was no Catherine Zeta, and could he talk? He was a charmer, and there was no getting around it. A few years younger than her but – what was she thinking! Silly old fool. No it was just nice to have a bit of male attention for a change. Even if he was just being—

'Constance, could you ask Stephen to pass the butter, please?'

'Constance, could you tell Wilson he should go easy on the butter before his fat ass explodes any more than it already has?'

'Constance, could you ask Stephen to shut his miserable little mouth before I banish him back to his poverty-stricken family and their ghastly two-up two-down in Kingsbury?'

'Constance, could you inform Wilson that I would rather live on a council estate in Colindale than spend one more night in the—'

'SHUT UP, THE PAIR OF YOU!'

They both looked aghast at this sudden show of sedition from the 'help'.

Wilson and Stephen bickered – it was what they did. They shot each other looks, shrugging in camp puzzlement at the extremity of the old woman's reaction. But the moment was brief as the other's face betrayed the seriousness of the fracture they were tapping. They were giving good bitch, but both of them knew it was different this time. The game was tainted with truth today. This was performance knife-twisting, except there were no tricks. It hurt.

Wilson was scared. And a scared Wilson was not good. Stephen knew that but he also knew that he was not going to back down.

'That little fucking bitch!' Wilson had said after Stephen had announced that Sapphire was sleeping in one of the eleven spare bedrooms.

Wilson, infuriated by the child's continuing presence in their lounge, had gone upstairs to sulk. Stephen had found him sitting up in bed ensconced in *The Scottish Ecclesiastical Hierarchy After the Reformation* with a pointed concentration that suggested he had spent the past hour stirring his simmering annoyance to boiling point.

'She is manipulating you, Stephen. She's just like her mother. You'll see! Ha, ha. You'll see!'

'She is a *child*, Wilson. She is *twelve* years old. What is *wrong* with you?'

'I don't care, anyway. You can do what you like. I just wish you could see what's going on. I hadn't taken you for stupid. I have just never taken you for a fool, that's all.'

Firstly, Wilson spent his entire life telling Stephen that he was a stupid sap. Usually when Stephen wanted something that Wilson thought threatened his supremacy. Secondly, oh fuck this – wrong time, wrong place – so just say it and get the histrionics out of the way.

'I want to stay on here for a while, Wilson. To train Sapphire for the local football team.'

Wilson took a breath as if he was about to speak then deflated painfully like he had been punched in the stomach. Defiant sarcasm washed across his face as he held his thumbs and forefingers in a 'W', shrugged and said, 'Whatever,' before lying down in the bed with his back to Stephen and pretending to go to sleep.

'Can we talk about this?' The words disintegrated as Stephen said them. He could feel that the end was nigh. Perhaps Wilson was done fighting.

Initially, the bitching over breakfast was a relief, except that they were both pretending. It felt scripted. Wilson was double-bluffing and Stephen was joining in because now *he* was afraid. Afraid of his sister's two-up two-down in Kingsbury; afraid of putting everything on the line for the principle of a moral responsibility that he wasn't sure how much he believed in. Stephen was afraid of losing everything, but mostly love.

Their moment of united surprise over Ms Heany's outburst was extended when her pinny pocket, or rather the mobile within it, began to ring and her face lit up with a girlish blush as she popped it back and said to the assorted company, 'I have a guest.'

A gentleman caller, Constance thought to herself as she put down the phone to her new friend and began walking towards the kitchen door to answer his rather mysterious request to 'open up for a surprise'. A flirty type, this Mr Fumble, and why not? She was answerable to nobody now that the Bishop was letting her go, and she had no ties to these two. No point in getting too excited at this stage but there was no getting away from it that Dennis had turned up at the right moment in her life. Constance was no romantic, but perhaps fate was not the—

'How long are you planning to stay in Killa?'

'How long have you known the Bishop?'

'Is the Bishop gay?'

'Wilson!' Click. 'Stephen!' Click. 'Wilson! Wilson! Wilson!'

Wilson got a shock. So did Stephen. Constance Heany was half-smiling like she hadn't quite got the gist of Mr Fumble's surprise yet.

The two seasoned celebrities were gaping like ingenues. So entirely unlikely was it that, at this stage of their celebrity, the press could have surged upon them in this way. In their home. Well, somebody else's home. Britain's premier gay couple were always coiffured, tailored, charming for the press. They were establishment now, the days of smutty tabloid interest well behind them, they staged and appeared at high-profile events with the full co-operation of the press. If anyone wanted to contact them they did so via an accommodating public relations person and generally enjoyed a level of co-operation for which the Wilson machine was, frankly, legendary. Certainly they hired security, but Stephen had always thought it was only for show. It gave Wilson a thrill to be flanked by a couple of besuited mercenaries, but it was just something else he liked to pay for that he didn't need. Stephen had believed that security was more of an ego trip than anything else. Unnecessary most of the time. Wilson's stalkers were half a dozen middle-aged women who hung about the gates of their estate on bank-holiday weekends eating packed lunches and drinking tea from flasks. The train spotters, Stephen called them. Wilson spent over a hundred grand a year protecting himself against the possibility that one of them might break into the house and spike him with a poisoned knitting needle. But the press? They had lost interest in them long ago. A couple of settled queens? Too tame for shame, surely. But add a bishop and what have you got? SCANDAL!

From the press boys' viewpoint, they were in the area anyway and poor old Fumble never could keep his mouth shut so they all followed him on his big exclusive trip. Between them, there had to be a way of knitting the tart, the rock star's wife, the transvestite priest, the Bishop and his homo house guests together. Or Dennis and his band of merry paps weren't fit to wipe their own arses.

And so Wilson in his silk robe, Stephen in his towelling one and their erstwhile housekeeper regarded with puzzlement the thirty or so journalists and photographers that were cluttering their kitchen, making no attempt to answer the questions being flung at them, or avoid the camera flashes. After a few minutes, in the face of their victims' seeming indifference, the press stopped.

There was a moment's silence, and an outsider would have observed in this stand-off a certain amount of trepidation in the faces of the press towards the ensemble they were facing. Wilson was the undisputed Prince of PR, and his impervious stance suggested he had reached a higher plane of annoyance that, with his unlimited funds and a professional and personal fan base that included at least one media boss, could mean trouble.

Then Sapphire appeared in the doorway. She was wearing a matronly flannelette nightie that could only have been borrowed from Constance. She was still half-asleep and barefoot.

'I heard a noise.'

It was too much for them. A child, two gay men and a bishop. Only Dennis Fumble knew that the Bishop was in America. The rest were running through that moral maze of personal tragedy, public responsibility and personal gain which only a journalist is able to negotiate.

The headline won. Perhaps this group was more tenacious than most, perhaps Sapphire was not a cute enough child to keep them at bay. If she had been daintier with bigger, bluer, wider eyes, wearing a pair of pink cotton lace-trimmed pyjamas, maybe they would have taken pity on her and left her alone.

'Where is the Bishop now?'

'What's your name, love?' The woman who had put her hand through Helen's letterbox pounced across the room and held her hand out. 'Here, sweetheart, you come over here to me.'

Cameras were flashing and people were calling and Sapphire was terrified. Stephen was shouting now, and prodding at a fat man: 'Fuck off and leave her alone!' He looked like he was going to hit him and that made Sapphire even more afraid. It was horrible to hear Stephen shout like that.

Constance Heany was behind him, and so Sapphire grabbed on to the nearest, safest thing to hand. Which was Wilson.

She put her arms around his waist and she pressed her head into his stomach and she wailed, 'I'm scared! I want my mum!'

And something happened then to this diminutive star. Something different.

Nobody had ever called out to Wilson in this way before.

I'm scared! I want my mum! God – that was the story of his life. In everything that Wilson did – his unnatural attachment to his slippers, the jealousy around Stephen, his love of scones and all things cake-like – he could trace back to those two statements. And yet, here was somebody now saying it to him. Challenging him, not in a bad way but in the same way he had called out so many times in his life.

Help me.

Not: 'Help me become famous/write songs/better my wardrobe.'

Just help.

It was simple and human and it was something that Wilson, for all his spoiled ways, understood. He wrote songs about being that vulnerable. 'Help' was the cornerstone of his career.

Wilson understood Sapphire's cry in the most innocent part of himself. The part that had driven him always, that had made so many millions of people love him.

But more than that, something protective in him clicked. A paternal gene which he had never known was there and which, furthermore, he was rather delighted to discover. This person, a child, seeking his protection, it made him feel . . . proud, invincible actually.

As Stephen was flailing his arms and screaming at the oncoming mass, Wilson put his hand on Sapphire's shoulder and led her, still clinging to his torso, upstairs where he had to make a very important phone call.

One hour later, Stephen was still holding them off in the kitchen. This was their second siege in two days. Why the fuck had they followed Fumble? They could all be back home skulling pints in their Notting Hill locals by now. No one likes children/Church stories. It's just when they come up, you have to deal with them. Tarts and rock stars? Lovely work when it comes, right, but this heavy-duty stuff? Depressing shit, but you can't just walk away. Fuck it – any chance of a coffee, mate?

Things had calmed right down. Stephen had sent Constance upstairs to Wilson and Sapphire (lest imaginations ran any more riot than they already had), and was loading the vast stash of home-made biscuits and bread into the assembled company. He had been through the whole thing a million times, but they did not believe him. It was too improbable, they decided, them just staying here in the Bishop's house and him not knowing. There was a connection. There had to be. Maybe the Bishop wasn't a paedophile, but let him come downstairs and tell them himself.

'HE'S IN AMERICA!'

We like you, Stephen, but, with all due respect, it wouldn't be the first time a celebrity has lied to us.

Fumble said nothing but took another slice of apple tart, part of him mournfully regretting that if he had a woman to cook like this for him maybe he might spend less time in the pub or chasing around after angry celebrities.

As he was filling the kettle for the fiftieth time, Stephen heard a terrible whirring sound coming from outside. He had not made it as far as the window to look out when four men wearing full combat gear and brandishing what looked very much like machine guns burst in the back door and one of them shouted at the top of his voice: 'GET OUT OF HERE, EVERY LAST MOTHERFUCKING ONE OF YOU, OR I'LL BLOW YOUR BRAINS OUT!'

Stephen wet himself slightly, Dennis Fumble fainted (or collapsed from a stroke) and the rest of them ran, leaving equipment and half-eaten scones behind them. Stephen instinctively headed up the stairs to see if the others were all right and found a scene of domestic bliss with Constance teaching Sapphire to knit and Wilson standing, one arm behind his back, gazing out over the lawn like a Victorian patriarch.

'I see my men arrived finally. I trust they saw the press hounds off the premises?'

Stephen was apoplectic with rage. Fear really, but rage was better.

'WHAT THE FUCK ARE YOU TALKING ABOUT – *YOUR* MEN?'

'*Para Security – uncompromising protection services for the pressures of the modern celebrity.* I knew they'd come in handy one day. Did you like the helicopter? Genuine US issue. I thought it was rather smart. Oops – off they go!'

The ferocious whirring started up again.

'HOW MUCH?' Stephen shouted over the noise.

'TEN GRAND!'

'CHEAP!'

'WHAT?'

'I SAID . . . oh . . . come here.'

And Stephen walked over to the window and took Wilson's hand.

'Stupid old queen,' he mouthed as the helicopter deafened overhead. Wilson squeezed his partner's hand back like he would never let it go and the two of them looked out over the lawn of the Bishop of Killa's palace.

Just in time to see the Bishop's car turn into the driveway.

33

'Yeah, right. Alfie Smith,' Fonzie said. 'You know what, Al? You are one mad son of a bitch, man.'

Once he had said it there was no going back because, well, Alfie *was* Alfie Smith. He had to argue his case.

'But I really *am* Alfie Smith.'

'You know what, Al? I thought you were a friend.'

'The rock star. Alfie Smith. I am him.'

'I am pouring my heart out to you here, man, and you are playing games with my head.'

'You must have read about it in the papers? I disappeared a couple of weeks ago, and I ended up here.'

'The girl I am in love with is doing me in, man, I turn to you for advice and you start saying you are this pop star or something and—'

'*That* is why Molly took me aside to show me the article about MoniKa – because she knows who I am, because, like you say, she is my biggest fan—'

'Shut the fuck up, man! This is not about you, yeah? This is about me – you know what?'

'But, Fonzie, I am *Alfie Smith.*'

'Right. Here it is. I don't fucking care *who* you are.'

A wake-up call right there. Not care that I am an internationally famous pop star, the very one whom your supposed girlfriend is in love with? Sitting here? In front of you? In the flesh? No. That can't be right.

'No one ever listens to *me*, man. I am just fucking foolish Fonzie Mallarkey, a useless gobshite that works in his uncle's poxy newsagent's shop. Good-for-a-laugh Fonzie. No-need-to-take-him-seriously Fonzie. You know what? If you were Alfie Smith that would just about make sense to me right now. That makes a pure haime's shite out of the whole thing.'

Fonzie looked at Alfie for a few seconds and the undercover celeb wondered what he was thinking. Was it sinking in who he was at last? The enormity of who he was? Did it put a different spin on the whole Molly thing?

'You do look kind of like the bastard.' Then he stood up and motioned Alfie towards the bike.

'It's no big deal. I am just kind of fucked right now and need to sort some shit out. I guess – well – I guess we haven't known each other that long, Al. You're a funny guy, yeah, but well, something's come up and, no offence, man, but maybe I need to work this one out with my homeys.'

◦

A breakage in male bonding is not always best expressed whilst holding on to the other person's waist during a motorcycle ride. And it is invariably the holder, in this case Alfie, who takes most of the pressure. Alfie was not a seasoned motorbike passenger and so sitting back and swaying independently was not an option. Rather there was a certain amount of clinging and clutching to a fellow male torso, which is not exactly balm to a diminishing male ego. And Alfie did feel diminished by Fonzie's rejection. He could not quite establish whether Fonzie did not believe he was Alfie Smith, which was annoying, or whether he believed he was Alfie Smith and didn't care, which felt, if Alfie was entirely honest with himself, hurtful. But why should it? Wasn't that what Alfie had been searching for? Anonymity? Normality? To shed all of that shallow celebrity shit and just be taken for who he was? Go to the pub, play pool, pick up girls at discos. Harbour an ambition to liven up the local radio waves with a dance show on K West FM. If the confrontation with Fonzie had proved anything, it was that all of that was possible. He could stay here and disappear from public life. Nothing to stop him. Karl and his record company couldn't sue another album out of him. Wilson was the big boss anyway, and he would back him if he thought this was what Alfie really wanted. His money could be re-routed. He could give it all away to charity – every last penny – and start again. In ten years' time, maybe he would have enough saved from DJing at weddings to put a deposit on a house. He would meet a nice girl, like Molly, and settle down. He would convert his small garage into a workshop for fixing up old guitars, and Fonzie and the boys would come round and discuss the bikes they were building in their garages. Their wives would all be friends, and on high days and holidays the women would make their husbands take them out for a meal, thinking they were dead sophisticated eating in the dining room of the local hotel instead of bar-bites in the pub. GP Geoff would still be holding out for the perfect woman at fifty, and they would all be slagging him for being a bachelor, and he would be flirting with their frumpy fat wives pretending he thought they were lucky to have found the love of a good woooomaaaaaaan . . .

Aaaaaaaargh! What had he done?

He had walked out on MoniKa – *MONIkA!* – officially the most beautiful woman in the world for this, this, this, nothing – *NOTHING* – of a life! *2Day, Hello!*, a weekly slagging from Honest Ron Parker was, he now realized, a small, small, *small* price to pay not to have to endure the poverty, the penance of an ordinary life. What the *fuck* had he been thinking?

In one grand swoop, Alfie wanted it all back. The hotel room service, the laundered sheets, the impulse-buying of cars, the beautiful wife – the adventure, excitement, madness pressure of a celebrity life.

And he knew, swerving round that wide bend in the road where the professionals' grand houses skirt the little town of Killa, that this was not where he belonged.

His beautiful wife. And not just beautiful.

Alfie was confused. Not all the time, but a lot of the time. Especially lately. He wanted an ordinary life, but not at the expense of being extraordinary. He understood what it must have been like to be Jesus, but he wasn't the son of God. He liked being one of the lads but only once they understood that he wasn't one of them really. There was a lot of conflicting stuff going on and sometimes – like now – it made his head hurt.

MoniKa was different. Mon always knew. What to do, what to wear, when to wear it, who to see, who not to see and when not to see them. Let *Hello!* cover the wedding and *2Day* do the house. She was decisive. Clear. Blue velvet curtains in the bedroom, maroon wool in the kitchen. It was one of the reasons why he married her. She was clear and confident and she knew where she was going, even if it didn't always fit in with Alfie's idea of himself as an earthy, giving, ordinary guy. Even if it meant not having your TV on wall brackets in the kitchen. That sureness, that bossy carry-on, the way she railroaded him into the *2Day* shoot was also the reason he left. But now, feeling stranded and alone, away from his own life, embroiled in some pretend existence, he wanted to be back there. In his new kitchen. Posing for *2Day*, popping bagels from their Dualit toaster if necessary. Anything to be back in a life that belonged to him with a woman who could provide the answers when it all got too much. He wanted her back, but Alfie knew that, even after this short time, it might be too late. MoniKa was not the type to hang around and wait. She loved him, enough to marry him. But women like MoniKa – you don't just walk out on them. The paper Molly had shown him had said she had a new boyfriend already. Honest Ron was an unreliable arsehole, but Alfie could not afford to disbelieve entirely that she might have met somebody else. The hardship of singledom was not in MoniKa's emotional vocabulary. He had 'stolen' her off a

Hollywood A-lister as it was. God! And he had left her! Alone! What had he been thinking?

'Shiiiiiiiiit!'

The bike swerved and for a second Alfie thought it was the end. Fonzie managed to stop them sideways with his boots.

'Whoah. *That* was close, man!'

It was Paud. He had run down an almost invisible dirt track at the side of a road and out in front of the bike.

'Whatthefuckareyou . . .?'

Fonzie was shaken. Alfie was having a moment. A near-death one. He had been on the point of throwing it all away, now it had nearly been taken away from him before he had the chance to get it all back. It was all too much. His head hurt. He wanted to lie down somewhere luxurious and be ministered to. Was there a health farm near here? Wilson would know. Could they just get back on the bike and get him into town where he could start planning his escape?

'Guys – it's all going off in Old Breslin's, man.'

'Yeah?'

Fonzie had pulled a muscle in his leg, but he was still curious. Paud was a quiet kind. It wasn't like him to come running out into the middle of the road like that, and what on earth could be happening in Aoife's great-uncle's place that could be that important.

'Aoife's home, yeah, but she's got this crew with her, right? Not like the usual gang, yeah? This freaky black guy who says nothing right? And a couple of – shit, man, you have *got* to see these birds! One of them reckons she's a journalist, yeah? Mad-looking English bitch but the other one – ma-an, you have *got* to see this other bird. She is like – whoah! – you have never seen anything so fucking steaming hot in your life, man, I mean in your *life*! So Derek's picked them up from the airport – in the fucking limo, man! And they've got Molly with them and – I can't tell you, man, but there is something going down with her I swear!' Paud was unemployed and he watched a lot of MTV. But when the jive talk went up? You knew there was something going down. Something in Killa, the place where nothing ever happens. The fashion show had been something, but the boys had distanced themselves from it on the grounds of it being girlish. Plus it wasn't theirs. It was a load of Dublin bastards sticking their noses in. This now, a happening up in Old Breslin's? This could be something worth talking about.

Fonzie was already walking up the narrow hill which led to Aoife's uncle's place, and Alfie had no choice but to follow. He was deeply pissed off now. Here he was walking into some parochial little mini-drama with Molly and her annoying model friend. He had been in Old Breslin's the week before with the boys and he had found it, honestly, quite frightening. The bar itself was nothing but the front 'parlour' of a freezing grey house up the steep tree-lined alley they were now walking. Old Breslin had silently passed around a bottle of obnoxiously strong, allegedly illegal home-brewed alcohol, which Alfie suspected was car-battery fluid cut with their good host's piss, while the lads all bristled with pride like they were initiating Alfie into a rare male custom. In fairness, at the time Alfie had thought it was pretty cool. But right now, he had no interest. He wanted to get away from this lot, get off somewhere on his own and think about his next move. About how he was going to get his old life back. He would call Wilson – he would know what to do. The most important thing was MoniKa. Getting her back. If he could get her back on side he could make everything all right again.

Alfie followed Fonzie and Paud into the parlour, and as his eyes adjusted to the dim light he identified a motley array of people. There was Molly, pert and pretty and all done up as if she was going to a disco. Aoife, with those long, loose gangly limbs that could only belong to a model. Between them, unusually, sat a young black guy. Good-looking beyond the realms of what was normal, his exoticism jarred in this rustic environment. Then there she was, although with the 'it can't be' factor it took a few seconds to sink in. .

'Alfie! Darling!'

Hettie fucking Flinthrop. Greeting him like this was *such* a coincidence. Was somebody having a laugh?

'What are you doing here? This is *such* a coincid—'

'Cut the crap, Hettie. What's going on?'

The ruthless little cow. She was Mon's self-appointed best friend. Except MoniKa said she was only hanging out with her for as long as it took to get a car out of her publishers. Which they were going to donate to charity. Of course.

'Alfie. Monny has been *so* worried about you! We *all* have! Where have you bee-een?'

Well, quite fucking obviously here, he thought –
although the mention of MoniKa's name in the context of
somebody who actually knew her softened his defences
sufficiently for him not to say it out loud.

Alfie's identity was finally revealed. His cover blown,
he stiffened slightly to gird himself against the reaction.
Hettie stood blinking at him, waiting for a reply. And that
was it. Nothing else. Molly waved over at him vaguely but
seemed absorbed with the black kid; Aoife and Fonzie
were laughing at some private joke. And the rest of the
lads – it occurred to Alfie that there was a very real
possibility they did not know who Alfie Smith was. A
group of people, after all, who did not read *Hello!* magazine, or *2Day* magazine or watch *Top Of The Pops*, if his
trip here went down in Killa legend he would probably be
as the DJ with the bad haircut who was pure poof on the
back of a bike. Or the pop singer who Fonzie Mallarkey's
girlfriend had a crush on.

It didn't feel right, this not being famous. It did not feel
right at all.

●

'How's MoniKa?'

Hettie smiled. That you-are-so-special-and-fabulous
smile that very clever celebrity journalists give to not-so-
clever celebrities.

'Well, you can ask her yourself.'

'You mean . . .?'

'Well, *of course*, darling! She's outside in the car!'

Derek Mallarkey's hired limo was out the back, and as

Alfie's hand reached for the door, he hesitated with – part excitement, part trepidation.

The reunion would be featured in *2Day* magazine. Of course it would. That was MoniKa. And if Alfie Smith wanted fame and fortune and a beautiful model wife – well, that was just a price he would have to pay.

ONE YEAR LATER

Helen sent

The divorce case of the decade followed by the biggest charity appeal since Live Aid – Helen Doherty has had a very busy year. Renowned for her dignified silence on the matter of her ex-husband's dalliances, *Irish Tatler* **met the elegant fundraiser near her Mayo home and discovered that if recent experiences have heightened her profile, they have done nothing to loosen her tongue.**

Killa – no disrespect to the people who live there – is in the middle of nowhere. A small sleepy seaside village along Mayo's northern coastline, a million miles away from the lush landscape of South Mayo where you might expect to find the odd (and some very odd!) rock star playing at country life in some grand old estate. Famous people may like to hide, but generally they like to do it in the company of other famous people. For a high-profile celebrity to buy a rambling estate in this area would be unusual. But for somebody of Helen Doherty's current profile and status as fundraiser, peacemaker and, let's face it, international celebrity, to be staying in a two-up two-down terraced cottage in the middle of Killa town? It's, frankly, unheard of. One cannot help but suspect that Ms Doherty is playing the humility card too hard.

We all know the Helen Doherty myth, of how she took her considerable divorce settlement from Godot's lead singer Mal Doherty and allegedly pumped every penny into the various charity projects she had been involved in over the years.

'I wouldn't bother fighting for this money myself,' she reportedly told the court. 'I can give a legal guarantee that every penny I earn from this settlement will be given to appointed charities. If my husband wants to write the cheques out to them directly, he can do so.'

Sources close to the family say that, despite his very public re-marriage to the Eighties pop singer Corrine Coen (aka Sapphire), Mal Doherty had never wanted the divorce and would 'take Helen back in the morning'. A sentiment one might dispute, had the second Mrs Doherty not protested as much as she did in that nasty newspaper column which accused Helen of every kind of machiavellian plot and greedy back-stabbedness. Her adversary's refusal to take action, or even comment on Corrine's slanderous column, some might say merely highlighted the author's own greed and bitterness.

I arranged to meet Helen in the bar of a local hotel. There were no secretaries, no PR people. I got her phone number directly from the charity. She did not offer to meet me in the small house which she reputedly shares with the ex-priest Enda Devlin, the constant companion she describes as 'a colleague and good friend', but whom sources have said is her lover.

She was dressed in jeans and a loose cashmere sweater; her hair was roughly tied and she was wearing very little make-up. It was a look that made it clear that looks were very much *not* the point. What was also very clear was that her personal life was off limits to journalists. We talked about her current project in Vietnam (featured in next month's issue), and anything that this interviewer did throw in the way of a dig was expertly fielded.

Where did she stay when she was in Ireland, for instance?

'My colleague Enda has a cottage in Killa which we use when we are in the country. It doubles as an office, although as long as I have the mobile plugged in I am working.'

'Some people say that Enda is your—'

'I have no interest in what people say about me.'

'Your life must be very different now?'

'From when?'

'From when you were married?'

'Yes, it is.'

'How is that?'

'Well, I am not married any more.'

'And you have less money.'

'By choice.'

'Yes, but . . .'

The questions ended there as Helen, quite politely, asserted that she was not interested in discussing her private life. We spent the next two hours talking about her work, and watching video footage on the bar TV in Donlan's Hotel, Killa, Co. Mayo. It was a bizarre experience sitting in such ordinary surroundings with this woman who seems to have come through the celebrity grinder if not unscathed, then at least, remarkably, with all of her dignity intact. In fact, it would not be going too far to say that in the past twelve months Helen Doherty has become something of a spiritual icon. The living embodiment of an ideal that is so very far from the celebrity worshipping of our everyday lives, Helen is walking proof that money, fame and all that goes with it do not buy happiness.

For that, it seems you need a big heart, a generous spirit and, if the look on Helen's face as I left her is anything to go by, a bearded ex-priest called Enda.

ALFIE AND MONIKA

**2DAY's editorial director Hettie Flinthrop visits
Britain's most famous couple in their beautiful
Holland Park home and talks about the difficult
times in the past and their plans for the future.**

**H: MoniKa, the decor in your house is beautiful. Tell me
how it came about.**

M: We owned the house for about six months before we
moved in and I worked with the decorators on the colours and themes for each room. Then in the last four
months since we have been living here, I have put in the
finishing touches.

H: Did you have an interior designer to help you?

M: No, I did it all by myself! Alfie's mother Sharon helped
me choose the curtains and tie-backs in all the guest
bedrooms.

**H: I can't believe you did all this yourself. It looks so
professional!**

M: It's funny you should say that because I am about to
open a shop on the King's Road selling beautiful things
that I have picked up on my travels.

H: So people can create this look at home?

M: Yes! I have seen so many wonderful carpets and bowls and things on my travels, and when I was in Morocco recently it hit me. Wouldn't it be wonderful if ordinary people in England could buy these wonderful carpets and things too, without having to travel abroad? The idea for the shop just sort of fell into place after that.

H: So is this the end of MoniKa the model/actress and the start of MoniKa the shopkeeper?

M: Ha ha ha. No, there will be ordinary people working in the shop. But I will have chosen nearly every item that goes in it. Just look at these little tea-light holders. They are my favourite thing at the moment. Aren't they adorable?

H: Just wonderful – a perfect adornment for any dinner-party table.

M: Exactly! Or you could just put tea-light candles in and arrange them around the side of your bath to create atmosphere.

H: Gorgeous. Alfie? What do you think of what your wife has done with the house?

A: It's great.

M: Alfie's not really into interiors – are you, darling?

A: No.

M: Hettie, I have to tell you this great story. Do you mind if I tell her the wall brackets story, darling?

A: No.

M: It was our first row. Alfie said that he wanted to put a television up on one of those wall brackets? Well, of course there was no way! As you can see, all of the televisions in the house are in custom-built cabinets.

A: There's nothing wrong with wall-mounted television sets.

M: So we compromised, because that is what marriage is, Hettie. Now Alfie has his own special den in the garden . . .

A: It's a shed.

M: . . . with his precious wall-mounted TV.

A: I am a very down-to-earth guy with very simple needs.

H: Alfie, despite your fame, people describe you as a very down-to-earth guy. Is that an accurate description?

M: Oh, it is *so* accurate. Alfie is very down-to-earth. Last weekend we flew over to Ireland and stayed in a bed and breakfast? A small one for thirty pounds a night? Like somewhere you'd stay if you were just normal? It was amazing.

A: Walshes' B&B in Killa, Co. Mayo. They're friends of mine. They have tea- and coffee-making facilities in the rooms and every room has its own television.

M: Wall-mounted!

A: Ha ha.

H: You guys are always laughing and joking! You are clearly still so in love.

M: Yes, we are, aren't we, babe?

A: Yes.

H: Congratulations on your first wedding anniversary!

M: One whole year later and we are happier than ever. Aren't we, babe?

A: Yes.

H: Alfie. MoniKa. The first few weeks of your marriage were clouded in controversy. Tell us about how you came through that difficult time?

M: Well, as everyone knows by now, it was just a big misunderstanding. Alfie was away working on an album with Wilson, and I was in Morocco on a photo shoot when this story broke that me and Alfie had split up. It was really horrible! And not in the least true. Was it, babe?

A: No.

M: So then *2Day* came along and did an article explaining to everyone that we were OK.

H: What's next for Alfie and MoniKa?

M: I am still modelling and we can now exclusively reveal that Alfie has been given the opportunity to go on the London stage, something which he has dreamed of since he was a child, haven't you, darling?

A: Yes.

M: So from next month you can see Alfie in *Joseph and the Amazing Technicolor Dreamcoat* before he leaves for its European tour!

H: Alfie. MoniKa. What is the secret of your happy marriage?

M: Give and take, Hettie, and we are still so very much in love. Isn't that right, babe?

A: Yes. Dear.

Next week, exclusive pictures of Alfie and MoniKa's first wedding anniversary celebrations

Extract from *2 DAY* magazine

It was the social event of the century, when singer/ songwriter Wilson hired the historic French estate for a formal life-time commitment ceremony to his partner Stephen Silke. Wearing matching powdered wigs in the style of their historic host Louis XVI, the two men positively glowed with pride as their spiritual advisor, Simeon Dunne, presided over the ceremony.

In the first of our six-part series, Hettie Flinthrop recalls meeting the happy couple a week before they flew to France to talk to them about their plans for the big day, and their plans for the future.

H: Wilson. Stephen. Why Versailles?

W: Because it is big and it's tacky and that's how much I love Stephen.

S: Really, darling – all this for *moi*? There's no need!

W: Yeah, right.

H: Tell me about the arrangements. Were you involved in all the details or did you hire a wedding co-ordinator?

W: Yawn. Stephen?

S: Jane Packer is on board as a consultant on the flowers – we're flying her over. Let me see, Giorgio is knocking us up a couple of going-away outfits . . .

W: What is this – an advertorial?

S: . . . but the wedding suits, they are genuine eighteenth century, so we have to hire them . . .

W: What, and give them back?

S: 'Fraid so, honey.

W: Oh, there is no fucking way! Who organized that?

S: Me.

W: Did I tell you to get somebody in to help you?

S: I did. Several people.

W: And still the best you could do was hire suits?

S: They are genuine eighteenth century.

W: Dry clean only?

S: No-clean only.

W: Arrrrrrgh! Are you mad? I don't know much history but I know they did not have anti-perspirant two hundred years ago!

S: They're fine. They have been hung outside for months. There's no smell off them at all now.

W: No smell? No smell?! Have you lost your mind? Have them copied! Ring Donatella, Giorgio – ring the people that did the wigs – I don't care – get them copied. I'm not wearing—

S: It's too late. Listen, Wilson, just—

H: **The ceremony itself. You are bringing your own personal spiritual advisor? Tell us about him.**

W: Is she still here? What the . . .?

S: Wilson, Hettie is here doing an interview.

W: She interrupted me!

S: She interrupted *me*, actually.

W: Now *you've* interrupted me!

S: No, I didn't.

W: Yes, you did!

S: When?

W: Just then.

S: No, I didn't.

H: Perhaps I had better come back another time?

S: No, Hettie, really. Wilson, go find your slippers.

W: But I—

S: Go! GO ON!

(Wilson leaves the room)

I'm sorry, Hettie – we're both a little stressed, the excitement, pre-wedding nerves. You know how it is. Now. Where were we?

H: Spiritual advisor?

S: Yes. Hilarious story. We were in Ireland and we ended up staying in this Bishop's palace while he was away on holiday. Then he came back right in the middle of this *big* drama where there were press everywhere and kind of paramilitary security people on his lawn. Not real ones, but they had helicopters and balaclavas and guns and everything – *anyway*. Bishop comes back, goes 'OHMIGOD!' and has a stroke on the lawn. Helicopters, hospitals, blah blah blah. When he comes out of rehab Wilson has only gone and bought his house off the Catholic Church. (Buying property off the Pope? Drama? Don't talk to me . . . but that's *another* story!) So we said to him, 'Look,

Simeon. We own the house, we love your housekeeper. We can't spend all year here because Hertfordshire, Cannes, la la la la. Why don't you and Connie stay in the house and mind it when we're not here.' Then when we decided to tie the knot, well Simeon still has all the gear – you know – the pointy hat and all – and we thought it would be fun for him to kind of do the ceremony. Make it more authentic. More churchy.

H: And was he instrumental in you and Wilson deciding to make this commitment to each other?

S: No, actually. That would be Sapphire?

H: Ah yes. Your daughter.

S: Well, she's not our *actual* daughter, but we are in the process of adopting her. The legalizing of our relationship will make things easier.

H: And Sapphire is the daughter of—

S: Whoah, bitch! Forget it. This is *2Day* magazine . . .

H: Sorry sorry sorry. And how are you and Wilson enjoying parenthood?

S: Very much! Sapphire spends school terms with either myself or Wilson in the Irish Palace, then holidays here – or Cannes – you know. We move around, although keeping to Sapphire's school schedule has tied us both down a bit. But we are loving every minute of it. Aren't we, darling?

(Wilson walks back in.)

W: Where the fuck are they? You've hidden them! Again! I thought we were over all this? I'm loving what?

S: Being a parent?

W: Oh yes. Well somebody has to take some responsi-

bility around here. Be the adult. What with all this
hiding of slippers and—

S: I did *not* hide your slippers!

W: La, la, la – like I believe you . . .

S: I am sick of this infantile . . .

W: Me? Infantile? Well that's just . . .

**Next week, Hettie joins Wilson and Stephen on
their chartered Commitment Cruise across
the English Channel**

To: Aoifebreslin@hotmail.com
From: Tangier!@hotmail.com

Dear Aoife,

I cannot believe I am *finally* in Tangier. I had to wait one whole
year to get my first *Vogue* shoot, but then I suppose that's
make-up for you! Still, Gary came through in the end and here
I am! Hettie came out yesterday for a couple of days. She's
turned it into a working trip (of course! She is *such* a
workaholic – bless), doing a 'shoot about a shoot'. She is
driving Favio absolutely mad, but like I said to him last night,
it's good for all our profiles. It may not be *Harpers* but *2Day* is
still England's best selling celebrity weekly! He looked at me
funny but then that's photographers for you, isn't it? 'All art
and no trousers.' (Sorry private joke. Backstage Betsy J?
Spring/Summer? Forget it, you had to be there.) But on to
more important matter. Aoife, I am thrilled about you and
Fonzie. I really and truly absolutely am. It is so weird me not
minding and how things have worked out. You are there quite
happy in Killa and here I am travelling the world. I used to
think Fonzie was the best I would ever do and now, here I am,
dating an England footballer! Sometimes I have to pinch
myself and say Wow! Can life really be this fabulous? I love
Ronnie and everything, but you know what the really
important thing is? If things don't work I know that my profile is
building and I will be able to meet someone else just as good
really quickly.

I don't know when I'll be able to get home next. Gary has me booked solid for the next three months – then it's Cannes. Hettie is pulling a freebie for me by insisting she needs to bring a make-up artist with her. She has turned out to be *such* a good friend.

Hugs hugs and kisses in tonnes, darling,

Molly.

PS It's a shame, but I know that I can't make it home for Eleanor Jackson's funeral. Will you get some flowers and send me the bill? U R a star.

OTHER BOOKS
AVAILABLE FROM PAN MACMILLAN

MORAG PRUNTY
DANCING WITH MULES	0 330 48491 5	£5.99
DISCO DADDY	0 330 48609 8	£6.99
POISON ARROWS	0 330 48610 1	£6.99

MEG CABOT
BOY MEETS GIRL	0 330 41887 4	£6.99

CLARE NAYLOR & MIMI HARE
THE SECOND ASSISTANT	0 330 42007 0	£6.99

All Pan Macmillan titles can be ordered from our website,
www.panmacmillan.com, or from your local bookshop
and are also available by post from:

Bookpost, PO Box 29, Douglas, Isle of Man IM99 1BQ
Credit cards accepted. For details:
Telephone: 01624 677237
Fax: 01624 670923
E-mail: bookshop@enterprise.net
www.bookpost.co.uk

Free postage and packing in the United Kingdom

Prices shown above were correct at the time of going to press.
Pan Macmillan reserve the right to show new retail prices on covers
which may differ from those previously advertised in the text
or elsewhere.